Outstanding praise for Peter Colt and his Andy Roark mysteries!

Back Bay Blues

"A classical mystery with an honor-bound detective and a keen sense of place… Besides having the P.I. spiel and the P.I. moves down pat, Roark is genuinely likable (not too tough, but not a patsy) and very much a character of his time."
– *The New York Times Book Review*

The Off-Islander

"Entertaining . . . Like Philip Marlowe—or Robert Parker's Spenser—Andy has a sharp eye for telling detail and male haberdashery. Those who enjoy newish reworkings of classic PI tropes will be satisfied."
—*Publishers Weekly*

"If you like your mysteries to be old-school in the vein of John D. MacDonald, or even farther back to Raymond Chandler or Dashiell Hammett, then you will appreciate this striking debut by Peter Colt. Long on atmosphere, detail, and character, it could place detective Andy Roark amongst the classic noir sleuths."
—Raymond Benson, author of *Blues in the Dark*

"By the end of the book . . . the reader has been taken for a long, exciting ride . . . We are told that this is not the last of the Andy Roark novels. I look forward to the next one."
—*Vietnam Veterans of America*

Books by Peter Colt

THE OFF-ISLANDER

BACK BAY BLUES

Published by Kensington Publishing Corp.

BACK BAY BLUES

PETER COLT

KENSINGTON
PUBLISHING CORP.

www.kensingtonbooks.com

KENSINGTON BOOKS are published by

Kensington Publishing Corp.
119 West 40th Street
New York, NY 10018

All Kensington titles, imprints, and distributed lines are available at special quantity discounts for bulk purchases for sales promotion, premiums, fund-raising, educational, or institutional use. Special book excerpts or customized printings can also be created to fit specific needs. For details, write or phone the office of the Kensington Special Sales Manager: Attn. Special Sales Department. Kensington Publishing Corp., 119 West 40th Street, New York, NY 10018. Phone: 1-800-221-2647.

The K logo is a trademark of Kensington Publishing Corp.

ISBN-13: 978-1-4967-2344-4
ISBN-10: 1-4967-2344-9
First Kensington Hardcover Edition: October 2020
First Kensington Mass Market Edition: September 2021

ISBN-13: 978-1-4967-2346-8 (ebook)
ISBN-10: 1-4967-2346-5 (ebook)

10 9 8 7 6 5 4 3 2 1

Printed in the United States of America

Acknowledgments

I would like to thank the following:

CME for tirelessly and heroically trying to bring some semblance of proper spelling and grammar to the stuff I write.

TFA, who spent countless hours trying to educate me about the inner workings of ships and listening to me tell him my ideas for stories for the last thirty years.

CLC, who is willing to answer questions about hypothermia, gunshot wounds, explosives, and many other esoteric things that Andy Roark should know about or experience.

Any mistakes that the reader finds are mine and mine alone.

Also, Cathy, who patiently lets me slip off to my office and write, leaving her to deal with everything and everyone else.

Lastly for Henry and Alder; there would be no point to any of this without you three.

BACK BAY BLUES

Chapter 1

November 1982 had been a hard month for me. I had witnessed a man killed, killed a man, and found out that an old friend had betrayed me. I could see if he had betrayed me for a woman, but in this case, it was just money. Not even a lot of money.

I had been worried that I wouldn't be able to find work without Danny Sullivan feeding it to me from his business as a criminal defense attorney. I had about a week in without work, and then it picked up. I put a new ad in the Yellow Pages, and that did the trick. It also helped that a lot of cops and lawyers knew me. A lot of former clients had sent referrals, and I didn't starve. After a time, I figured out that Danny's referrals had been nice, but I didn't need them, and the last one had almost gotten me killed.

November had slipped into December without much fanfare. Christmas came and went, and New Year's passed without resolution. February found me cold and worn out. I had been hired by a lawyer for a big shipbuilding company to investigate a workers' comp case down at the shipyard in Quincy, Massachusetts, at the end of January. It was a couple of days that wrapped up quickly.

That case led to one involving union agitators. The shipyard did a lot of work for the navy and operated on close margins. Too many union problems could shut them down. There was always a fear that the Soviets would pay agitators to do that at the shipyard and that the giant crane called "Goliath" that dominated the Quincy skyline would fall still.

For me, it meant a lot of time hanging around the docks, the yard, and the bars that the shipyard workers went to. It meant a lot of time trying to figure out who was who in the world of shipyard labor. February down on the docks by the Fore River was cold, damp, wind-driven cold, the type of cold that started at my feet and worked its way up into the very center of me.

I was dressed for the weather, plenty of wool, and on the colder days a peacoat and watch cap. I had good gloves, but they could only keep my hands warm for so long. I had a .45 caliber Colt Lightweight Commander in the pocket of the peacoat, in the special pocket the navy had designed just for it.

It was a big gun that shot a big, slow .45 caliber bullet, but if I needed a gun down on the docks then I would really need a gun. I had two spare magazines in the other pocket. I had a big folding Buck knife stuck down in the pocket of my faded jeans. I could flip the blade out fast, and it was sharp enough to shave the hair off my arm. I used to carry a Colt 1903, but for legal reasons that was now in a safe deposit box in the basement of a bank in

Providence, Rhode Island. I am not telling you which one, but it looks a lot like the building Clark Kent works in.

Detective work is a lot of boredom: waiting, watching, and trying to make sense of what you see. Sometimes I was on foot, and other times I would park the Subaru Brat that I was borrowing from a friend. The Ghia wasn't good for surveillance, so it stayed at home. The Brat was tan and had a cap on the back. The jump seats had been removed, and I could lie down in a sleeping bag in the back. It would get cold, but it let me unobtrusively take pictures of people in and around the shipyard. The downside was I ended every day cold, stiff, and hungry.

One night when I was fighting traffic trying to get back to my apartment in Boston's Back Bay, I saw a brightly lit restaurant in a strip mall on the outskirts of Quincy. It had red curtains and lacquered lattice woodwork in the windows. There was a yellowing menu in the window, and a bright neon sign that said, THE BLUE LOTUS, formed into that weird faux Asian version of the English alphabet you could only find in Chinese restaurants. It looked inviting, and the tickle of the cold starting in my throat made me think of Hot and Sour Soup.

It had snowed lightly that day, adding to my need for warmth. I pulled the Brat through the slush and slid into a parking spot. When I pulled open the door, I was greeted by the wonderful smell of cooking food and exotic spices. There was a small counter in front of me with a cash register, and a ceramic golden cat with one raised paw was next to the register. To my left was an unused coatrack and a small shrine with a ceramic Buddha and incense. Behind the cash register was a dusty bar with dusty liquor bottles that ran half the length of the restaurant. There were two booths by the window that the Brat was facing and then a series of tables that ran the room's length opposite the bar. Behind the bar were three red vinyl booths. The chairs were all black metal with red vinyl cushions.

Two of the tables were taken up by older Asian couples: Chinese, Vietnamese, it was impossible to tell. There was a young white couple sitting in one of the booths by the window. A skinny Asian man with black slacks and a checked shirt with rolled sleeves walked up to me from somewhere in the back. He wore aviator-framed prescription glasses and was smoking. He said, around the cigarette burning in the corner of his mouth, "You wan table?" His accent was thick but not indecipherable. He could have been thirty-five or fifty-five, I couldn't tell.

"A booth, if you don't mind." He shrugged and, taking a menu from the stack by the register, led me to a booth. I sat down, the peacoat folded next to me on the booth, with the pocket with the Colt facing up. He took my order and, later, brought it out without saying much or taking the cigarette from his mouth. The restaurant and its menu were Chinese, but I had spent over two years in Vietnam and knew that he was about as Chinese as I was. He could have stepped right out of any restaurant, bar, or club in Saigon.

I turned down the bowl of bread rolls and Chinese mustard that every Chinese restaurant seemed to insist you eat. He merely grunted something that sounded like approval. I asked for chopsticks, and he answered with another grunt and put a paper sleeve with two wooden chopsticks down in front of me. He seemed genuinely shocked when I ordered tea instead of a drink; by that I mean he raised his left eyebrow a millimeter higher than the one on the right.

The food was excellent. The Hot and Sour Soup did its job, and the dumplings I ordered were perfectly steamed and pan seared. I managed to eat Lo Mein with the chopsticks without wearing much of it or embarrassing myself. He brought the check on green paper on a plastic tray, pinned down by two fortune cookies, which I ignored. I left enough cash to pay the bill and leave a tip.

When I stood up and put the peacoat on, he was at the table, moving on quiet catlike feet. "You din have fortune cookie. You no wan?"

"No, I learned my fortune a long time ago." He grunted, which seemed to be his preferred method of communicating with me. I wondered if he smelled Vietnam on me. I walked out past the ceramic cat, which was waving its frozen paw at me.

Chapter 2

The case seemed to have little end in sight, and the weather in Boston wasn't going to get much warmer until the end of March, which to a true Bostonian meant May. I spent a lot of time down by the Fore and Weymouth Rivers, always in the shadow of the Goliath. I found myself stopping at The Blue Lotus once or twice a week. The only recognition that I was becoming kind of a regular was that the skinny Vietnamese man stopped bringing me bread rolls or fortune cookies. One night when a young, slim woman whom I took to be his daughter tried to bring me some bread rolls, he barked at her in their native language, and she whisked the rolls away.

One day when I came in my peacoat and watch cap, the Asian man looked at me and said, "What are you, sailor? You in navy?"

"No, I've been working down at the shipyard." My hair was still pretty short. I was getting used to it being not shaggy anymore. My mustache, on the other hand, I had let go a little. It was good but it wasn't Magnum good.

"No, you no sailor. Hands too soft. Sailor have rough hands." He held out his and showed me his palms, which were calloused and rough. The fingers were gnarled like tree roots and nicotine stained at the tips. They spoke of rough work done with stoicism and little else.

One day in early March, I was the only one other than him in the place in the late afternoon. A car squealed into the lot and parked across two spots. It was an asshole move no matter how you looked at it. The car was a green Chrysler from the Carter years, and the four kids who got out looked like high school football players. Two had on team jackets from Quincy High, and two had baseball bats. I slid the Colt out from the peacoat and into the small of my back. The Asian man heard the bells on the door and came out.

The tallest of the boys, with long dark hair, said, "We're sick of you gooks coming here to our town."

One of the others added intelligently, "Yeah."

"We are gonna bust up your gook restaurant, then your gook face, and you are gonna leave."

The Asian man stood still and quietly, almost at a whisper, said, "Fuck you" in the clearest English I had ever heard him use. His anger seemed to radiate off of him. It was incandescent.

"What did you say, gook? We are gonna trash the place and teach you a lesson." This one had long blond hair and looked like he bench pressed small cars when he wasn't stuffing smaller boys into lockers or dropping lit M-80s in the toilet. I saw his feet shift and I stood up.

One of the others looked at me and said, "What the fuck do you want, faggot," with all the toughness that a seventeen-year-old bully can muster.

I pulled the Colt out with little hurry and flipped off the safety as it was on its way up. It made an audible clicking noise, but by then the restaurant was very still and very quiet. I pointed it squarely between the eyes of the first kid. His eyes widened but not as big as the barrel of the .45 must have seemed. "It isn't nice to call people names, like faggot. Also, I don't like the word *gook*. I especially don't like it when a bunch of limp dick high school jocks say it to a friend of mine."

"You won't use that gun, mister. You won't shoot anyone," from one of the team jackets. His voice cracked with his lack of confidence.

"My fren, he kill before, lots of times. He in Vietnam. He kill lots of gooks." I was not expecting him to speak, much less say that.

"Gook, round eye, it's all the same to me. Okay, who's first?" My turn to sound like a wannabe tough guy.

"Come on, guys, let's get out of here. My dad will want the car back." Like that, they fled out the door. They couldn't get in the Chrysler fast enough and almost caused an accident pulling out of the parking lot.

"Okay, you put away you gun. Looks like something you buy in Tu Do Street. Like some Tu Do Street pimp with shiny gun."

My pistol was stainless steel with stag horn grips, and Tu Do Street was in Saigon, famous for its fleshpots and other forms of vice. If you had the money, you could have it on Tu Do Street. A pimp on Tu Do Street would have a chrome or nickel pistol.

"How did you know?" I asked him. He held out his hand to me and I took it.

"Old fren, my name is Nguyen. I am from Saigon. I have seen lots of American boys with guns. You different, your face, your eyes, you a killer. I have seen men like you." He then smiled and laughed. He was right. He went to the dusty bar and poured us each a snifter of very old, very good cognac. We toasted in Vietnamese, French, and then English.

From that moment on, when I went in the restaurant, he insisted on making me Vietnamese food. No more of the bread roll and fortune cookie variety of Chinese food that littered the South Shore; from then on it was pho so hot and spicy it would clear out my sinuses and water my eyes. Bee bong that was cool and filling and always good. I never saw an egg roll again, because nime chow displaced them on my plate. Sometimes it was something simple like rice and vegetables with a little meat in nuoc mam and soy sauce. He insisted on giving me the sweet, cloying Vietnamese coffee, made with condensed milk served over ice. If it was dinnertime, it would be Japanese beer in a silver can. There was no more Vietnamese 33 Beer to be had, and if there were they probably wouldn't sell it in Quincy, Massachusetts.

A few weeks later, I stopped into The Blue Lotus on a night when the April sunset had given away to an India ink sky. It was chilly but not raw. My case was wrapping up. The shipyard had offered me a permanent job as a security consultant. The money would be regular, but it would mean having a boss. I hadn't much liked that in the army and even less so in the cops. The shipyard's man paid me and told me if I reconsidered . . . but we both knew that I wasn't going to.

Nguyen waved me over to a booth toward the back when I walked in. He motioned me to sit and somehow without saying so indicated we would eat together. Two cans of Asahi arrived with chopsticks and napkins. A plate of nime chow arrived, translucent tubes of rice noodles, bean sprouts, cucumber, cilantro, and shrimp all in a rice wrapper. Nguyen sat down across from me, tapping the ash of his cigarette into an old cracked saucer that he placed not quite between us. He took off his silver-framed aviators and put them down next to his ashtray. His daughter brought out two steaming bowls of pho, spicy noodle soup. She placed a plate heaped with thinly shaved slices of rare beef between us. We each picked up a slice and put it in our soup.

Nguyen's daughter, Linh, looked at me, smiled, and said, "Enjoy your pho, Andy." She pronounced it the Vietnamese way, "fa," not the stupid white guy way, "fo." I thanked her, and her father grunted one of his usual commands. I knew I had achieved status as regular when Linh started using my name.

"I think she has a crush on you, Round Eye," he said between slurps of pho. He seemed to enjoy calling me by the mild racial slur. In his mind, it probably made up for all of the times I had referred to his people by racial slurs. It was easier in Vietnam not to think of them as people, to be dismissive, to dehumanize them. That was Vietnam.

The war was over, and I had grown up enough to be ashamed of things like that.

"I'm too old for her." It was always a thorny point when someone tells you their teenage daughter has a crush on you. We each slid more beef into our pho.

"You not rich enough, either." He laughed.

His laugh was the laugh of a much fatter man. It started somewhere in his stomach and positively rumbled out of his wiry frame. I ate my pho, alternating between chopsticks and the shallow spoon that you can only get in Asian restaurants. I managed to not drip too much broth on my shirt. When the soup got to be too hot for me, I bit into a chewy nime chow for a break from the heat, washing it all down with the excellent Japanese beer.

When we had finished eating, he leaned back contentedly and grunted another command. Linh brought two more beers, didn't make eye contact with me, and began clearing away the plates and bowls. "I hope you liked your pho, Andy." She had the habit of overusing my first name, the way that teenagers do when they start dipping their toes in the world of adult acceptance. I assured her I did, and she cleared everything and left.

"That was good, Round Eye, wasn't it?"

"It was." My mouth was still burning, and I was still dabbing my nose with a napkin.

"Were you in Vietnam in '75 for the fall?" Nguyen asked.

"No, I was home by then." I had watched the helicopters on the roof of what everyone assumes was the embassy, but the famous shot was really of a CIA safe house. I sat in front of the TV with a can of beer warming in my hand and tears running down my face. The Vietnam War had gone on for so long that we all assumed it would go on forever. I had thought that I could always go back if I couldn't cut it in the world. Then it ended, and I wept. I would never be able to go back to the war; I could never go home. My true home. The only place I felt that I belonged. I would never go back to being a Recon man, the only exceptional thing I had ever done. From that point on, I would always just be some guy, some shmuck.

"It was . . . *ho'o lan*"—he paused searching for the English word—"chaos." He sat across from me, looking through me to almost a decade before. The smoke from his menthol cigarette curled up in front of us. "At first, no one wanted to believe that it was happening. We thought, there is no way the Americans will let the communists have it all after spending so many of their young men's lives here. Then it became undeniable that you had abandoned us. That is when the panic started. It finally occurred to people that the NVA were coming, with tanks, artillery. They were coming, and they were going to destroy everything we knew.

"As they got closer, you could hear the artillery, could hear it getting closer and closer. Every day, more and more refugees poured into the city. Every day, more and more of our soldiers fled into the city. Each day, more chaos. Each day, more young men with short hair and civilian clothes, their uniforms thrown away, trying to blend in.

"People trying to flee, people trying to plan. Money changed hands. No one wanted piasters. U.S. dollars weren't even that popular. Everyone wanted gold or diamonds. The markets that sold them were raising prices per ounce and still getting cleaned out.

"I was lucky. I was a sailor. Not important, but lucky to be on a ship. I was able to get my family on board: wife, son, and Linh. Ship had important people on it. Important people who brought their important things with them. Papers, jewels, money, and gold. We had many who were fleeing, they had paid to get on ship. Paid everything they had. Bought gold and paid it all just to stand on deck. Some tried to barter their daughters, Linh's age, to the important men on board.

"The night of April 29, 1975, we slipped away from the pier. Saigon was burning, and the smoke was thick. We were trying to sneak out of the city to the sea. We were afraid that they would shell us or bomb us from planes. But there was nothing. We slipped down the river to the sea. We were the flotilla of defeat: rich man's yachts, navy ships that would not fight, and merchant ships like mine. Some of the ships were in such bad shape we ended up towing them to sea. We were packed with refugees and those who had been important people in government. Not the most important. They could afford to buy their way onto airplanes and helicopters. No, these were the somewhat important and the unimportant but not the poor. There was no room for the poor on the boats.

"There were stories about how we were carrying the people who were going to start the government in exile. Some thought we were going to Taiwan or the Philippines. People said we had gold on board, enough gold to start the government in exile. There were rumors that all of the gold bullion from the South Vietnamese treasury was on board. Some of the crazy fucking generals thought that we would start a counterrevolution and topple the communists. Can you believe that the same assholes who just lost a war through their greed, corruption, and bungling thought they would topple the government that had just sent them running? Assholes." He snorted.

He barked at Linh again, and this time two more beers and two cognacs arrived. The nice thing about not having a boss, a wife, a girlfriend or even a pet that cared meant that I could stay and drink with Nguyen. No chance of getting fired or dumped. Just a hangover in the morning to remind me that I am not twenty anymore.

"I stayed with the ship, the *Adams*. It was a ship the Vietnamese government was loaned from the Americans. It was an old cargo ship. What you call it? A Freedom ship . . . no Liberty, a Liberty ship. We sailed on the *Adams*. People got off the ship in the Philippines. We stay a long time there. I stay with ship because I know about engines, fixing them. Then we told ship will go to America. San Francisco, California. We will get to stay in America. In California, I am able to find some work in garage. Working on engines. The pay is small, but it is job. My wife work in restaurant. Kids go to school. We live in small apartment, kids sleep in bed, wife on couch, and daddy Nguyen gets floor or bed if no one in it.

"I find second job, washing dishes. I am always hungry, never enough. And kids, kids get most, then wife . . . then daddy Nguyen. That is why I like good food now. So long, I eat nothing or what I can get from dishes I wash in restaurant. Americans . . . you throw away good food. Waste so much."

I had been hungry before, but he was describing a type

of hunger that I would never know. I lit another Lucky and looked at him. "How did you come here, to Quincy? Seems like California would be nicer, warmer?"

"In Vietnam, in navy, I make friend. American sailor. He from here. He told me about snow. We don't have snow in Vietnam, but snow sound beautiful. Clean and nice, not like Saigon, not like panic. Snow sound . . . *bing yen* . . . peaceful. I wanted to see snow. To touch it. I wanted everything to be peaceful."

It was hard for me to picture Quincy, Massachusetts, as a mecca of peace and quiet, but compared to war-torn Saigon, it would do. Who am I to judge? He seemed happy enough. More beer and cognac arrived, and the neon light was turned off, and the door was locked.

"We come here, kids go in school, and I work. Again, two jobs. We save money and save, and I still eat last. I work down on docks for Domino sugar, unloading sacks of sugar. I work in restaurant. Wife work in factory making clothes. Kids go to school. Then finally have enough money to buy house, not big house, but ours. Then end up buying restaurant. Now, Nguyen never hungry, never have to eat last, never have to eat other people's throwaway food." He smiled and patted his belly, or where a fat man would have had a belly, but he was rail thin.

His story was like a lot of those of immigrants who came here fleeing their wars, their persecution. Not unlike my mother, the teenaged German war bride who married my father, the paratrooper, who had stayed behind after the war to be part of the occupation. Married him so she wouldn't starve or be raped by Ivan. My mother who looked at me one day when I was six and said, "I love you, *Liebchen,* but Mama must go." I heard the kitchen door swing shut on its hinges and I never saw her again.

"What did you do in war? You no sailor."

"No, I was in the army. I would try to find the NVA on the Ho Chi Minh Trail, then call in planes and artillery to kill them." We had gathered intelligence, taken photographs, and made reports. It was dangerous, so fucking dangerous, and often ended with us running and fighting for our lives. The NVA were always hunting us, and even though we were supposed to gather intelligence, it seemed like we did an awful lot of fighting.

"That sounds dangerous." He smiled. His teeth were crooked and nicotine stained, but, nonetheless, his smile was charming.

"Yes, many of my friends died. I lived." Recon, in MACV-SOG (Military Assistance Command Vietnam, Studies and Observation Group) had the highest per capita casualty rate of any unit or activity in the war.

"That is how you know your fortune?"

"Yes." Fighting, killing, and not dying when my brothers did, or even worse, they simply disappeared. I knew my fortune. I had lived. Survived it somehow. I had been cursed.

"*Trung Si* Roark." He used the Vietnamese for sergeant, more or less my old rank. "We don't choose who lives or dies. We simply act our part; some men live, some die. Men like us, Round Eye, we are like those cats outside behind the restaurant. They don't live in house. No one feeds them or is nice to them. They just scratch around. What you call them?"

"Strays. Stray cats."

"Yes. That is us. I have no more home in Vietnam. Only home here. Only family here. You, you have no home since war over. We stray cats."

Nguyen and I talked about Vietnam, the Vietnam that had been before the communists. He had been from Saigon and spent much of the war there. I had been in the northern part of South Vietnam but got to the city for R&R enough to know some of its geography beyond Tu Do Street. It was hard for most people to fathom but I had fallen in love with Vietnam. The place was exotic and had history. The women were slim and beautiful, with gentle mannerisms. It was about as far from Southie as could be.

We talked about the war and how fucked up it had been. We got angry about the politicians and the generals and we drank good cognac until it ran out; then we drank mediocre cognac. When he started to pass out with a lit cigarette in his hand, I packed him into my car and drove him home to his modest house in Weymouth.

As I drove to Weymouth the Doors were on the radio, and the Ghia bumped along the pothole-pocked roads. The jostling and rocking reminded me of the beat of the rotor blades of the Huey taking me on my first mission in-country. It was the mission that showed me that war was random.

Recon work was dangerous, very dangerous, and we all had known it. We were playing the biggest game of hide-and-seek in the world while being hunted by the best the enemy had. We were being hunted in their terrain and vastly outnumbered.

Our casualties were staggering. Sometimes, the best, most experienced trained and equipped men died. Anyone could be unlucky. Many men better than me had been killed. There was no rhyme or reason for it. It was hard to accept that you could be well armed, equipped, have the best training, and work with the best men in the business and still get killed.

I was still green, but Tony's team had been short one American. The mission was supposed to be a milk run to check sensors that the air force had dropped on the trail from the Wild Blue Yonder. A milk run . . . I wasn't old enough to realize what a lie that was.

By rights they shouldn't have taken me. I was so green I should be in comic books. Tony convinced his One-Zero to take me on the milk run to get me some training. I sat in and watched as they meticulously planned the mission. Tony and his team leader, Jim, taught me the team drills for breaking contact if we met the enemy. We practiced the Australian Peel, where a line of men meet the enemy and hit the ground. The point man fires a whole magazine and gets up and runs to the back of the line. The next man does the same but gets up and pivots to the opposite side of the man before him. Then each team member does the same, alternating which side they run down. When done fast it looks like someone is un-peeling a green, heavily armed banana. The team moved back like that, breaking contact and giving the enemy something to think about. We practiced other drills and we practiced and then practiced some more. When Tony and Jim were satisfied, we were ready, we went.

We rode in the Slicks, beating the sky, with the *WHUP-WHUP-WHUP* of the rotor. We approached the LZ and we got out and stood on the skids. The rotor was blowing humid air tinged with the smell of aviation gas in my face. I was tense, my stomach trying to fold over on itself from the inside. It was a miracle I didn't puke from the stress.

We looked at the One-Zero, he stepped off the skid into the elephant grass, and we followed. We moved away and formed a loose circle, weapons at the ready. The Slicks flew away, heading back to the launch site. We waited listening to the jungle, trying to hear any sound that might be the enemy.

Jim radioed, "Team OK." We stood up and formed up to move out . . . and it seemed like the very jungle itself opened up on us. AK rounds started pouring in on us. Whipping by my head, giving me every chance to end up on some war memorial. Grenades and RPGs began to explode. Jim died radioing the choppers to come back. He never felt the blast from the RPG or the pieces of hot metal that ripped through his head.

Rounds whipped by and hot pieces of metal cut into flesh. There were screams and I almost forgot about the god-awful heat and humidity when the coppery smell of blood overwhelmed me. Tony rallied us, organized us to start shooting back. We didn't do the Australian Peel that we had practiced to the point of boredom.

We took turns firing and moving back. The Slicks came in to pick us up when the heavy machine-guns opened up on them. The slow, heavy beat of Russian-made 12.7mm machine guns gave cadence to our flight. The 12.7mm rounds pissed through aluminum skin and plexiglass windows. Everything was moving in slow motion for me as I was firing my M-16, trying to find targets. Tony seemed to be everywhere at once. He threw grenades and rallied men. Tony got the wounded on board. I covered him when he went back to get Jim. Then he pushed me on board the Slick and we lifted off.

The bird limped back to the launch site like a prize-fighter who is still standing at the end of the fight with a much bigger, better opponent. When we touched down someone pushed a cold beer into my hand and people clapped me on the back. I looked at Tony and he looked at me. "You did good out there, Red."

"Thanks, man. Jesus. You saved my life."

"No worries, man. You'll get the chance to return the favor someday." He was right—I would. It was another memory I kept packed away in my mind full of unhappy memories.

Then I made my way back to my empty apartment. Leslie had been gone for over a year now. The hole she left in my life was more than just missing things from an apartment.

We had met at the Brattle Book Shop. The Brattle was the closest thing that I had to a church. Rows and rows of used books just waiting to be picked up and read. I had been in Detective fiction—where else would a private eye be? Leslie was a grad student, English lit, who was working on a theory that in fiction private eyes were the twentieth century's version of cowboys, who were the nineteenth-century version of the knights of old. Imagine her surprise when she met one in the flesh. She was trying to reach a book on a high shelf, and I happened to be there.

Which led to coffee and we started dating shortly after. We went to dinner and she took me to movies at the Coolidge Theater. We saw *Casablanca* there, and when Bogie punched the bad guy, everyone in the place called out, "Hit 'em, Bogie!" Popcorn flew everywhere.

Sitting in the dark, holding hands, and whispering, I felt that some part of me was being restored. I was getting something back that had been missing for a long time. Later there were nights under the covers, watching the Movie Loft on channel 38. Laughing at Chevy Chase and Goldie Hawn as an unlikely police detective and his imperiled love interest. For a time, it was good.

Then we were living together, and things had soured. She had been able to live with the nightmares and my being irritable. She had been able to put up with my coming home bruised and occasionally battered from work. She had put up with a lot of crap.

But in the end it was the long silences, my unwillingness to talk to her about it. She suspected that it was another woman. In truth it was Vietnam, the place, the war. Almost every night I was transported there in my dreams. It wasn't just the war but the parts of me that were trapped there, never able to leave, the ghosts of my friends or the memories of war. I was afraid of what she would see, looking at me, if I told her about it. I was afraid of the look on her face when she realized that I missed the war. In the end silence was safer. Then one day, there were tears and the next she was gone. I had a chance to be normal, to be happy, and I had blown it.

I wasn't so out of touch with myself to realize that I didn't want to be six years old saying good-bye to my mother all over again. Women had come and gone in my life, and I was grateful for their attention. No relationship ever seemed to turn into anything more serious than shacking up together for a while. I had never met anyone whom I wanted to worry about their leaving me. Until Leslie I had never met anyone whom I wanted to be close to, could see staying with.

I had slowly replaced most of the things she had taken with her: furniture, books, records, and things for the kitchen. There was no replacing her warmth, the gentle way she would take my face in her hands after making love. But by the end, the warmth had ebbed, slipping away from us. Then I dreaded walking up the stairs to the silence and tension that had become our relationship. Then it was over, and she had left. Another casualty of my shabby little war that no one wanted to talk about.

Chapter 3

Over the next two years, cases came and went. One girlfriend came and went, and one cat, named Sir Leominster, came to stay. I picked up a couple more scars and bruises. I would make a point of stopping by The Blue Lotus every other week if I could. Every few months, Nguyen and I would get rip-roaring drunk talking about the war and the communists. He understandably hated them, and I wasn't a particular fan of them. I was invited over for Christmas, which they celebrated as a nod to their adopted home, even though they were Buddhists. Then the Christmas after that, I was sitting in the living room with Nguyen after everyone had gone their separate ways. We were drinking cognac, admiring the small silver Christmas tree and its twinkling lights. We were talking about what we hoped 1985 was going to bring. Nguyen got up suddenly, leaving me to look at the snow outside and the lights on the neighboring houses. He came back in and handed me a small wrapped package. "Happy Christmas, Round Eye." This was a slight breach of our protocol because we got each other bottles of booze, and I had already given my gifts to the family.

"What is this?" I asked as I looked at the wrapped package in his hand.

"A gift for you." It was obviously a paperback book.

"Thank you." I took it and unwrapped it. It was a paperback copy of Dashiell Hammett's *The Maltese Falcon*. He had written something on the inside cover in Vietnamese, which he knew I didn't read.

"I read this book on ship from Vietnam. Now I know real Round Eye Private Eye." It was amazing that English was not his first language, but he effortlessly made a pun out of a racial slur.

"What does it say?" I said, pointing to the inscription.

"It says, Merry Christmas, Round Eye Private Eye, you still not rich enough to marry my daughter." He then laughed his rich belly laugh.

I was invited for Tet, the Vietnamese lunar new year. It was a big deal in Vietnam, imagine Christmas, New Year's Eve and the Fourth of July rolled into one holiday. It was such a huge holiday that in 1968 the Viet Cong attacked every major city in South Vietnam knowing that they would catch the ARVN off guard. It said a lot about how close I had grown to Nguyen's family that they invited me to their Tet celebration. I got to know Nguyen's wife, An; his son, Tuan. Tuan was a graduate student studying for his MBA. Linh was halfway through a BA at Northeastern. It was nice, after so many years in the cold, to have something approximating a family.

* * *

March in Boston is cold. People start thinking about spring, but in reality, it is more cold and wet weather. Sometime toward the end of April, spring finally shows up like a guy late for a date with his wife; he meant to be there sooner, but something came up . . . you understand? Other than making some old wounds ache, I didn't mind it. I walked to the office, dodging puddles of slush and avoiding patches of ice.

I had on duck boots from L. L. Bean and a Pendleton's wool button-down shirt that was some sort of blue plaid only a lumberjack could love. I had my Colt Commander in a holster on my hip. I was wearing my peacoat, and a silk houndstooth scarf that An had given me for Christmas. I was as prepared for March in Boston as one could be.

I stopped at the corner store across the street from my office and bought a *Globe*. There was a new coffee shop next door, and they were happy to sell me a coffee and corn muffin. I managed to cross the street without getting killed or splashed with slush. I went into the pizza place downstairs. Old Man Marconi always insists on giving me a cappuccino in the morning, even though I like my coffee black. I have learned not to argue with him.

After the cappuccino and talk about the weather and talk about boxing, it was time to go upstairs. The only sport Marconi liked to talk about was boxing. I hung my coat on the coat tree and sat down at my desk. The only messages on the machine were about people who wanted money from me and none from the people who owed me money.

I drank my now cold coffee, ate my corn muffin, and read the paper. It was the usual mix of depressing news.

British coal miners had ended their long strike. The other international news was bad. Russia still had nukes. We still had nukes. We were still pointing them at each other. We wanted to spend millions on a new type of missile. There was still a war going on in Afghanistan. The city news wasn't much better. Everything seemed to be getting more expensive. A man was stabbed in his car in Chinatown a couple of days ago. The police weren't saying much, other than it was fatal. They had no leads in last week's murder in Quincy where a Vietnamese man was shot leaving a Vietnamese newspaper that I had never heard of. Then again, I was not an expert on Vietnamese publications. The police didn't have much to say about that one either. Maybe it stood out because I had Vietnam on the mind. April was coming up, the tenth anniversary of the fall of Saigon. The end of my war.

I folded up the paper and brushed the crumbs off my shirt. The newspaper went out into the waiting room, on the table. It helped the illusion that I was so busy that people had to wait to see me. I spent the next couple of hours catching up on paperwork: bills that had to go out and reports that had to be written. I did all this while smoking a pipe of tobacco; it was a rich blend of Latakia cut with Virginia and Cavendish. I had the window cracked to let the smoke out and some cold, fresh air in.

The bell on the outer door tinkled, and I stood up. Most people called ahead, but I had the occasional walk-in. I put my hand on the Colt, just to reassure myself that it was still there. I was pretty sure that no one was actively trying to kill me right now.

She was standing in my waiting room wearing a blue winter coat that reached down to her calves. Her boots

were more practical than fashionable. She was putting a
knit wool cap into the pocket of the parka. Her hair was
black and fashionably clipped by someone who had been
well paid for it. She saw me and smiled hesitantly. She
had one of those bags that looked like a large leather
sack. She was Vietnamese.

"Mr. Roark?" I had been expecting the patois of pidgin
English mixed with Vietnamese. Instead, her accent was
decidedly California.

"Yes, I'm Andy Roark." My brain was trying to catch
up to my eyes and ears.

"The detective?"

"I hope so; it was expensive to have it painted on the
door." The bad joke fell flatter than Mrs. Sullivan's pan-
cakes.

"Yes." She dragged it out, and I was vaguely disappointed that she hadn't laughed.

She had unzipped the parka and put it on the rack next
to my peacoat. She unwound a long silk scarf and put it
over her coat on the rack. What was revealed sans parka
was an odd mix of slim and curvy. She wore blue corduroys tucked into her sensible boots and a cashmere
sweater in a shade of green that worked with the pants.
She wore no rings, and the only jewelry she did wear was
a pair of diamond earrings. She was elegant in a world
that seemed to think that women with safety pins in their
cheeks and purple, spikey hair were all the rage.

"Mr. Roark, I need a detective. I am hoping that you
are available?" I assured her I was. She held out a hand
that was long and slim. I took it in mine and felt the pressure of her fingers as they briefly squeezed my hand.

"My name is Thuy Duong." Her name could have

been Minnie Mouse, my heart would have been racing just the same. "You read this morning's paper?" She pointed at it.

"Yes." It had been almost the most productive part of my day.

"I am concerned about the murders. The Vietnamese man at the paper was my uncle, Hieu. He was a journalist, and lately he was scared of something or someone." Her lower lip trembled as she said it, and I was having unprofessional thoughts about it.

"The newspaper said the police think it was a mugging gone wrong."

"No, he was shot several times. There was no attempt at robbery."

"Okay, you said murders?" I left the question out there.

"There was a Vietnamese man stabbed in Chinatown. I do not know what the connection is with my uncle, but it seems unlikely two Vietnamese men are murdered so closely together?" I was stumped at that one.

"You don't know the second victim?" It seemed intelligent to say the obvious thing.

"No, but how could it not be related? How many Vietnamese live here in Boston? Also, how many police are Vietnamese? You at least were in Vietnam."

"Good point. Okay. I am not the police. They have lots of resources. Lots of men, labs, etcetera. On the other hand, this will be my only job while they will have to deal with every crime in the city."

"You will take the case." It is impossible to describe the way she said it or bit her fleshy lower lip, but it made me weak in the knees.

"Yes, I will." I then explained my fees and how I worked. She nodded and opened her bag and took out a large stack of cash.

"I have been traveling. I cashed some traveler's checks on the way here." She counted out ten one hundred–dollar bills and handed them to me. "If this runs out, you can call me for more." She handed me a card that said she was a language tutor. It had her number on it. She wrote out her uncle's full name and address on the back of her card. I told her I would call her when I had something. She went to the rack to get her coat. I watched as her body shifted under the cashmere sweater and corduroys as she slipped on her coat and wound her scarf around her neck. She left and the show was over.

I breathed normally again. It wasn't physical exactly. I knew that. It wasn't just that. There was something about talking to her, being around her. . . . It felt like the beginning of something that had nothing to do with the case. It was possibility. She was Ms. Unknown Variable, that tall/short, skinny/curvy woman who might offer a respite from the loneliness of a lonely life. I hadn't felt that since I handed Leslie *The Raymond Chandler Omnibus* from the top shelf in the Brattle Book Shop.

Chapter 4

Now in the movies or TV, I would call up an old buddy from the force and buy him lunch and ask for a favor. In reality, it didn't work that way. I would need to go to the police headquarters at 154 Berkley Street, inform them that I had been hired by the family, and see what they would share with me. It wouldn't be much. I would be lucky if anyone would talk to me.

Police headquarters wasn't far, and the weather was not quite Arctic, so I decided to walk. I locked up and went out into the street and the cold. By the time my eyes were watering, the tip of my nose was numb, and my ears hurt, I was standing in front of police headquarters. There were cruisers parked out front, and the building loomed above me. There were many taller buildings in Boston, but the stone and cement monolith that was built in 1920 seemed to tower over me.

I made my way in and waited my turn to speak to the desk sergeant. He was rumpled and weathered and straight out of Central Casting's request for an Irish police sergeant. He was chewing on a cigar that had gone out and looked like he impersonally hated every human being in the world. He took my card, looked at my license, and snorted when I told him why I was there.

"Son, are you having me on?" I was pretty sure that my skull would be dented by a nightstick if I were.

"No, Sergeant."

"Did Solly or one of those other limp dicks upstairs put you up to this?" I assured him I was serious and didn't know anyone named Solly or any of the limp dicks upstairs. He picked up the phone in front of him, and, looking suspiciously the whole time, dialed a number.

"McCourt here, sir. No, you are not gonna believe this. No, sir. An actual Shamus. No, sir, he says Solly isn't behind this. Yes, sir. His name . . . hey, Shamus, what's your name?"

"Roark." He repeated it, and the conversation they just had. Then he put the phone down with a bang and a "Ha."

"Captain will see you." He handed me an orange badge to pin to my coat that said, VISITOR. He flagged down some passing patrolman and told him to take me to Captain Johnston's office. The young cop motioned me to follow him, and I was reminded of my own time working for the police.

"You really a private eye? Like Magnum?" I was trapped in an elevator with him and it didn't seem the time to tell him what I thought of TV private eyes.

"Yep, except this is Boston and I don't drive a Ferrari." He laughed. "Too much slush and too many potholes."

"Also, you're too short." Everybody is a critic.

We spent the next few minutes talking about the Celtics. Then we were up in the detective bureau in front of a door that said, CAPTAIN D. JOHNSTON. The kid knocked, and when the voice inside said to come in, he opened the door, explained who I was, and ushered me inside. Captain Johnston was not what I was expecting. Instead of the usual corned-beef-and-cabbage-fed cop, he was black. Black cops weren't anything out of the ordinary, but a black captain of detectives was a bit of a novelty. When I had started on the job, Italians were considered minorities and Hispanic cops were downright exotic. There had been some black guys, but the force had been mostly corned beef and cabbage.

He was taller than me with a fastidious air about him, with hair that was cropped close to the rounded curve of his skull and shot through with curls of gray. Above his lip he had a mustache that was neatly trimmed. Johnson was well dressed in pressed gray slacks and a white shirt. The square butt of a large revolver stuck out of his waist band. Next rode a gold shield; literally his badge of office. He stuck out a hand and shook mine. He had enough self-confidence that he didn't feel the need to try to crush the life out of my hand when we shook.

He motioned me to a metal chair that looked like it was a veteran of World War II. Johnston sat down behind a desk that was a battleship. His desk had a gooseneck lamp that shone on a series of piles of papers and folders. He had a black push-button phone off to one side, and an electric typewriter took up most of the middle of his desk.

"What can we do for you, Mr. Roark?" His eyes were brown, and under the left one he had a triangular scar the size of a pencil eraser.

"I was hired to look into the murder in Chinatown and the one in Quincy to see if they are in any way related." He looked at me, his face motionless, flat as a calm sea.

"Of course, they're related. Two Vietnamese men killed in two days a few miles apart . . . how could they not be related?"

"That is my client's thinking."

"Or they are just two unlucky idiots, killed in two separate, unrelated incidents, in two different towns." Now he cocked his head, and I realized that the eye with the scar was lazy. "Why should I help you? You are just going to make a mess of things, and I will have to clean them up."

"Because I will have to investigate no matter what. Sharing what you already know means I won't go back over territory you've already covered. If I find out anything new, I would be obligated as an officer of the court to share it with you."

"You used to be a cop on this job." It was most definitely not a question.

"Yes, sir." I was wondering if it would come to this.

"I asked around. People said you were good but too smart for your own good."

"That sounds about right."

"I see." I was glad he did because I was still figuring it all out. He picked up the phone and summoned a detective with an Irish-sounding last name. The detective came in, handed him a file, and looked at me. I don't know why—I surely didn't know anything.

"Kelly, you have the Chinatown stabbing. Does anything stand out?" Kelly looked like his name implied. His suit was Jordan Marsh and crumpled.

"No, sir. It is all in the report. It was pretty straightforward. The victim, named Pham Duc Dong, was parked in his car near the Chinatown gate a little after ten at night. His car was running and in park. He was a smoker and had his window rolled down. We think he was waiting for someone. A person or persons unknown reached through the window and stabbed him once in a downward fashion through the collarbone area, severing the subclavian artery. Death happened in seconds. The blade, according to the doc, is a thin, sharp, double-edged knife. No weapon was recovered at the scene. There are not a lot of forensics to go on."

"Double-edged knife. Like a commando knife?" I asked.

"It could have been. Like in the old movies. We can check. Either way, Mr. Dong didn't bleed much."

"Mr. Pham," I clarified. "Vietnamese people use their last name first, then middle, then first."

"Oh, yeah. Well, whatever order he puts his name in, he is just as dead." Detective Kelly left the office to see about his other cases, one of which might actually be solvable.

The captain handed me the file. "You can look this over and take notes, but you can't take it with you. I am going to go get a cup of coffee. Leave it on my desk on your way out."

I read through the report and looked at the black-and-white crime scene photos. There was not a lot to be learned from it. A Vietnamese businessman from Virginia in his Mercedes sedan was killed, quickly and efficiently. There wasn't a lot of blood. The blade had severed the artery and punctured the top of the left lung. He bled out into his own lung. It would have been quiet and taken seconds. There were no fingerprints, no clues, no forensics. Just him, a pile of cigarette butts outside his car, and a neat, clean killing. To the casual observer it wouldn't have looked like much. Just another drunk passed out at the wheel.

I scribbled some notes in my notebook, made a copy of the dead man's property form and his address in Virginia. I also made a note of his business address, a suburb in Virginia that I recognized as housing a lot of people who make money from the U.S. government. Then I put the file back on the captain's desk. I took out one of my business cards, wrote my thanks on it, and left it on top of the file. That done, I made my way out of police headquarters.

I was not going to walk to Quincy, so I made my way back to the Ghia. The weather hadn't warmed up much in the time I had been at headquarters. She started with limited protest, and, after a bit, a thin stream of heat made its way from the heater to me. I took the southern artery, which brought me right to the police department. As buildings go, it was an uninspiring hunk of gray concrete and stone. It was WPA era but had none of the artistry that went into other WPA buildings: no eagles, decorative moldings; no sense of the importance of combining art and structure. Just an ugly gray box with windows.

I parked in the visitors' area and made my way inside. There was a glass window, beyond which was a clerk with permed hair and the look of perpetual boredom that they all have. She looked at the photostat of my license and ID. I told her I was hoping to talk to someone about the Hieu homicide. She told me to wait and indicated a bank of plastic chairs that looked uncomfortable and nearly indestructible. I was right about their comfort level. It only took me two of the twenty minutes that I was sitting in one to figure it out. I never had the chance to see if it was indestructible.

The door opened, and a middle-aged man, sagging around the middle, badge and gun on his hip, looked at me. "You Roark?" Resisting the urge to point out sarcastically that there was no one else waiting, I assured him I was. He held out a perfunctory hand and said, "My name is O'Brien. I'm a detective. Come on in." We walked back into an office area with the usual mix of desks, cops, and cigarette smoke. On the walls were posters of wanted people, occasionally broken up by pictures of guns.

We went to his desk, and I sat down where he indicated. He pulled out a slim folder and passed it to me. "There isn't much. Hieu Tam came here from Vietnam in 1980. He was a journalist and worked for the *Globe* as a part-time translator. He also edited a local Vietnamese paper whose name I can't pronounce. He was leaving work a couple of nights ago and someone shot him with a .380. He took four in the chest and three to the face. No witnesses, no one around. Someone heard the shots and called it in. Took the patrol guy a little while to find him."

"Was anything taken? Anything unusual or out of place? Any evidence?" I like to ask the really obvious questions.

"His wallet was on the ground, no cash. They left his briefcase, which had papers in Vietnamese, which no one here knows. Miscellaneous papers and maps, whatever those are. There was a tape recorder, tapes, a 35mm camera and film. The crime scene guys found seven .380 shell casings. The ejector left a slightly off-center mark on the casings. That was it. No one saw anything and, other than his widow, no one seems to care."

I looked at the photos. They cataloged the awkwardness of death. There were pictures of his body where he landed, contorted. His open coat, blood, and the wallet. There were pictures of his hair out of place and the permanent grimace that the pain had left on his face. The three rounds were clustered around his left eye, eyebrow, and forehead. There were pictures of shell casings and little numbered tents next to them. There was not much to be learned from the photos, and there was less to be learned from the uncaring, overworked Detective O'Brien. I wrote down Hieu's address and thanked O'Brien and I left.

I lit a Lucky in the parking lot, cupping my hand around the cigarette. I inhaled deeply. I was not exactly upset about seeing pictures of the dead Vietnamese man. It didn't exactly remind me of Vietnam . . . except that it did. It wasn't that we got used to death over there, killing, seeing people killed. It was that we had grown casual about it. It took me a while to realize that I didn't like that. There was a time that a dead Vietnamese was just a number to me.

One night, I had been on R&R and was staying at the MACV SOG compound in Da Nang. My teammates and I were on a special pass. We had snatched a prisoner. Management had been happy. We got a pass and I went to the beach, where I linked up with two old friends, Chris and Tony. That night, after a day of lying on the beach and a night of drinking, I passed out with a sunburn and head full of Chivas and Budweiser.

I woke up to the sound of explosions, communist B-40 rockets and AK-47 rounds. We rolled out of our racks in the guest quarters: huts down by the beach, the army's version of a tropical resort. A new guy, a first lieutenant, ran to the door and threw it open. AK rounds plowed into his bare chest. Tony grabbed a CAR-15, and Chris picked up a sawed-off pump and killed the VC Sapper who appeared in the open door. The blast from his grenade bundle rocked our hut and peppered it with hot metal. I found a CAR-15 and a bandolier of ammunition and grenades.

"It is a fuck-show out there." Tony was from New York.

"Sure is." Chris drawled the two words into a whole sentence in deep Alabamese.

"Fuck it." I was the eloquent one.

We were through what was left of the door. Red and green tracers, enemies in the lethal color war between communists and Americans, were whizzing by. Buildings were on fire and naked VC Sappers were everywhere. We split up. Tony said he was going to find the mortar pit and put up some illumination rounds. Chris said he wanted to go find a machine gun. I just started moving forward with no plan other than to kill as many of them as I could. The place was a madhouse, and I knew that I wasn't going to survive the night. It didn't matter. I was happy. I was simply acting, pure action. No thought. I was the freest man alive.

As Sappers appeared in front of me, I shot them with short bursts from the CAR. If I saw a cluster, I threw a grenade. I wasn't sure if I was still drunk or it was the euphoria that comes from knowing you are going to die and suddenly be free from life's worries. There is freedom in knowing your fate. I was stepping toward the battle. When my CAR ran dry, I rolled under a hut and reloaded. I heard moaning, and there was an American there. I couldn't do anything for him.

"Don't worry, pal. Help is coming. The cavalry is on the way. You will be all right." It was bullshit. His chest had rosettes where the bullets had gone in. His head was leaking, too. I was lying as much as if I had said that the Red Sox were going to win the World Series. I rolled out and found more of the enemy to kill. I was euphoric; some sort of Viking berserker rage distilled down through the generations of Irish had taken over my senses.

Then the place lit up like day. Tony had found the mortar pit and the illumination rounds, essentially giant parachute flares launched from a mortar. That turned the tide. Now guys could tell friend from enemy without having to be nose to nose with them. The element of surprise was gone, and the attack lost its momentum.

Later in the morning, when it was done and the offshore breeze was keeping the flies away, Tony and I were sitting against the sandbags of the mortar pit, my CAR-15 with its last magazine across my knees. I had a hand grenade, which I had planned to blow myself up with when I ran out of ammunition. Fortunately, it hadn't come to that. I looked ridiculous in jungle boots, skivvies, and an empty cloth bandolier, covered in sand, ash, smoke, and blood.

Tony had sported me to a cigarette. I had no idea where he had gotten a pack. We were contemplating a dead Sapper. He was wearing a loincloth, painted in charcoal and his chest stitched with bullets. His face forever frozen, wincing from the pain of the bullets I had pumped into him.

We sat together contemplating the dead gook. Me and Tony. Companionable.

"Wanna sport me to another smoke, pal? Sure, you don't mind?" I held my hand out. He ignored it. I reached into the unbuttoned pocket of the fatigue shirt and took

out the pack. I shook two out and lit them. I put one between his lips on his good side. "We're just gonna sit here
with our friend the gook and enjoy a beautiful morning
by the beach. Just like a couple of normal American kids.
Just like Cape Cod . . . well, with guns and shit, but you
know what I mean." Tony was smiling on his good side
and his face was caved in where the Sapper had shot him
on his bad side, the AK's rounds leaving a mess of his
once handsome face.

Chris came up a little while later.

"Hey, bud, come on. We gotta get you some clothes
and then we gotta *di di mau*. Come on, bud, we gotta go."
He said *bud* like it had two syllables. He was right. We
had places to go. Things to do. Our war wasn't over yet.

"Good-bye, bro. I will see you in Valhalla." Tony didn't
answer.

"Come on, man, don't do that pagan shit. Heaven,
man. He is going to Heaven." Chris was from the South,
and his god was a vengeful one.

"Yeah, but warriors go to Valhalla. Come on, we gotta
go fight Charlie." We stood up and started to walk away,
leaving our dead friend and the man who had killed him
to keep each other company.

Chris said, "Hey, man, do you think he will go to Valhalla?"

"Tony, of course. He was a Green Beret, a Recon man . . .
Valhalla was meant for guys like him. Filled with mead and
Valkyrie pussy for guys just like Tony."

"No, man, the Cong who got him. The gook, does he
go to Valhalla, too?" He was serious because nothing in
Southern Baptist Alabama covered this theological point.
I had to think about it for a minute. Nothing in my Boston
Irish Catholic upbringing had covered this either.

"Yeah. I think he does. Little Cong, he was hard. He was a motherfucker, had to be hard to zap Tony. Little fucker deserves to be in Valhalla trying to get some mead and Valkyrie pussy, too."

"Yeah, I can see that. Makes as much sense as the rest of your pagan shit."

Chapter 5

Hieu's family lived in an apartment building in Quincy. It was the same standard three-decker tenement that populated the mill towns of the Northeast. Three levels, three porches, wooden frame, filled with almost a century of near poverty and disrepair. The doorbell didn't work, and the mailbox indicated they lived on the third floor. In the cops, especially during the hot summers, it seemed as though every call was on the third floor.

I opened the door and walked in. I went up the stairs. It reminded me of a thousand tenements that I had been in. In the cops, it was to stop a fight or take a report or tell someone a loved one was dead. This time, someone else had done that. The feeling was the same. This time, I wasn't bringing them the unbearable heartbreak and grief, lives ripped asunder by devastating news brought by men in blue uniforms. Here, I was just intruding on a family's grief in order to get some information.

The building smelled the same way they always do, of poverty and hopelessness. When I was a kid, that was the smell of burnt flour, cooked cabbage, and stale cigarette smoke. Now, it smelled vaguely oily and fishy, like stale *nuoc mam*, the ubiquitous Vietnamese fish sauce that went into most dishes. Cockroaches skittered around, away from the sound of footsteps.

The landing was narrow and crowded, and the apartment was crowded. It smelled of incense and cigarette smoke. In the distance, I could hear wailing. No one here was going to talk to me even if I knew more Vietnamese than I did, and my command of Vietnamese wasn't suitable for condolences and mourning. I could say words in Vietnamese like *flamethrower* and *anti-personnel mine*, or order beer or a girl for the night. My language of death was very different from what they were speaking. I was just another awkward white guy, out of place and with no understanding of their grief.

I turned and started down the tenement steps, leaving behind a version of my own poverty experience. I had been to thousands of these apartments, people grieving after the wakes: Irish music, whiskey, beer, and cigarettes. There were always a fistfight, tears, and a relative who was hurt until the morning brought semi sincere apologies. This time, the language was different and the smell of *nuoc mam* was overpowering. It was ubiquitous in Vietnam, and I had thought that I would never smell it again. It was different in a restaurant, but here in a hot, crowded apartment house, it was too much.

I was grateful for the lungful of Quincy's freshest air. I

looked toward the ever-present Goliath and lit a cigarette. "Like you could have done any better." I wasn't far from The Blue Lotus, and the thought of a cold beer was not the worst thing in the world. I could use a dose of Nguyen's sly humor.

I navigated the Ghia through the streets of Quincy. I couldn't always see it, but Goliath was always towering above the skyline. It didn't take me too long to get to The Blue Lotus. I parked and went in, the bell on the door tinkled marking my passage. The restaurant was as warm and comforting as the first time I had been in. The smells from the kitchen were welcome and seemed a world away from the family grieving not far away.

I started toward the back. Nguyen wasn't in his usual booth. Linh wasn't anywhere in sight. I slid out of the peacoat and put it on a hook on the outside of the booth. I moved toward the kitchen; Nguyen had an office in the back. Through the round windows, I could see two Vietnamese men talking to Nguyen and Linh. I could hear over the kitchen noises the sound of angry, high-pitched Vietnamese.

I undid the bottom two buttons of my shirt in case I had to pull my .45, and then I pushed into the kitchen. I plastered a stupid look on my face and said, "Is this the way to the men's room?"

The two Vietnamese turned to me. One was average and looked like he dressed out of a ten-year-old catalog. My age, he was in good shape and had a cigarette in the corner of his mouth. He didn't say anything. The other was a teenager, maybe twenty at the oldest. He was dressed in an Adidas tracksuit, a black one. He had Adidas shell toes on his feet and a Kangol hat on his head. He looked like the Asian knockoff of Run-DMC. He started to reach into his pocket, but the other man put a hand on his arm and said something in Vietnamese. Asian Run turned to Nguyen and said something. Nguyen handed him a white envelope. Then Asian Run and Vietnamese Old Catalog Man left.

"Linh, you take Andy to table. Get him a beer and something to eat. I will join you in a minute." Linh led me out by the arm and did as her father told her. When she brought my beer, I asked her to sit down. She did with a look around the restaurant that spoke of years of having worked in it and of her parents' expectations.

"Linh, who were those men?"

"Them . . . they are gangsters. Bad men, Andy." She said it flatly. No anger, no affect, just statement of fact.

"What did they want with your father?"

"Money . . . they always come looking. . . ." She stopped. Nguyen was making his way from the kitchen. He barked at his daughter in Vietnamese, and she jumped out of the booth like she had been scalded. He sat down with me, and Linh brought him a beer. He said more to her in Vietnamese, which I took to be his ordering our dinner.

"Nguyen, who were those men? Were they shaking you down?"

"No, Round Eye, it isn't like that. They are part of a charity, a nationalist charity that wants money. They go to Vietnamese business owners, family, friends and ask for money to go back and fight in Vietnam. They want money for nationalist papers here. They are like you, sad that the war is over."

"They are shaking you down for money to fight a war we lost ten years ago? That seems pretty stupid." He smiled.

"Yes, it must. They aren't shaking me down. I believe we should fight the communists. I give them money when I can."

"But you were arguing with them?"

"No, I was arguing with the boy, because he was rude. He is always rude. His father is an important man within the Committee. Trin thinks he is a colonel because his father is."

"If they are shaking you down or threatening you, I can help. I would like to help."

"There is nothing to help with. They ask for money. I give them money. If it hurts the communists, I am happy."

"They were carrying guns?" Adidas tracksuits are comfortable but don't hide anything. Old Catalog Man had his in the small of his back.

"They carry a lot of cash; it is sensible to have a gun." The food came, and I knew that there was no more discussing the issue, not that I was making any headway with Nguyen. The food was good, *pho* with beef and *nime chow*.

"Nguyen, do you know a man named Hieu? He used to work for a Vietnamese newspaper."

"Why, Round Eye? All Vietnamese in Quincy must know each other?"

"He was murdered. I was hired by his niece to look into it. I went to the house, but they are mourning, and they are not going to talk to a white guy."

"I know Hieu. Not well, but I see him around. He didn't escape in '75. He wasn't lucky."

"Not lucky enough to be in the Vietnamese navy?"

"No, Round Eye, not lucky like me. He was arrested

and sent to a reeducation camp. He was reeducated and was able to get here in 1981. He was a good writer."

"That must have been rough." I could only imagine what a communist Vietnamese reeducation camp would be like. "What did he write about?"

"Politics. He wrote about the struggle to take Vietnam back from the communists. Initially, he agreed with Colonel Tran and the Committee, but lately he started writing articles that were critical of the Committee, critical of the struggle to free our home. People started to say that he was a communist. He lost his job. Then this . . . very sad."

"What was he writing that was so critical of this Colonel Tam?"

"Tran."

"Yeah, what was Hieu writing?"

"Hieu, when he first came here, first started writing, said we should go back to Vietnam. We should run around the hills fighting like the Cong did. Then, as he was here longer, he started to say that there was no point trying to fight the communists directly. He felt they were too strong. He started to write about needing to find a political answer, a negotiation. Hieu felt that Vietnamese people are basically like Americans. He felt we need to give it time and that we would be able to influence Vietnam to accept noncommunist government." He was saying this as though it were a bedtime story, nice to hear but total fiction.

"What do you think?" I was curious. To me, the communists had been our enemies. The Viet Cong, the NVA, were trying to kill me, and I, them. It had been very simple. They had won, and the country had fallen. It seemed impossible that after fighting such a long, bloody war the two countries could ever be anything other than hostile toward each other.

"I think Vietnamese in South are like Americans. They like good life, Coca-Cola, beer, nice things, but Northern people now in charge. They like Ho, they like Mao, Lenin . . . can't like America. Even if they could, they fight for so long, struggle for so long, they couldn't ever be friends with America again."

"So, by suggesting a political solution, he was also making people angry?"

"Yes. For Vietnamese in America, there is no compromise with communists. Anything other than fighting them is compromise." Nguyen's eyes behind his clear aviators were dark and hard, like marbles. "Here, Americans forget war, forget the dead, forget their soldiers. Men like you, Round Eye, forgotten in your own home." His voice had risen, higher in pitch, and he was angry.

"Americans try to pretend it didn't happen. At least Colonel Tran and his people don't do that. That is why I give them money. That is why people angry at Hieu. He wants us to stop fighting the communists. It was like the last thirty years never happen for Hieu . . . except he was tortured, reeducated. He lost everything. Then he come here. Wife and kids, they here. Here he have freedom. Here!"

"Was anyone angry enough about what he wrote to kill him?"

"Why would someone kill a writer for writing? That doesn't make sense. Not in America. In Vietnam, nationalists and communists would kill each other all the time—writers, politicians—but not here."

"I will take your word for it. I am sure that there are

plenty of writers at the *Globe* and the *Herald* who would love to take a shot at each other." He laughed and the tension, the passion was gone. Linh came back with noodles mixed with vegetables and meat, *nime chow* on the side, and more beer for Nguyen and me.

"Did you know the other Vietnamese man killed?"

"In Chinatown?"

"Yes."

"No. His name very common. Paper said he was from Virginia."

"I wonder what he was doing up here?"

"I don't know. Not all Vietnamese share travel plans with each other." His sarcasm was palpable, but his tone was gentle.

"No, but you don't think it is odd that two Vietnamese die in the same area around the same time, much less are murdered? This is weird. This isn't some gang thing in the projects or the Irish and Italian guys whacking each other. . . . When was the last Vietnamese murder in the state?" I didn't know because the Vietnamese community, like most immigrant communities, was insular.

"What, now I am like Quincy on TV? I figure out and solve murders? No, Round Eye, you private eye . . . you been to Vietnam . . . you figure it out." He slurped a particularly long noodle into his mouth. The noise was loud and drawn out sounding like a raspberry.

We spent the rest of the night talking about Saigon, the city he was born in and loved. We drank and talked about the war. He had joined the Vietnamese Navy before it existed; it was the French Colonial Navy then. He loved the Vietnamese Navy when it came into existence, loved the Americans who had been assigned to train and help them. His stories were hilarious and sad. We drank some more and he told me about what he had loved about his country, his home, and his beloved Saigon. He spoke about it with much more passion than I ever spoke of Southie. Many beers later, I drove home thinking that guys like Nguyen and Hieu were passionate about their lost country. I was just sad about my lost war.

Chapter 6

The next morning arrived filled with bright sunshine and the promise of spring that most people from Boston know to be little more than a cruel hoax designed to test our resolve. Up in Bangor, they expect winter to last almost to June, and down in Providence, the people were too tough to admit the weather bothered them. In New York, winter is something that makes Central Park look magical. Down in New Haven . . . well, I didn't know anyone who cared about what people in New Haven think. After all, it is home to Yale and steamed cheeseburgers.

I went through my morning rituals involving getting up, getting presentable, and making my way to the office. I was thinking of poor Hieu, his hard life and bad luck and then to come here and get murdered. Was there a connection to the man from Virginia, or was it just dumb luck that two expatriates thousands of miles from home get murdered miles apart, a couple of days apart?

Hieu had lost everything once. He had been painfully reeducated and escaped Vietnam and made his way here. He took a stance that was unpopular and seemed on the brink of losing everything all over again. I never met him, but he seemed like a guy you couldn't knock down and keep down. Nguyen was like that, too, eating out of bus trays and working two jobs, sleeping where he had to so his family could rest, get an education.

I often wondered about the people I had worked with and known. The Montagnards who had fought alongside us and then we split. Did they fade back into the mountains? Did they keep fighting? How many of them had been "reeducated"? How many had been killed? We abandoned them. There weren't many things that my nation did that I was ashamed of . . . not Nixon, not Watergate. But that, leaving the Yards to fend for themselves, was unforgivable.

The office was the same as I'd left it. I drank my coffee from the Styrofoam cup and wrote up my case notes to date on a yellow legal pad. There were a lot of question marks and lines leading to other things on the page. I was no closer to solving the case than I was when I had taken it yesterday. I was a good detective, but I had never solved two murders in one day . . . not unless there was a butler lying around to blame.

The Yellow Pages gave me an address for Hieu's paper in Quincy. It was in a strip mall not far from the shipyards. I went out to the Ghia, and as a nod to spring, I optimistically left my sweater at home. The peacoat went over the Commander on my hip.

The Ghia started as though it was under duress. Thin

trickles of warm air came out of the vent when I turned the heater on. The rock-and-roll station was playing the Velvet Underground, and the day looked pretty fine. I was feeling pretty good. There was something about being on a case, a real mystery, not just taking pictures of people cheating; cheating on their spouses, cheating the insurance company, cheating themselves. I was in my cool car, listening to cool music, in one of the coolest cities in the world. I was going to investigate something. I was going to, briefly, be productive again. I was going to feel like I was relevant again.

The strip mall was where I remembered it, and the front door of the newspaper looked familiar from the crime scene photos of Hieu. The paper's office was the last suite in the row of businesses. It was bounded by an open dirt lot where the blacktop of the parking lot ended. There was a pole with one light, and I imagined that at night the place was pretty desolate even though it was a hundred yards from the street.

I parked. The lot in front of the paper was bare except for the Ghia and one of those boxy little Hondas. The Honda was dented and rusty and made the Ghia look like a slightly less dented princess parked next to a frog. Farther down by the other businesses there were plenty of cars. It was a pretty good place to murder someone. It was a shitty place to die, but then they all were.

I tried the door, but it was locked. I knocked and waited and knocked again. After a few minutes, I saw a man approach. He was young, in his twenties, Vietnamese, with a wispy mustache. He was wearing jeans, a paisley shirt, and a blue jean jacket. If he had on boots and a Stetson, he could have been a cowboy.

"Yes?"

"My name is Roark. I'm a detective. I was hoping to talk to someone about Hieu?" My voice was raised to penetrate the glass door.

"Where is your badge?" He was understandably suspicious; it seemed like everyone was suspicious of me. It must be the mustache.

"I'm a private detective. Hold on." I dug out the photostat of my license and held it up to the glass. He appeared to study it intently. All it would have told him besides my name and vital statistics was that I was licensed by the Commonwealth of Massachusetts as a private investigator.

"All right." He unlocked the door and opened it for me. I stepped into and onto a sea of wreckage. Paper was everywhere, and it looked like everything of value that could be broken was. Someone had spray-painted "Gooks die," or words to that effect, everywhere they could. My nose twitched at the smell of dry, rancid urine.

"You're not a cop." He was looking at me with hostility. It was an occupational hazard. Someday my very presence will not make people angry. Someday.

"No, I was hired to investigate Hieu's murder by his family." I was looking around the wreckage.

"You don't look like a cop."

"I used to be one in Boston a long time ago, if that makes you feel better. Do you mind if I smoke?"

"No, what's the point?" He shrugged but took the cigarette that I offered. I rolled the wheel on the Zippo I had started carrying again. It was battered. It had my call sign and our team name on one side. It had an engraving of Vietnam on the other.

"Mike . . . who is that?" A girl emerged from a back

room. She was slim and pretty, older than Linh, but I wasn't sure how much older. Her hair was long and straight. She was wearing a sweater, red corduroys, and looked at me with unguarded suspicion.

"Thien, he is a detective. You know, like on TV."

"He doesn't look like a cop." Her suspicion was not unwarranted.

"I used to be. Now I am a private investigator."

"Like Magnum," Mike added unhelpfully, but a cigarette does buy some loyalty still.

"He's no Magnum. . . ." I was clearly too short and far too inadequate. I didn't even want to contemplate their criticisms of my mustache.

"I get that all the time. Listen, do you guys work here?"

"Yes, Mike and I are journalism students at Northeastern. We intern here." She was clearly the boss.

"Did you know Hieu?" As soon as I said his name, they both looked pained.

"He was such a . . . sweet man." She crumpled against Mike and started to sob.

"I'm sorry, they were close." He was used to holding her but a little embarrassed by the sudden intimacy in front of a stranger.

"No need to apologize. Grief right now is understandable."

"It's just . . . well, we both liked Hieu. He was . . . was so sincere."

"Sincere?"

"Yeah, like he tried hard to teach us stuff about journalism. Not writing, not telling stories but digging into things, getting facts, then turning them into a story." His passion overcame his youth, and I could see that he was going to be a real journalist, not just someone who majored in it in college.

"He wanted us to write about things that were relevant to the Vietnamese community." This was from her, and each word was punctuated by sniffles. "He said he wanted us to be great journalists . . . not good, great."

"He said any asshole could write about flowers or clothes or human-interest shit like puppies. He said real journalists wrote about stories that impacted people. Journalists were the ones who brought the truth to light for the people. They challenge governments and corruption and are the backbone of democracy." Mike looked at me almost as though he wanted to fight me.

"Was he working on anything in particular? Was he excited about anything?"

"Why? Do you think he was killed because of a story?" From her.

"I think that the police are happy that this was a mugging gone wrong. Maybe it was. On the other hand, I know that Hieu was writing things that were making the Committee unhappy with him."

"You know about the Committee?" Mike, raised his voice and started toward me. She took a step to the side.

"Yes, I do."

"You wouldn't understand."

"Wouldn't understand what?"

"What the communists are like. What they have done to our country. We need the Committee. We need to fight them." His voice was rising.

"No, we don't. They are a bunch of assholes, Mike." Her voice had lost all the weepiness. "If we are going to

beat the communists, it will be through promoting demo-
cratic ideals, like Hieu taught us: journalism, freedom of
press and expression. We already lost when we tried with
violence."

"What the fuck would this guy know. You, what did
you lose?" He couldn't yell at her, so he turned to me.

"Mike, I fought the communists. I was there when you
were just a little boy. My blood was spilled on the ground
in Vietnam. Most of my friends are dead. Please don't
lecture me about sacrifice, because I have had a bellyful
of it." I wanted to be angry but couldn't summon it. His
youth and certainty just made me sad.

"Yeah . . . where, what did you do?"

"Do you want to see my scars or should I dig out my
discharge papers? I fought the NVA and the Cong. They
killed us and we killed them."

"Yeah. All right."

"What was Hieu working on?"

"We aren't sure. He said it was big. It was going to
show what assholes the Committee were. Lately, he had
gotten secretive and disappeared for a few days."

"Disappeared?"

"Yeah, he showed up again after a few days and then
he was murdered." He crushed the cigarette butt out.

"Mike, I know you guys don't know me, but I'm a
friend. I only want to know who killed Hieu and why."

"Well, when he first started writing, he was very pro
Committee." From Mike.

"He had been tortured in Vietnam. He was angry,"
Thien weighed in.

"I can understand that. Torture does that to you."

"He started off thinking that the Committee was the

way, that they were going to finance and lead this glorious counterrevolution. They were waiting for when the time was right to strike. A crop failure. A political implosion. They were training saboteurs or training new fighters . . . but somehow . . ." Mike trailed off.

"The time was never right." I could see where it was going.

"Hieu became disillusioned. He said that they took money from Vietnamese in America. He said they stole Vietnamese money. They promised much, talked about training camps in Thailand and showed slide shows of men in camouflage, but yet the time was never right. Each Recon mission didn't bring back quite enough information."

"He started to think it was a scam?"

"Yes. He felt that if they were asking for so much from us here that they should be doing more. Then he said it was just some sort of con."

"Did anyone else think so?"

"If they did, they didn't say. It was very unpatriotic. We grew up hating the communists. Everyone had to be against them, or you were one of them. That, in our community, that is worse than being a leper or having the plague."

"When did he get labeled as a communist?" It was hard to imagine that there could be so much passion for labels and ideologies after a decade. On the other hand, as much as I had run away from Southie, no one took it from me. No one had tried to reeducate me.

"A year ago. Then he lost his job, and the paper was all he had. No one in the community would talk to him or his wife or his kids. He didn't say anything to us, but you could tell it hurt him," Thien said, her eyes shiny with tears that were waiting to come. "Imagine going through all of that and then here in the land of democracy he is painted Red and his community turns against him."

"It was bad for his family. His wife couldn't go to the Vietnamese stores, and his sons were always getting in fights in school. The funny thing was that Hieu hated the communists. He hated them more than anyone I know."

"What changed recently?" One of the most critical skills of being a detective is to know when to insert a relevant question.

"He said that he had found someone, someone he knew from Saigon. He said that he could get proof, that he would make them look like fools." Mike said it with conviction.

"Did he say what it was?"

"No, only that they, the Committee, were liars, not patriots, and that he would show them for what they were. He was going to clear his name."

"Did you believe him?"

"Yes, absolutely. You have to understand, Hieu didn't just say things. He was different. He said only things he meant. For him each word he spoke had meaning, purpose. That was just who he was."

"Do you think that is why he was killed?"

"I don't know. Hieu is killed, then your people vandalize our office. . . . Who can tell anymore?" His passion had deflated, and the moment was gone.

"My people?" I knew where he was going.

"White people. Whites did this."

"Uh-huh. Was anything taken? Or was the place just trashed."

"How can we tell? Look around you, man." Mike was in that place where anger and defeat intersect.

"Please find out who did this to him. Hieu didn't deserve this." Thien clutched my arm and looked at me with brown eyes so sincere it hurt to look into them after my lifetime of sin. I gave them each my business card and unrealistic promises, and I left them to clean up.

Chapter 7

I drove back to Hieu's house, the three-decker that they specialized in, in every mill town in New England hadn't magically transformed into a mansion in my absence. There was no crowd today. Death is like that. The mourners decrease by day in inverse proportion. You lose the most in the first day until it is just family and die-hard friends.

I stepped onto the creaking porch and rang the bell to Hieu's third-floor apartment. I heard footsteps on the stairs and then a Vietnamese woman in her forties opened the door. She was wearing black and had a cigarette in her hand. She reminded me of so much of Vietnam that I greeted her in Vietnamese without thinking.

"*Sin Chow.*"

"Hello." She dragged on her cigarette.

"I'm sorry. My name is Andy Roark. I'm a detective. I

was hoping that someone would talk to me about Hieu?"
I showed her the photostat of my license. For all that she
seemed to care, I might have shown her the top of a car-
ton of Chesterfields. I took out a cigarette of my own and
lit it.

"I am his wife. I was coming down for a cigarette. I
wanted . . . needed to get away from . . . everyone. Family and friends are all trying to say nice things, trying to
make me feel better, but, how can they?" She was not a
pretty woman, but she had presence and bearing. Her
English was accented but flawless.

"Is Hieu's family here?" I was hoping that Thuy might
be there.

"No. My family did not get along with his. We aren't
close," she said, and it seemed as though she had said it
often in the past.

"I was hired by his niece to try to find out who murdered him and why."

"I see. Why would she do that?"

"She was concerned that there might be a connection
between Hieu's murder, and another Vietnamese man
murdered in Chinatown recently."

"Do you think there is a connection, Mr. Roark?" It occurred to me that what was nagging me about her speech
was that it was educated. I had expected pidgin but instead received mildly accented Oxford. Her English had
been professionally taught. Her family had money once.
Her English was the product of expensive schools and
being taught the language from a young age.

"I don't know. That's why I'm here. I don't mean to
disturb you while you're mourning, but I am worried that
the police will treat Hieu's death like a mugging, that
they will not look at all of the possibilities."

"Why should that worry you? You did not know Hieu."

"No, I didn't, but it seems that after all that life had dealt him, he deserves better than to be written off. Treated casually."

"Hieu did not deserve to be murdered. Shot down like that."

"No, ma'am, he didn't. Do you have any idea why anyone would want him killed?" It was a question that I hated to ask but had to.

"Of course. Anyone who knew him from Vietnam who couldn't escape with him. Anyone from the Committee who painted him in a bad light recently. Anyone who believed them when they say that he was a communist."

"He wasn't a communist, was he?"

"No, Hieu hated the communists. The Committee has used that as a strategy for years. Denounce anyone, destabilize their lives, take away their friends, and Hieu was no different."

"Why did Hieu get this special treatment?"

"He wrote about the Committee. He didn't agree with their politics or actions. He didn't like that they coerced people into giving them money. He felt that they were frauds, that each year the generals got fat, the colonels got a little less fat and so on. Hieu hated watching it. He hated the way they distorted the truth, and he especially hated that they would denounce people here in America. He felt that they were doing everything that we had come to America to get away from. He wrote about it and them. They hated it."

"He sounds like an incredible man."

"He was. We met at university. Even then Hieu was . . . intense. He was the type of person you had to pay attention to. When he spoke, people stopped talking to listen to him. I was not very pretty, and I was sure no one even noticed me." She took a drag on her cigarette and I took a drag on my own. "Everyone else would talk about who should be in power: Catholics, Buddhists. . . . Everyone talked about the war. Hieu, he wanted to talk about the English language, Thomas Jefferson and the Declaration of Independence. He loved reading the Constitution and the Gettysburg Address. He said that English was the language of democracy . . . of freedom."

She stopped to cry, and I gave her a few minutes. I leaned against the post that helped prop up the porch above and watched cars drive by on her street. Most of the cars were nothing special, five- or ten-year-old metal monsters with dust and dents. They were mostly American with a couple of Hondas mixed in. Then there was a cream-colored Ford that circled the block twice, then settled in somewhere.

"I'm sorry," she said after the squall of tears had passed.

"You just lost your husband. I would be shocked if you weren't upset."

"He loved journalism. He felt that journalism was the highest form of democracy. His calling was telling stories that illustrated democracy. He was always amazed that the government in this country revered journalists. He said Watergate would never have happened in Vietnam, then or now." She dabbed at her eyes.

"Tell me about him and the Committee?" That is me, ace detective with the probing questions.

"When we left Vietnam, we were separated. I had the children. My father was an important man in the government. Not the army but a bureaucrat. When he realized the communists were getting close to Saigon, he got us out. Hieu, he stayed. He said he had to stay, to write about what was happening." She looked off in the distance, then lit another cigarette. "I was always angry that he did that. In fact, I never forgave him for staying behind when he could have gone with us. Then he was captured and put in a reeducation camp."

"That must have been hard, for both of you."

"Mr. Roark, he survived on a handful of cold rice a day. Sometimes a bowl of soup made from fish heads. Some days there was no food. For the first month they would beat the soles of his feet with bamboo sticks. The next month, they beat his arms and legs every night and day, for days at a time. When they found out he was a writer, they broke his fingers. Every finger. Can you imagine? Here, in the winter his feet would ache and sometimes they would swell.

"After a time, they would beat him every other day, then it was weekly, then once a month. After a year, they let Hieu go. Now he has no money, no family. He wandered Saigon, he made friends and was eventually able to escape. He found us here." She paused and spread her hands and arms wide for a second, then clutched them around her chest, like she was hugging herself.

"I was so happy. The children were happy. We were a family, and I had my Hieu back. He still loved me. I was so . . . so afraid he would be mad at me for leaving . . . for not going through . . ." She was starting to choke up a little.

"For not being reeducated? No. If you described Hieu accurately, he was glad that you were safe. He would have endured anything knowing you and the children were safe."

She looked at me, my face.

"Thank you. That was a very nice thing to say."

"What was it that made him mad at the Committee?"

"When he came here and started to get better, to work, he liked what they had to say. As time went on, it began to change for him. He saw them as arrogant. He didn't like the way they demanded money from Vietnamese people. He said they talked of a counterrevolution but that nothing ever happened with them. In the end, he said they were the same corrupt military that lost the war; now they were in America, the same ones who lost the war. He started to write about them and would show the world who they were and what they were about."

"I went to the newspaper, and a young man and woman there said that Hieu had disappeared for a few days before his death. Do you know where he was or what he was doing?"

"Yes. He went to Virginia."

"Virginia?"

"Yes, he went to look at boats in the James River."

"Boats in the James River, that was it?"

"No. There was a man from Vietnam that he knew and wanted to see."

"Who was the man?" I am known for my complex questions.

"He didn't say who he was, just that he knew him from Saigon. He had been a friend of Hieu's growing up in Saigon. His friend had gone into the navy. His family had been wealthy, and he was some sort of officer. He did not fight, though. He had a job in Saigon."

"Did Hieu say what this was about?"

"Hieu called it a 'river of lies' and said that he was going to untangle it. That he would expose the Committee for the frauds they are. He was excited for the first time in months."

"Where in Virginia was this man?" I was never going to be famous for the questions I ask.

"A place called Fairfax . . . wait, I have a card." She disappeared upstairs and came back down after a few minutes. She handed me a card for Global Sea Transport. The name on the card was that of the dead Vietnamese man in Chinatown, Pham Duc Dong. I thanked her and left for the cold comfort inside the Karmann Ghia. As I was turning off her street, headed back toward town, I noticed a cream-colored Ford Thunderbird bobbing up and weaving through traffic behind me.

Chapter 8

The Ghia's heater eked warmth into the car with all the efficiency of a leaky seal on a refrigerator door. I fought the clutch and traffic back into the city. I stopped at a gas station to use a pay phone. Ma Bell connected me to Thuy, and we agreed to meet near her office in Cambridge in a couple of hours. I know Ma Bell didn't exist anymore, but I liked to think she was still at the switchboard. I was comforted by continuity. I got back in the Ghia and began to nudge and bump my way up the artery.

A long time ago, the army had spent considerable time and money teaching me things like how to follow people on foot and in cars. One of the first rules of following someone in a car is to pick one that doesn't stand out. They taught us that a three-year-old car locally made—Opel in Germany, Ford in America—that was blue or black was the ticket. Ideally, you use three or four cars connected by radio.

A cream-colored Ford Thunderbird with a blue leather hardtop was not subtle. The driver wasn't trying to be. I let the flow of traffic buoy me along like a fish in a stream. Every now and then I would make a turn or do something to make sure that I wasn't being paranoid. The guy in the Ford was sticking to me and the Ghia. He stuck to me in traffic, through the city and all the way to Back Bay. He followed me down by Mass General Hospital and the city jail.

He took a left with me onto Charles Street and slid past me when I stopped and maneuvered the Ghia into a parking spot outside of a copy shop that I sometimes use. I locked the Ghia and went in. I greeted the owner and told him what I wanted. I was just going into the back of the store when I saw the Ford park across the street.

I made my way into the employee area. The owner led me by word processors, a computer, printing presses, and his office. He opened the door and let me out into the little alley behind his place. The alley led to a courtyard, and across that, another alley and then back to Charles Street, but three blocks down. The Ford was still idling where it was parked, and I made my way to the elevated platform of the Red Line.

I put tokens in the turnstile and waited for the train where I could see the stairs up to the platform. No one came, and I was blending in with the mix of students, professors, and whoever else was going to Cambridge that day. The train came and still no sign of anyone looking for me.

The ride into Cambridge is nice. You start up on the elevated portion, and you cross the Charles River, which at sunset on a nice night gets lit up fiery orange. The Red Line hurtles underground, a fast ride, until the train brakes hard to make its turn before it pulls into the gleaming, science fiction station of Harvard Square. I stepped out onto the platform. I went past the glass and concrete of the modern-looking station, up the stairs, and emerged by the kiosk selling newspapers next to the tiny shop that sold publications from around the world, just in case one needed *Der Spiegel* to go with my copy of the *Globe*.

I walked to the entrance of the Harvard Cooperative Society, known affectionately by all who owe it money as "the Coop," as though it housed chickens instead of books and necessities. The Coop was expansive. The second floor straddled an otherwise inoffensive street, which was where I popped out after looking at books for a bit. From there I went to the Asa Wursthaus. I had a quick apple schnapps at the bar to ensure that the chill was being fought off and no one was following. From there, I took a rambling, illogical route to Bow and Arrow Streets. Not far from the Harvard Lampoon, I stepped into an anonymous doorway and down into the Café Pamplona. The café was dark and packed tightly with small wooden tables. It could have been Spain instead of Cambridge.

I was able to find a small table and ordered a *café con leche*. For some reason, a cappuccino just tastes better when called by its Spanish name. Thuy came in a few minutes later and sat down at the table across from me. Across was an overstatement. The Pamplona was small and crowded and we were so close as to almost be touching. She shed her bulky coat and ordered a coffee. I started to tell her about the last couple of days. She brushed errant strands of her hair behind one ear. It felt intimate even if the subject wasn't.

"You were right. There is a connection between Hieu and the man in Chinatown." I was eager to tell her and reassure her that we weren't on some sort of wild goose chase.

"What was it?" She was leaning in, and I caught the hint of some sort of perfume. Not overdone or overpowering, something expensive.

"Have you heard of the Committee?" Her eyes were brown, and her skin was flawless.

"The Committee?" Sitting close to her in the café, I was reminded a little of Leslie. It wasn't in an obvious way. Thuy was Vietnamese and the only thing Asian about Leslie was her love of Dim Sum. It sort of snuck up on me that she was pretty, and she was smart. She was the type of woman my old friend Danny Sullivan's wife, Maryanne, would have approved of for me. Leslie had been the only other one who fit that bill.

"It is a group of crazy ex-generals and colonels running around collecting money to start an armed counter-revolution in the People's Republic of Vietnam."

"They sound . . . they sound nuts." She shook her head. Then she bit her fleshy lower lip. I wanted to bite it, too.

"I guess they are. They only operate in Vietnamese communities. Hieu was their darling as long as he was writing things that they wanted to read. Then he broke with them. He started advocating for a more political approach to dealing with the People's Republic of Vietnam. They blacklisted him."

"Blacklisted?" She was wearing lip gloss. It was subtle but shiny and mildly distracting. Her sweater was a V neck, and there were hints of lace, and I wondered what her breasts would look like. Instead, I focused on her eyes and the diamonds glinting on each earlobe. I kept on telling her what I had found out.

"They spread it around that he was a communist. The Vietnamese community turned their back on him, and his family. Can you imagine that? He suffered through reeducation camps in Vietnam. He was tortured, and then they did that to him here." I found that I was annoyed with them for doing that to Hieu.

"I can't imagine. Poor man."

"Anyway, Hieu found a man that he had known growing up in Saigon named Pham Duc Dong. Pham had been from a wealthy family. He had gone into the Vietnamese Navy but wasn't in combat. Hieu found him or got word or something that the man was from Fairfax, Virginia. Hieu went to look at boats on the James River and to talk to the man. It is the same man who was murdered in Chinatown. He was connected to a company in Virginia. Did he ever talk about his work?"

"No, we weren't that close. He was here and my family was in California. . . . Maybe that is why this is so important to me? What else have you found out about him?" She had looked down and then back up at my face.

"Not much more than I told you. I have to go to Virginia to follow up on this."

"Okay, that makes sense. I will give you money to pay for the expenses."

"Thank you."

"Andy?" She was biting her lower lip again, and I was feeling like a boy again.

"Yes?"

"You were a soldier, right? You fought in Vietnam?" She was searching my face. I was being judged, and I was sure that I would fail. My hands are not clean.

"I was, and I did." I didn't like the slight tightness in my chest.

"What did you do?"

"It doesn't matter. My country asked me to fight for it, so I did. I am lucky to be alive, and that is all that matters."

"What did you do? Lots of people were there, there were different jobs."

"I was in Special Forces, a Green Beret. The Vietnamese would consider me a war criminal if they had their way."

"What did you do? Specifically?"

"It doesn't matter anymore. It is over. That life for me is over. Now I just try to help people."

I paid for the coffees, and we each went our separate ways. I vaguely wondered if her way led to a bright apartment in Cambridge and a boyfriend. My way was leading me to a still empty apartment, excepting, of course, Sir Leominster, the cat.

No one followed me to the T-station in Harvard Square. No one got off of the Red Line with me at Charles Street, and no one followed me past the darkened alleyways as I made my way up Charles Street. I took my time but no one was following me period.

When I got to the print shop, the Ghia was listing to the left on two flat tires. The antenna was broken and someone had keyed the car. I stepped closer to look at the damage. I was so intent on the car that I forgot my surroundings. I heard a shoe scrape, leather on pavement, and someone punched me in the kidneys. My legs went to jelly but didn't buckle until the second and third shots to the kidney.

When I hit the ground, I rolled toward the Ghia and the kicks to my back and the stomps to my arms were the worst of it. The pavement was cold, and they weren't trying to kill me, because they left my head alone. My gun was under me, but it would not have been any use. From my vantage point on the cold pavement, I noticed that both the tires on the Ghia were slashed and that I didn't like being kicked in the back. I didn't like being kicked in the arms either, but it was better than being kicked in the back.

"Listen, fucker." A command. "Stop poking your gook-loving nose in where it doesn't belong. Next time, I will fucking kill your ass dead. Forget about Pham. Forget about Hieu. Forget about the paper and especially forget about the Committee." He punctuated each command with a blow to my kidneys, not enough to do real damage, just enough to hurt like hell. His voice was calm, like ordering a coffee calm. He wasn't winded; he was management. I could hear the other two, the ones who had tried to play soccer with my kidneys and ribs. They were breathing heavy. They gulped for air when they complimented each other in Vietnamese on the job they were doing.

After their footsteps receded into the night, I heard a large engine start. Like on a Ford. I retched a little, then gingerly got into a sitting position, leaning against my equally battered Karmann Ghia. We had been to the wars the Ghia and I. I found a cigarette that wasn't crushed too badly and lit it. The smoke wound its way into my lungs and calmed me down. I would have offered one to the Ghia but that would have been silly.

There was no point in taking the car. I would call the auto club in the morning. I heard a car engine revving as a car came up Charles Street. It was a big one, and I had had enough for one night. It wasn't that I minded the beating . . . but the Ghia, the princess among paupers, she was an innocent. I gingerly eased the Colt Commander out of the holster. It took me a minute, a century, a lifetime to flick the safety off.

The car pulled up and stopped. I was slowly trying to raise the pistol, which seemed to weigh ninety pounds.

"Andy, put the gun away. Oh God. Andy . . ." Thuy walked over to me. I put the gun on safe and in its holster. She wrapped an arm around me and helped me to her car. Her hair smelled nice, and her body was warm next to mine. I wanted to tell her I loved her. It was an irrational response to the beating I had just received. That tends to make me want to tell pretty women who rescue me that I love them. I usually grow out of it.

I told her my apartment wasn't far, and she drove us there. She parked and helped me, on my jelly legs, up all four flights of stairs. The apartment was the same. The cat, Sir Leominster, meowed incessantly at me. She kicked at him faintly. He backed off only after more accusatory meows.

We got my coat off. I was able to get my pistol off and put it away in the bedroom. I wanted to lie down and sleep. She insisted that I go with her to the bathroom. She peeled bloodied and dirty clothes off of me with the efficiency of a combat medic. She ran her hands over me in the least sexy way a woman has ever touched me. She didn't say anything about the state I was in.

She ran a bath in the old clawfoot tub and guided me into it. If I had anything left in me, I would have screamed when the hot water touched me. Instead, I slid in and gritted my teeth. She left and came back without her coat. I momentarily forgot about my bruised body as I watched her walk. Thuy was carrying a large glass of neat whiskey.

"Drink this. It will help. Nothing is broken. You will be sore, and I think your kidneys and ribs are bruised." I took a big sip of the whiskey.

"I was hoping our first date would be more romantic." She smiled at me a little uncertainly. I have that effect on women; they are uncertain if I am a good bet or not. Usually they err on the side of caution and I go home alone. "Oh, you must have hit your head, too. Did they say anything?"

"They told me to drop the case and to stop having Vietnamese friends."

"Oh." Her eyes widened comically. "So, what will you do now, Andy?"

"I am going to go to Virginia. That is the next step. I need to know who Pham was, who he worked for. There must be some clue as to what Hieu found."

"Do you think it was important?"

"Yes, he thought whatever he found was the key to this whole thing."

"That is very important."

"It certainly was to Hieu." He had died for it.

"What was he looking for?"

"I dunno. His widow said he was looking for a boat."

"You aren't in much shape to go to Virginia by yourself."

"I'll be fine."

"I don't think so." She proved me wrong by helping me out of the bath and into bed. She brought me more whiskey, and I almost spit out a mouthful of it when she shimmied out of her jeans. She had fantastic legs, and her sweater didn't come down far enough to be discreet. She slid into bed next to me. Her bare leg was smooth and impossible to ignore against my own.

"I am not in any condition to be romantic." I wasn't— between the bruises on my head and the whiskey I was feeling a little out of it.

"Oh, I am not worried. But there is only one bed and you are in no condition to sleep on the floor." She was right. I wasn't in any shape to do anything.

I concentrated on trying to finish the whiskey, all too aware of her next to me. Her fingers were tracing my old scars: the AK-47 wounds, the shrapnel marks. I shouldn't complain. Women—I hadn't met one who wasn't fascinated by the scars. I hated them. She pushed and probed with her fingers; the map of my war written on my body. It left out diseases, dysentery, and the profound sense of loss I felt for my friends. Years of bad dreams, night sweats, and wondering why I lived when better men than me hadn't. She listened, fascinated, as I answered each question she asked. The whiskey and exhaustion were better than truth serum.

"Were you drafted?" Her face, not far from mine. Uncomfortable eye contact and the smell of sex and perfume.

"No. I volunteered. My country was at war, and I wasn't doing anything . . . anything that was making a difference." It seemed silly trying to explain years later. I woke up one day and felt like I was wasting my life. I was on a one-way ticket to the rest of my life in Southie, in a mill or as a criminal. I had heard rumors of a whole wide, exotic, exciting world out there. Also, other kids were being made to go. Their lives, their promises, their potential weren't any less than mine.

"You volunteered to fight in an immoral war? Was it worth it?"

My answer was more whiskey and a noncommittal grunt. How do you explain it?

"You saw a lot of combat." Slim fingers, pushing and prodding the scar tissue on my body and my past.

"Yes." Recon work was, ideally, boring. You got in and out undiscovered. A good team leader, known as a One-Zero, would plan it that way. Usually there was some sort of contact with the enemy, gunfire, and the tape you placed on the muzzle of your weapon to keep moisture and crud out of the barrel was shot off. When I had been a Cherry, a Greenie, watching guys come and go while I was being trained and quietly assessed, I secretly wanted to be one of those guys who came back from a mission with the tape shot off his muzzle. How I ached to be the guy on the landing pad, to have someone thrust a cold beer into my hands and pound my shoulders for coming back alive. Then it happened, and after a while, I wanted nothing more than to come home with the tape still intact.

"Did you like it? The war, the killing?" She was holding my face in her hands.

"The killing, no. No sane person likes that. The war . . . it isn't that I liked it. It was the only place in my life that I felt I belonged. I was good at what I did. It was the only time in my life that I felt that . . . felt important. Also, for the first time in my whole life I had brothers, a family." It had never occurred to me that what I had been desperate for as a child had been provided for me by the army, the war.

"Were you an orphan?" Her hand was lazy, turning on my chest, among the scars, burns, and hair.

"My father was a solider, a paratrooper. He stayed in Germany after the war as part of the occupation, because Europe fascinated him. He loved the art, the literature, the architecture, and the culture. He was from South Boston, born and raised. His world was summed up by several square blocks: the mill, the church, a library, and Fenway Park. Even bombed-out Europe with its piles of rubble was more exotic and interesting than home.

"His father came over from Ireland by way of New-foundland. Grandpa became a citizen after he joined the army and was sent to fight the Germans during the First World War, minutes after his feet touched the docks in Boston. Grandpa came home from the trenches, and life in the mill, the block, the church . . . all of it seemed pretty good. My father didn't much like the mills, but it was work when a lot of others didn't have any. Then the war came, and he volunteered to jump out of airplanes. He had wanted to be a writer; write poems and stories about the things he saw. The war was his chance.

"He met my mother at a museum, or what was left of one. She was young and pretty, a teenager, really. She had blond hair and green eyes. He said she was so hungry and skinny she reminded him of a stray cat. He was twenty-eight, a sergeant, and had chocolate and cigarettes. They got married and then moved home to South Boston. He went back to the mills. Then, a few years later, I was born. Then, when I was six, my mother left. Then, it was just Dad and me."

"Why did she leave?"

"Ah, that is one of the great mysteries of my life. Who knows? I am sure she had a good reason. Maybe she was more like Dad than he could have guessed. Anyway, I ended up in the army and Vietnam. Vietnam seemed better than life in Southie, working in the same mill as my dad, having kids and dying in the same few square blocks. The cycle of life for us. So, like my dad I ran off to war to get out of the neighborhood." She had lit us both cigarettes, and I still had some whiskey to finish.

"Andy?"

"Yeah." Andy Roark, intellectual conversationalist.

"We should take the train to Virginia."

"Why the train? It will take all day."

"Because the men who did this to you"—she accentuated her point by pushing on a bruised rib and listening to me grunt and inhale sharply—"will be looking at the airport or the bus station. They might be watching your apartment." Her point was good.

"Why won't they watch the train station?"

"There are two, and the T feeds into them." She was right.

"That is pretty sharp thinking."

"Well, no one beat me up tonight . . . well, not even you." She giggled and smiled into her fist.

"Ha . . . don't make me laugh. It hurts." It reminded me of lying in bed with Leslie, talking, joking around, moments that were more intimate than lovemaking. I drifted off wondering what the rest of it would be like with Thuy.

That night, the dreams were simple. I was back in Vietnam, in the mist, on a paddy dike. It was quiet. I was alone. My team was missing. I was missing. I had the

Swedish K gun with the huge silencer. I was crouched down, and when a Vietcong came running down the dike at me, I emptied the K gun into him. He kept coming and bayonetted me, again and again. Then, at the other end of the AK was Thuy, laughing at me. I woke up sweating and aching. She was curled on her side away from me, snoring softly like a cat.

Chapter 9

The next day, the sun woke me up. The smell of coffee in the kitchen was welcome, and if I could have moved right away, I would have. It took a few minutes to get sore muscles to respond to the commands from my brain. I winced and got up to make my way to the bathroom. The pinkish urine in the bowl was not surprising giving the work they had done on my kidneys. I managed to brush my teeth without hurting anything, but only just.

I went into the kitchen, and my heroics were rewarded by the sight of Thuy. She had made coffee in the stovetop espresso pot that I picked up when I last had a girlfriend. I had just read *Serpico* and thought that it would impress her if I knew how to make espresso.

"Good morning." I didn't want to say anything, because she was lovely to watch. She moved around the kitchen on light feet, like a dancer. Her movements were precise and elegant.

"Andy, you are up. Good." She smiled and pushed strands of her dark hair back behind an ear. Her smile, if the advertisers could get their hands on it, would have sold toothpaste by the ton.

"I tried to make breakfast but . . . you don't have much?" She frowned and then shrugged.

"No, I usually don't have breakfast here."

"Well, I hope coffee and toast will do."

"Perfect." Black coffee, toast, and cigarettes. I can think of worse breakfasts to share with a pretty lady. We talked about her family. They had come here before the fall of Saigon, the end of the war. Her father was a doctor and her mother a housewife. They moved to California and, with some effort, her father was able to practice again.

After breakfast, I used the telephone and arranged to have the Ghia towed to my garage. I had done some work for the owner concerning a daughter making bad life choices. He agreed to fix the tires and replace the antenna, then would park it outside my place. I offered to pick it up, but he wouldn't hear of it. "You need a body buried; you call me. I gotta shovel." The bad decisions had revolved around heroin and a would-be pimp. I thanked him.

The next call was to Amtrak. I listened to the schedule options and weighed the countersurveillance issues against how much extra time it would take me to move around in my current state. Also, I figured a day to travel, a day or two in Virginia, and then a day back by train. Thuy needed clothes, and we agreed to meet on the ten-o-five, which would get us into DC in the early evening. She was going to get on the train at South Station, and I would get on at Back Bay. We would meet in the club car closest to the front of the train.

I packed my faithful postman's bag with changes of clothes, a pint of bourbon, a couple of packs of cigarettes, my shaving kit, a box of .38 hollow points, and a Spenser novel by Robert B. Parker. It was raining, so I put the trench coat on over my jean jacket, which was over a blue oxford shirt and khaki pants and good solid walking shoes from Bean's.

In the right-hand pocket of the trench coat, I stuck a Smith & Wesson Chief's Special, loaded with 125 grain hollow-point bullets. It was a light round but that made up for the short barrel of the snub nose. This one was blued, that deep Smith & Wesson blue, with a five-shot cylinder and an abbreviated hammer. It wasn't a .45, but it was a lot easier on the tailoring and was well hidden. Also, I didn't relish the thought of the Commander digging into my side for eight hours on the train, given the state of my ribs. In the left pocket of my trench coat, I put a speed loader with five bullets and another one in the front left pocket of the khakis. My Buck knife went into the front right pocket.

I locked the Commander away in the safe and put out extra food for Sir Leominster, who looked at me accusingly and meowed for a solid five minutes. I rubbed him under the chin. I locked up and made my way downstairs. The cream-colored T-bird was parked across the street. I turned left and headed toward the office. By now, they must have another car involved. I walked slowly, staying on large, open, well-traveled streets. It took an effort of will not to clutch the .38 in my pocket. I do not like getting beaten up. It brings out emotions in me that are uncomfortable: fear, anger, violent rage at those responsible. It fucks with my sense of Karmic balance.

I eventually found a T-stop and put the tokens in and caught the first train. I spent the next half hour riding the color-coded T around. Red Line to Orange Line to Green Line, flirted with the Blue Line but those days were over for me. I ended up taking the Orange Line to Back Bay. I was running away via railroad rainbow. If I was being followed, they were James Bond good. Even I was confused when I paid the Amtrak agent for the trip to DC.

She found me sitting in one of the booths of the dining car. Apparently, the phrase "club car" went out with the movie *Strangers on a Train*. Although the Amtrak trains looked like wingless Boeings, I still loved the train. I could ride for hours just staring out the windows, imagining all the stories, the little private dramas, happening as we whizzed by.

She was wearing the same jacket, and her giant handbag was accompanied by a sensible canvas duffel bag. I had discreetly moved the .38 into the inner pocket of the jean jacket, and the trench coat was flopped over my bag. She threw her bags on the seat and slid into the booth.

"I didn't know if you were going to make it." Her eyebrows knitted into a cute frown.

"I am an ace detective—it was just a matter of switching trains a lot." For some reason I wanted to show off a little. She sat across from me. It was nice, like a date or something. We rode on the train, talking about the things you talk about on first dates. Massachusetts turned into Rhode Island, whose two stops, Providence and Kingston, passed in the blink of an eye. Then we were sliding through Connecticut. Unlike driving through Connecticut on the highway, it was nice by train.

Somewhere in Connecticut, we put the dining car to the test. A prepackaged tuna salad sandwich for her, the kind that was cut in half and came in a triangle of plastic. Being the all-American type, I went with the cheeseburger, which was microwaved and chewy but not exactly bad. We both washed it all down with cans of Coke. We paused in New York, then New Jersey slid by, Philadelphia was a stop, Delaware and Baltimore, and then we pulled into the new Union Station in Washington, D.C.

We made our way past the neat shops and ignored their offerings. We moved past homeless, who stood in stark contrast to the shops and the people in suits. Both wanted money but some weren't in a position to earn it, others were. We made our way out to the taxis. We found one and told the driver to take us to the Hay-Adams. It was expensive, but Thuy didn't care. It was her money. As the cab wove a circuitous route to it, Thuy looked out the window at the city in awe.

"First time in Washington?" I asked.

"Yes, but I think I love Washington, District of Columbia." She was smiling, and her eyes were bright.

The Hay-Adams is an impressive edifice. It screamed of a time when wood paneling and marble weren't extravagances but expectation. Based on their commitment to wood paneling, large swaths of Virginia forest had been cleared to feed the hotel's need. It spoke of Rockefellers and Roosevelts, the diplomacy of expensive whiskey and cigars. The driveway and entry made every girl, even Vietnamese girls from California, want to be princesses. It made me briefly wish that I was worthy of a set of army dress blues, my pile of ribbons, and a sabre. Even I wouldn't mind a turn at being Prince Charming. A chance to show off a little.

We went through the process of checking in. The desk assured me that they could have a rental car there for us in the morning. They had maps on hand for the asking, one of the city and one of Virginia and Maryland. For what the Hay-Adams charges, I wouldn't have been surprised if I could have ordered a hit man from the front desk. I am sure someone tried it once.

The room was a single. Thuy held my hand at the front desk and there didn't seem to be any need to discuss our accommodations. Our room was elegant and tasteful. Wood paneling, nice art that wasn't quite museum quality, and a four-poster bed big enough that the marines could have landed helicopters on it if it were floating at sea. The floor was wood with real Persian carpets instead of synthetic wall-to-wall. Our room had a color TV in an armoire and a fireplace that I was pretty sure hadn't seen a fire in decades. There were two antique love seats in case the overstuffed armchairs by the fire weren't good enough. I hadn't been in a hotel this nice, regal, or tasteful since my fateful trip to San Francisco two years ago.

We showered and never made it out for dinner. We were not tasteful nor elegant in our efforts. In the end, we were a hot sweaty mess, and the room looked like a bomb had gone off. The effect was only heightened by the smoke from our cigarettes. Room service brought food, and the mini bar provided lots of booze. If I thought that Thuy was going to go easy on me because of the beating I took, I was dead wrong. She turned out to be a woman of appetites. I was lucky there was whiskey and Anacin.

We woke up the next morning. The sun was streaming

in, and if the weather couldn't make up its mind in Boston, in Washington, D.C., it was without hesitation sunny and warm. We showered and ate breakfast in the hotel restaurant. The food was excellent, and the love of wood paneling extended to the columns in the restaurant. It made me wonder if the architect really hated trees, hated them to the point of a vendetta. Then we collected our rental car and maps and headed for Alexandria. We decided that we would try the widow first, and then go to the company that Dong had worked for.

We found the street on the map and made our way out of the city proper and into the suburban sprawl that was its extension. We made it to Alexandria after fighting Washington's perpetual traffic. We found the house, after a few wrong turns in a series of neighborhoods that all looked the same containing houses that all looked the same. The one we wanted was at the end of a cul-de-sac.

We parked on the street and went to the door. We rang the bell, and after a few minutes, a Vietnamese lady opened the door. She was dressed in a dark pantsuit, some color that wasn't really blue or black, and a cream-colored blouse. She had a piece of amber jewelry pinned to her lapel that had the quiet, tasteful qualities of truly expensive things. We introduced ourselves, I showed her a photostat of my license, and she invited us in.

"Ba Pham, I would like to express my condolences for your loss and apologize for bothering you while you are in mourning."

"You are from Boston. I am not sure how I can help you." Her hands were small and neat as she directed us to sit in the living room. "Coffee?"

"Yes, please." She slid away to the kitchen and came back a few minutes later.

I took the time to look at the pictures in the living room. They had the usual pictures of children and family portraits, but in one area was a picture of a young Pham in a navy uniform. There were others, and then one caught my eye. It showed the same man standing next to a man in a Vietnamese Navy uniform, wearing mirrored aviator sunglasses. They were facing the sun and something glinted on his chest above his ribbons. There was another man in the picture who wasn't in uniform but was in a madras shirt and had long hair. The man with the madras shirt was a young Hieu. Mrs. Pham came back into the living room with a tray with cups of coffee, cream, and sugar. We all sat down. I took my coffee black, but Thuy took hers with a lot of cream and sugar.

"How do you think I can help you, Mr. Roark?"

"I think your husband's murder is related to Thuy's uncle's murder." I laid out the trail of breadcrumbs that had led us to Virginia. "I am hoping that I can find something that connects them. I just don't know what it is."

"I still do not see what my husband has to do with this?"

"Hieu had contacted him. How did your husband know Hieu? He had your husband's name and the name of the company he worked for."

"I see. They were friends in Saigon, what the English would call schoolmates. They went to the same lycée and *école*. There were a group of them that went to school together and then ran around Saigon when they were young. Then the war moved closer and closer, and they grew apart."

"When did you come here to the United States?"

"We left Saigon the night before it fell. My husband was an officer in the Vietnamese Navy. He was young, but he was well thought of and gained rank quickly." She was smiling at the thought of his career or perhaps a time that was not, a decade later, ancient history.

"What did he do in the navy?"

"He dealt with logistics, moving supplies but at a high level. They sent him to American military schools. He had a good understanding of what it took to move large amounts of cargo around the world. The Americans adored him. He helped them with moving freight. He brought much war material into Vietnam for the war."

"What did he do when he came to America?"

"He was hired by an import/export company. American friends who thought well of him from the war. His knowledge of shipping was a large help, also his knowledge of Southeast Asia. His company does work with the government."

"I see. Was he involved in anything else? Was he active in the Vietnamese community here?"

"He was active in the Committee to Restore the Republic of Vietnam."

"The Committee?"

"Yes."

"What was his role with the Committee?"

"He was very important, very senior. He helped move the gold out of Saigon."

"Gold? What gold?" Few things pique a man's interest like gold.

"Well, when we were evacuating Vietnam . . . we weren't going to leave the communists our gold." She said it like I was the slow kid in class. "We took it with us, on the ships that fled Saigon, the night before the North arrived. It took days to load them. It wasn't just gold, but that is what my husband wanted to protect.

They were going to need it to start a government in exile. He was trying to protect the dream of our Vietnam."

"That was what funded the Committee? Gold?"

"Yes, I mean, there was a lot of it. Gold, U.S. dollars, lots of it."

"Blended to fit in with a convoy of refugees."

"Yes, so that one day, one day, the Committee could raise an army, and go back and destroy the communists. My husband was an important man." We asked her more questions but, ultimately, we just went in circles for a few more minutes. She didn't know anything more or she became lost in the narcotic-like memories of her husband as much as the Valium she must have taken. We thanked her and left. We sat in the parked car in the sunny Virginia morning. It was spring in Virginia—birds chirping, plants blooming—and I didn't notice any of it.

"Andy, how much gold do you think she is talking about?"

"I don't know, Thuy. How much could one country have in its treasury ten years ago? That is even if it made it here. . . . They stopped in a lot of friendly countries along the way. Hieu was looking for a ship here. Pham was here. The navy has a presence here as well."

"Do you think it was the ship with the gold?"

"What else could it be?"

"Let's go find Global Sea Transport."

Chapter 10

Virginia in March is the very opposite of Boston in March. In Virginia, it was slowly warming, there were buds on some of the trees, and the daffodils were bright yellow. The air held the promise of warm summer days to come, of dogwoods and cherry blossoms. The one rainstorm had come and gone with little fanfare. Virginia hadn't felt the need to punish us for hoping for spring.

We drove through suburban Virginia, home to all of the bureaucrats and spies who kept Washington, D.C., running, with the windows lowered, which you would only do in Boston at this time of year if you had a burning desire to fill your car with slush. We smoked, and the tendrils whirled out the window like Chinese dragons. We talked about gold, Vietnamese gold. We tried to guess how much the Vietnamese treasury would have been worth then and now.

Global Sea Transport was in an unremarkable suite in an unremarkable strip mall that was just off the highway. If it were a car, it would have been a Ford Escort. Feeling paranoid, I took a couple of turns through the parking lot. I was thankful for the .38 poking me in the side. I parked a few spots away from the door. I got out of the car stiffly.

"Are you all right, Andy?"

"I'm okay. Feel like a million bucks." I was good at bundling my lies together.

We walked to the glass door that seemed like it belonged more to a convenience store than an import/export business. It was tinted, as many were; the sun in summertime Virginia could be as unforgiving as winter in Boston. The door was locked, but there was a sign that told us to ring the bell for help.

After a time, the door was opened by a heavy man who had a face like a canned ham. Pink, fleshy, and didn't have a lot going for it. He had a blond crew cut, sunburn, and blue eyes. I wanted to call him Hammy. He was thick, running to fat, and wore a blue suit that I was pretty sure was made of special NASA-designed space age fabric. His tie was a combination of tan and gray striping that was wide and had been new at the end of Jimmy Carter's presidency. He was wearing black wingtips on his feet; "low quarters," we called them in the army. The toes were polished to a mirror shine, and I was sure that Hammy spent his youth in the service of Uncle Sugar. I could relate.

"Hey there, can I help y'all?" His accent south of the Mason Dixon line.

"Yes, we were hoping to come in and talk about imports and exports." I tried to sound Southern. I have to believe that my mustache helped.

"From Asia?" he said, looking at Thuy.

"Is there any other kind?" Then I did my best guffaw.

"C'mon in. Y'all want some coffee? I'd offer y'all some doughnuts, but the danged Krispy Kremes just don't last around here." He showed us through a waiting room that was so generic that the Ficus trees couldn't tell each other apart. The carpet running throughout was a unifying theme of nausea-inducing burnt umber. He showed us into a wood-paneled office with pictures of ships and planes on the wall. Here and there were pictures of men in uniform. Vietnam was prominently featured. We sat in chairs that were chrome and leather and designed by someone who knew nothing about comfort. His desk had a nameplate that said JEFFERIES. He had a pen set, what looked like a framed family portrait, a brass letter opener that looked like a knife, and a solid crystal globe a little bigger than a baseball. He had a phone with a lot of lights and buttons across from me.

"What brings y'all in here to Global Sea Transport?"

"Well, we're looking for a boat. Something good size. A friend of ours told us to look at the James River and told us Global Sea Transport was the place to go." Thuy seemed content to let me do all the talking.

Hammy looked confused for an instant. "A boat, on the James River? For what? Mister, we don't deal in pleasure craft."

"No, we are looking to do some importin' and exportin' from Asia mostly, some from Asia Minor if business is good." I was Southernizing my voice. There was something about Hammy that was annoying me. He screamed military officer, and it was irrationally triggering my irrational dislike of authority.

"Well, sir, we can help you with a boat. The James is

only navigable to oceangoing vessels from Richmond on down. We mostly lease ships and planes to facilitate international commerce. Depending upon your needs we can set you up with some inexpensive options. What are y'all—" He was interrupted by the phone ringing. "Excuse me, my girl, Doris, is at lunch."

He was making a lot of "yes" and "aha" noises into the phone while turning. He would glance at us then away. He said into the receiver, "Yes, he is." He started to open the middle drawer of the desk. I leaned forward in my chair, and we made eye contact. I shook my head from side to side. He looked at me and stopped. He said goodbye and hung up the phone. He carefully put both hands on the armrests of the chair.

"I am thinking that before the gun in the drawer cleared the desk the letter opener would be in my subclavian artery." That was a very specific way to kill someone, but it seemed to be following me from Boston. It was a technique taught to OSS (Office of Strategic Services) commandos in World War II because it was fast and efficient.

"The paperweight, into your forehead. Not the temple. I don't want to kill you, but I don't want to get shot, either. What is it—a .45 or a Magnum?"

"Magnum, a Ruger .357. It's heavy, and you are faster than me. . . ." It wasn't a question. We had just been there, and he had his answer. The fight had been decided when I shook my head.

"Yes. You shouldn't keep it in the drawer."

"It digs into my side when I am sitting. I wasn't expecting you, Mr. Roark. My colleagues just called me to tell me that I shouldn't have answered the door."

"They called just to tell you they told you so. Look, we are just here investigating two deaths. We aren't looking for trouble, and we are no threat to anyone." He laughed, short little barking laughs that didn't make me like him any better.

"Mr. Roark. We know you. We know you intimately. You are actually a very dangerous man. You know it and we know it."

I shrugged. It seemed like he and I spoke the same language, learned in the same schools. "Okay. Well, tell me about boats on the James River and Global Sea Transport."

"We arrange for transport of cargo mostly to and from Asia, South and Central America. We facilitate the movement of cargo that U.S. government would like moved but doesn't want just anyone to move. If necessary, we can supply ships and planes."

"Shit."

"Yep."

"Air America, except now Sea America, too?"

"Something like that. Except we are a private entity that has one client."

"You guys were supposed to have closed up shop in 1976."

"Sure, I heard that, too. I also heard that every December a fat guy shimmies down chimneys all over the world to bring kids toys. Don't make it true." He had gone all Southern and folksy.

"What did this have to do with Hieu?"

"Nothing. He was an annoyance but not our annoyance."

"And the guy in Boston, Pham . . . he was your guy?"

"Yes, Pham knew shipping. He knew Southeast Asia. He had been very helpful to us in Vietnam, especially at the end." Suddenly the pictures on the walls were making more and more sense. They were pieces of a jigsaw puzzle, but only pieces. Some of them showed rows of cargo ships, Liberty ships lashed together. Some of them showed Jefferies in Navy khakis, arm and arm with two Vietnamese Navy officers. One was dead in Boston. One was wearing mirrored aviators and something reflective on his chest.

"Shit. You knew him."

"Yes. God help the son of a bitch who murdered him, if I get to him. If you find out who . . . I would appreciate it if . . . Pham . . .we were shipmates, friends. We had a lot of miles together. . . ." He trailed off. I knew what he meant. His friend had survived the war only to be murdered in America. It wasn't fair . . . but death rarely is.

"There is a mothball fleet on the James River?" I pointed to the pictures.

"There is. Mostly rusting hulks from two wars ago. All of it about as exciting as a bowl of soggy cornflakes." He looked at me, and I knew that was as far as it was going to go. I tried, but, in the end, all he said was, "I have nothing left to say to you. Go back to Bahhsstin, Mr. Roark; Virginia isn't for you. Go back and find out who killed my friend." Thuy and I left.

We consulted and found that we should head back to the city. It would be too late for lunch, but a drink and early dinner might be nice.

"Andy, what is Air America?" The way she said it made me feel old. Her generation didn't care about the war. To them, it was ancient, embarrassing history. It reminded me of the old joke where the punch line is, "You mean Paul McCartney was in a band before Wings?"

"Air America was a CIA operation. It was an air transport wing that they developed in the fifties to help out

Chiang Kai-shek. It was called Civil Air Transport then. But in Vietnam, it was used to fly resupply missions or cargo missions that were secret, and the U.S. Air Force couldn't do them."

"They still exist?"

"Yeah, I am pretty sure they do."

"Andy, what did he mean when he said you were dangerous . . . that he knew?"

"He was referring to the war. He was there, too. He was in some advisory or clandestine position. He was telling me that he knew what I had done in the war."

"What did you do in the war?"

"I did Recon work in Special Forces."

"Recon?"

"Yeah, short for Reconnaissance. My job was to go up to the Ho Chi Minh Trail and spy on movements and report back. It was very dangerous, and many times we had to fight our way out."

"Oh . . . did you kill . . . kill many men?" Her eyes were big, and her lower lip was quivering.

"I don't know. I killed men. It was a war; they were trying to kill me. They killed a lot of my friends." This was not a conversation I wanted to have with a pretty Vietnamese girl, winding our way through the streets of suburban Virginia. There was no way to explain it all.

"Was it bad?" It was a question that was impossible to answer. No one wanted to talk about the war. Despite *Magnum P.I.* being on TV or the occasional movie about paralyzed vets, America wanted to forget Vietnam the way you want to forget having a one-night stand with a girl your buddy is now dating. You all knew what happened, but no one wanted to talk about it. When someone did ask about it, they didn't really want to hear the answer. Women, they always asked me if it was "bad." Nobody wanted to talk to a vet or to admit that they had spit on us or called us baby killers.

"It wasn't good." That was only partly true. I had loved Recon work. It was exhilarating. I was good at it. I felt alive. It was a giant, deadly game of cat and mouse. It was the only thing in my life that I had been exceptional at.

The problem was that as the game went on, I noticed that the faces of my friends kept changing. Guys would get killed or go missing, and new guys would show up. It wasn't just that the old hands were disappearing, but new guys were, too. Recon had a ridiculously high casualty rate. Each loss took a piece out of me. Then, one day, I realized that there was no one left that I started with. . . . Then I wondered when I would buy it. When was it my turn to go to Valhalla? When you start thinking like that . . . then it is over.

We were making our way back into the city. The afternoon was giving way to early evening, and we were contemplating food. We were passing all of the monuments when she said, "Have you been to the memorial?"

"The Lincoln Memorial?" I could hope.

"No, the one from your war. The Vietnam Memorial."

"No." In 1982, when the memorial was dedicated and opened to the public there had been a big push to get the Vietnam vets to go. I thought about it, but I couldn't bring myself to go. I couldn't stand to see my brothers' names on that wall. I still couldn't understand why their names were on it and not mine. They didn't deserve to be killed any more than me and I didn't deserve to live any more than them.

"We could stop there. It is close."

"No thank you."

"Why not? You should see it. It celebrates your war dead."

"No. I am all set with that."

"But . . ."

"No. I don't want to go, and I don't want to talk about this anymore." My voice had steel in it, and I had not heard that version of it since leaving the army.

Later that night, we tried dinner. The mood was tense, and we were snipping and sniping at each other like dogs fighting over the scraps of our fight. We ate and drank and smoked. That night we lay awake in bed, the stony silence lying between us like the walls bisecting the New England countryside. There was no lovemaking, tender caresses, or soft words, just two bodies in a bed trying not to touch. Peace offerings and a hand on her back were both rejected.

In my dream that night, I was moving slowly. Quietly. Moving down the paddy dike in the mist. Everything was indistinct. But I was back in Vietnam . . . back in Recon. I was moving quietly on my jungle-booted feet, bristling with weapons: silenced Swedish K, Hi-Power on my hip, knife on my web gear. Weighed down by grenades, little Danish ones that were cute—a little bigger than golf balls and smaller than American ones. A White Phosphorus grenade the size of a soup can taped to the left shoulder of my web gear. I was carrying a United Nations' worth of weapons. I was weighed down with ammunition but light on my feet. I moved like a fucking Baryshnikov, a bad-ass, deadly ballet dancer.

The garrote is simple and, like most of my weapons, inelegant: wood handles and piano wire. I whipped it over the sentry's head. Crossed my arms fast, hard, and pivoted on the balls of my feet, a deadly version of "about-face," under the wires, dance moves. Disco of death.

I pulled him off the ground, back to back. He flailed against me. We were an obscene version of Shakespeare's "two-backed beast." He couldn't make any noise. . . . The piano wire was fast and unforgiving. His windpipe was just flesh and cartilage. Physics was unarguable. He was slightly built, like a lot of VC. I felt the life drain out of him. When it was done, I lowered him to the ground. His head lolled to one side and let out a rasping noise—air, gas escaping. He looked at me with Thuy's face, distorted by a horrid death. Somehow, I managed not to scream in the middle of the night in the bed in the Hay-Adams. I managed not to wake her. I tossed and turned the rest of the night but never really slept. Thuy lay next to me, snoring slightly, like a kitten.

Chapter 11

When we woke up the next morning, we were polite to each other. We were wary about fighting. She was being nice, overly polite, and I was being polite and noncommittal. We got dressed and made our way downstairs for breakfast. I was tired after a night of nightmares. I wanted coffee and plenty of it.

The restaurant in the Hay-Adams did not disappoint. The tablecloths were of the whitest linen, and the floral centerpieces were tasteful bouquets of real flowers. The waitress brought us coffee and menus.

"Andy, what is a milkshake?"

"What, are you kidding? You grew up in California. . . . You must have had one. Milk and ice cream all mixed up. You drink it through a straw. Do we have to have your parents arrested for child neglect?" Her smile faltered.

"No. I just never had one. My parents were very . . . very strict." She bit her lower lip.

"Oh, if you have never had a milkshake you should have one. . . . It is a life-changing experience."

The waitress came and we ordered. Thuy ordered the fruit bowl and a coffee milkshake, and I ordered a cheese omelet, breakfast sausage, and wheat toast. The waitress was unsure of making a milkshake for breakfast but that was the nice thing about being in a five-star hotel. They reluctantly do what you ask them to, then charge you a lot of money for it. My plate was garnished with a half slice of orange and a bit of parsley, which seemed an odd marriage. She enjoyed her milkshake. We ate in companionable silence.

"What now?" she asked.

"I am not sure. We know that your uncle and another man were murdered. We think it is about gold that was smuggled out of Saigon in 1975. We were just at a front company for the CIA, and they know about us." I was summing up the obvious bits.

"The gold must exist. Why kill two men if it doesn't?"

"Someone doesn't want anyone to know what happened to it?"

"Or find it?" She was looking at me over the straw of her milkshake, head slightly tilted down but eyes up, her black hair framing her face, all of it making her look like a teenager.

"Or maybe someone wants it to fund a counterrevolution. I bet the Committee would love to get their hands on it, Colonel Tran and his boys."

"The Committee is like a club for veterans of the war.

Or maybe a bunch of old criminals. Who knows?" She was right. There was no great uprising, no big political movement either.

"Maybe they don't have it. Or do you think they are still sitting on the money? Why?"

"They can't do it without America. They weren't going to do it after the fall of Saigon. Jimmy Carter wasn't going to help them invade the People's Republic of Vietnam. But Ronald Reagan . . . Reagan might . . . he hates the communists." She looked very serious as she said it.

"So, they have been waiting for the right time, which you think is now."

"Yes."

"But where is the gold, the money? I can't see them putting it in a bank."

"Andy, what if it is still out there? What if Hieu figured out where it is? What if that is why they killed him?" She put her hand on my arm, a warm gesture after a very frigid night.

"What about the other guy?"

"He knew too. They had to silence him."

"Okay, it's a stretch, but okay. Where would you hide the South Vietnamese treasury and not put it in a bank? We know it fit on a cargo ship or ships. . . . That is a lot of gold."

"I don't know. Would it be hard to unload by hand? Or at a pier?"

"By hand, probably not practical. On a pier, it would be crated, but there is a much higher chance of being seen. Was it in crates or pallets?" I was chewing over the idea. It was hard because we had no idea how much gold there had been. There had been a run on gold leading up to the collapse, but much of that had been sold, stolen, or purchased from Chinese currency dealers, banks, or in shady spots on Tu Do Street. How much had there been to begin with? "Maybe it is in a storage unit in some small town. The South Vietnamese gold behind one of those orange doors with a padlock." She giggled at the thought of it.

"Andy, that would be funny. Bars and bars of gold in some nowhere town protected only by a padlock." I had to admit the idea was amusing.

"What do we know? We know that there was gold loaded onto a ship or ships sometime around April 27 or 28 of 1975. We know that the flotilla of ships made its way down the Saigon River and to Can Tho island during the evening of April 29. From Can Tho, they would have steamed under their own power or been towed east to the American fleet." I had this vision of the former Vietnamese Navy, then the ragtag flotilla of cargo ships, Liberty ships, and yachts that comprised Nguyen's "flotilla of defeat." I wondered what he was feeling as dawn broke on the deck of the *Adams*, the sun coming up, angry, orange, and hot, and he realized—knew—that he had survived but had forever lost his home. Poor Nguyen.

"What are you thinking about?" It was a singularly feminine question.

"I was imagining what it was like to be on the flotilla of boats leaving Saigon. Could they hear artillery landing? Were they close enough to smell Saigon burning? What did the morning look like to them as they neared Can Tho and the American fleet? Were their eyes filled with defeat, or were they filled with hope for a new chance?" For men like Nguyen, it must have been bittersweet. He had saved his family but lost his war and lost his home.

Did he weep privately, like I did in front of the small black-and-white TV? Watching the helicopters on the embassy roof over and over again. Each jolt of Chivas making Walter Cronkite and Dan Rather look a little more human as they talked numbers, statistics in front of their increasingly red-colored map of Vietnam. Cronkite and Rather, two trusted names, reeling off the manifest of defeat, manifest of towns and cities fallen to the NVA. Their manifest of woes.

"That's it!" The thought, when it came to me in a moment of clarity, hurt my tired head.

"What is it?"

"Records."

"What?"

"There will be shipping records. Each ship. Maybe not as complete as peacetime, but ports of entry, etcetera. There are maritime records that can be checked, and then we can check all the corporate records for Global Sea Transport imports. We might even be able to cross-reference ships that they have now to ten years ago."

"It seems like a lot of work." She said it doubtfully.

"Oh, it is," I assured her cheerfully.

The nice thing about being in Washington, D.C., was that we had access to the world's best libraries. The Smithsonian would put the Great Library of Alexandria to shame if it were still around. It took a little work with the telephone and phone book to figure out where to go to find the last ten years of maritime registries and shipping records. We were also on the hunt for the business incorporation records for Global Sea Transport, and they were here in DC also.

We ended up at the public library. It was a huge task, and I expected it would take hours. We split up. She went to look for anything to do with Global Sea Transport in the old business records. I went to the national ships registry and looked up Liberty ships that we transferred over to the Vietnamese Navy. The list wasn't very long, and I noticed that the *John Q. Adams* was one of them. She was renamed in Vietnam, but her name was changed back in 1976.

The *Adams* and the rest of her cohorts left Vietnam in 1975. One was scrapped in the Philippines. The other two were sold to a Panamanian cargo line that seemed to specialize in cheap ships that ended up at the bottom of the ocean floor.

But the *Adams* and one other ship made it to the United States. There the *John Q. Adams* reverted to her old name. She ended up in the National Defense Reserve Fleet, the Mothball Fleet in Suisun Bay, California, where she appeared to stay for the better part of the last decade.

The Mothball Fleet were a bunch of ships that the navy kept around in case there was another full-scale war and the government needed to rapidly enlarge its sealift capabilities in a hurry. Depending upon the ship's age and upkeep, they could have old ships seaworthy in weeks or months. The ships were moored in rows and rows in different bays and rivers in the lower forty-eight.

It might also be a neat place to secure a bunch of gold

you didn't know what else to do with. The fleet was patrolled and guarded. They had maintenance crews that kept them afloat and ensured that they could be brought back to seaworthiness. It would be simple to leave some cargo on board and to guard it. It would keep it away from prying eyes, away from people who watch government facilities and warehouses. It would keep it out of banks and gold exchanges, where there would be records. In short, it might allow it to become an invisible type of currency.

Later in the afternoon, she found me in the library, hunched over a table with copies of registries open and photocopies of various pages. She told me what she had found out about Global Sea Transport . . . which was not much. It had been incorporated in 1980. Before it was Global Sea Transport Import Export it had been called Near East Imports, then before that Far East Imports, and before that it was US-Asia Export, Inc. They had the office in Fairfax, and they had an office in San Francisco. Suisun Bay was part of the San Francisco Bay, but it was to the east or inland of San Francisco. Also, the army had the Presidio army base in San Francisco, and the navy still had some real estate there, too. They had Treasure Island, which was a man-made island. It had been made for the San Francisco World's Fair, but the navy grabbed it during the outbreak of World War II. Neither branch was giving back precious San Francisco real estate. If the company and some version of Air America was involved, they couldn't have chosen a better place to be. Travis Air Force Base was across the bay as well. There was also Naval Air Station Alameda just outside of Oakland. The Mothball Fleet made more and more sense. It would be close to government facilities, government support, and Southeast Asia. It was an excellent version of hiding in plain sight.

"You did good work."

"Thank you. How about rewarding me by taking me to dinner? I haven't had anything to eat in hours." She was right; we had worked through lunch.

"Of course."

It had taken us all morning and afternoon to find out not very much. We decided to head back to Boston in the morning. She said that she wanted to enjoy the Hay-Adams hospitality for one more night. I think she was a little taken with the four-poster bed and the wealth of pillows. I certainly had never slept in such luxury. Or maybe it was the hope of tonight being better than last night.

We gathered up our photocopies and notes and went outside for a cigarette and to find a cab. We got one and went to the hotel to drop everything off and freshen up. In the cab, she leaned against me and held my hand. Her head was against my shoulder and she smelled faintly of cigarette smoke and shampoo. It was nice to hold hands in a cab with a pretty girl. It had been a while.

The cab took a circuitous route, as they do a lot in Washington, D.C. The city, in its infinite wisdom, had set up zones for fares instead of making it mileage based; you paid by the number of zones you went through. If you were going from one zone to the end of another, it might be a long trip, but they couldn't charge by mileage. This led to either cabbies not wanting to go to certain locations or driving around to ensure they hit enough zones to make it worth their while.

We decided on Chinese for dinner, and the hotel recommended a restaurant a short walk away. Thuy had changed into a black dress that was clingy without being too clingy and low heels. She threw on a denim jacket that came down to the bottom of her rib cage. I changed my shirt and washed my face. I slipped the .38 into the waist of my khakis and wondered if the gun would leave oil on the light blue shirt. I had on my denim jacket and trench coat.

A light spring rain had started to fall and huddling under an umbrella for the short walk felt romantic. For some reason, Washington in the early evening always felt like a romantic city to me. It wasn't Paris or even Boston, but it was romantic. Maybe it was the cherry trees and their pretty blossoms? As an added bonus, we weren't being followed, as far as I could tell.

We found the restaurant. If The Blue Lotus celebrated its tacky, faded, New England take on Chinese food then Jade Dragon took itself very, very seriously. There was no cliched neon but instead a sign that was simply a green dragon, swinging above the door. The door was flanked by what were supposed to be two terra-cotta dogs that sat chest high. Inside, the lights were soft, and the black lacquered wood shone. There were koi ponds and water effects, paper lanterns, and green bamboo seemed to grow strategically around the room. There was the ubiquitous golden cat, one paw raised, looking for a high-five that would never come. This one was two-thirds the size of the one at Nguyen's.

We were seated at a table, and Thuy and the waitress, who could have been twenty or forty, hit it off. Thuy spoke to her in what I assumed was Chinese. I was no expert, but it seemed that she spoke fluidly with few pauses.

The waitress wrote things down, laughed politely, and turned on her heel and headed for the kitchen.

"Do you speak Chinese?" I was curious.

"I speak some Mandarin but not fluently."

"You could have fooled me. Where did you pick it up?"

"Oh, growing up in California there were still big Chinese communities. I learned it there."

"Oh. Cool." I was not a linguist. I spoke German, because of my mother; English, because of my father and Our Sisters of Perpetual Piousness; and some Vietnamese, because of the army.

"I ordered for us. I hope you don't mind." The waitress arrived with a glass of scotch for each of us, then a steaming wooden container of dumplings.

"No, not at all. I trust your judgment."

"Andy?" She was looking down at her dumplings.

"What?"

"Can I ask you a question?" She looked up at me with large, brown eyes.

"Sure."

We both used chopsticks, each of us nimbly, and dipped the dumplings in soy sauce with ginger and scallions before eating them. They were fantastic. Balls of steamed pork mixed with garlic and scallion, inside chewy dough. The sauce brought out the flavors, and the ginger rounded it all out.

"You promise you won't get mad?" She looked at me with an earnestness that even Meryl Streep couldn't perform.

"Well, I . . ." Never, in my short life, had that request indicated something good was about to happen.

"Andy, do you promise?"

"Sure, doll." My best Bogie to the Vietnamese equivalent of her Bacall. I liked her. Possibly a lot.

"Why don't you want to go to the memorial?" Her large brown eyes looked at my face, looked in my eyes for something that wasn't there.

"It's complicated." I wasn't ready for this.

"Does it remind you of the bad things you did, had to do? The people you killed?" She was so earnest she didn't realize what a raw nerve she was tugging on.

"No . . . not so much that. That was war. The NVA and Cong were doing their best to kill me. . . . I am pretty sure they don't feel bad about that or the friends of mine they did kill. I am not saying I don't think about that, but it is just one part of it."

"Then what . . . ? You seemed so angry yesterday," She was persistent.

"Thuy, it is tough to explain." It wasn't tough to explain. . . . Having to think about it, talk about it . . . give voice to it, that was tough.

"Please, Andy, please try. . . . It is important to me."

"Okay. . . . It isn't about what I did or had to do. I am not proud of it, nor am I ashamed of it. There is no glory in killing. That was just the war, my small part of a small war."

"Then why don't you want to go see it? It looks magnificent and haunting."

"Thuy . . . I don't want to see it because I lived, many of my friends and brothers didn't."

"Isn't that good? You are alive."

"No, it is . . . and it isn't. Most of my friends, men who

were my brothers, . . . they died. Their names are on that wall. Why did I live? Why me? How come I am not on that wall instead of them? I wasn't any better than them or any more deserving than my brothers. Or, for that matter, just the average guys who got drafted who are on that wall. Why them and not me?"

"Andy, you couldn't control that. Any of that."

"No, I couldn't, but that doesn't change anything. They are dead and I am alive. They didn't particularly deserve to die, and I didn't particularly deserve to live." I didn't add that I was trapped with memories of them, that I saw a lot of my old friends at night when I should have been asleep.

More whiskey arrived without my asking for it. The empty bamboo steamer was removed and a dish with rice arrived. Shrimp in a brown lobster sauce packed with vegetables, and strips of chicken in a sauce that had flecks of red pepper in it fought with broccoli for room on another platter. Thuy served us both, putting a bed of fluffy white rice on my plate then hers, then covering the circle of rice half with shrimp and half with chicken.

"Is that what you are dreaming about when you wake me up in bed at night?"

"Usually." There were some dreams from when I was a cop, but they were not as vivid.

"Do you talk to anyone about it?"

"A shrink?"

"Anyone?"

"No."

"Why not?"

"It isn't my thing."

"It might help?"

"It isn't for me. My father and his generation, guys who fought the Nazis, jumped into Normandy, friends of his who had been in the Pacific . . . they had it far worse, and they didn't talk to anyone. They didn't need to. They came home and went about the business of starting to live their lives."

We spent the next several minutes eating and the conversation was limited to the food, which was excellent. We didn't need to talk about the war, my role in it or my dreams about it. I was happy for the respite. I needed R&R from a war that I wasn't even fighting in anymore.

Another scotch later and dinner was done. I had turned down my fortune cookie. I knew what my curse was. She ate mine.

We walked back to the hotel arm in arm. We talked about the things that new lovers talk about as we made our way back to the land of four-poster beds. We shared a cigarette under the umbrella in the rain and generally said romantic things to each other.

We decided against the hotel bar in favor of the mini bar and bed. In the elevator up to our room, she kissed me deeply and clung to me. Once inside, she took off her jean jacket, started to undress me, then, satisfied with the results, peeled her dress over her head. She led me to the bed and pushed me on my back. She put her mouth on me and after a few minutes, she climbed on top of me. She rode me, moaning, hands on my chest until we both came to a shuddering climax.

Later in bed, legs intertwined, drinking mini bar whiskey from mini bottles and smoking cigarettes, she said, "Andy?"

"Yes, Thuy."

"The war? Did you ever get over it?"

"Sort of . . . It is over for me, but it is also a part of me. It's like cancer."

"What about killing a person, do you ever get over that?"

"I don't know. I know that it got easier to do it after the first time. I know that I never liked it. Maybe it isn't that it got easier—it was just better than being killed. I know that as I got older, I learned to live with it but . . . my hands will never be clean. You don't get over it; if you are lucky you learn to live with it. The men I killed were try-ing to kill me, my friends, or other Americans."

"Women." Her cigarette tip glowing in the dark.

"What?"

"If you killed Viet Minh, you would call them Viet Cong. If you killed them, you probably killed women, too."

I knew that. Intellectually I did. I had memories of it. I didn't like to think about it. What type of shitty war puts you in that position, to kill women?

"I'm sorry. I shouldn't have said that." She was look-ing at my face as though there were answers to be gleaned.

"No, it is true. I just don't like to think about that part of it."

"Why is it different?"

"I don't know. Most of the women I knew were either wives or kids of the Montagnards; we loved them. Or they were Vietnamese women who cooked and did laun-dry near bases, or they were whores. It seems shameful now, but there it was common. You are the only Vietnamese woman I have slept with who I didn't pay." She didn't recoil in horror, at least.

"I am not surprised but . . . I don't want to think about that."

"Good, me neither."

She pushed her face into the hollow of my shoulder. Her hands tracing my old scars, probing old wounds until she found her way down my body. My breathing changed as she took me in her hand. Then when I was ready, she pulled me on to her, and we made love again slowly, gently, sweetly.

Chapter 12

The next day the sun stabbed into our four-poster cocoon. She was wrapped around me, and it felt fine and warm. I was getting used to having her around. We got up and showered. We decided that we had time for breakfast and coffee.

We were smiling and giggling like little kids at each other. We held hands on the way to Union Station and bought our tickets to Boston. We sat in the main part of the train in our airline-like seats. We snuggled close and watched the scenery flick by as we made our way back to Boston. We traded stories about our childhood. We held hands in the station and then outside, where we found a cab to take us back to my apartment.

It was early evening by the time we got home, and I didn't think anyone was following us. I wasn't sure I even cared. The garage had done me a favor, and the Ghia was parked in its spot in front of my apartment building. The keys were in my mailbox along with a few days' worth of bills and a supermarket flyer.

We went up into the apartment. Sir Leominster let out a plaintive howl to let me know that he hadn't enjoyed being alone for a few days. Thuy hung her big puffy coat on the hook on the wall. I put my bag down by the bedroom door, and she dropped her shoulder bag on the table. Her duffel bag went on the floor. I threw the keys on the table and hung my jacket on the back of a chair.

She went to the bathroom, and I went to get a whiskey. "Do you want a drink?" I asked the bathroom door. Her voice came from the other side of it. "Sure, whiskey and ice."

I poured the drinks and then went to get a cigarette. My pack of Luckies was empty. I crushed it and dropped it on the table. I picked up Thuy's handbag hoping to find some cigarettes in it. It was heavy, and after rummaging, I found out why. There was all the usual purse stuff— money, wallet, make-up—but also a zippered pocket that wasn't able to close. It had a flap, and if it hadn't been open, I would never have seen it. I would never have seen the butt of a pistol.

I pulled it out mostly out of curiosity. It was a CZ, a Czechoslovakian copy of the Walther PPK in .32 ACP. It was the Iron Curtain's version of the James Bond gun. They were also known as *Czeska,* and outside of Langley or maybe Fort Bragg they just didn't exist in this country. This one had a long, thick silencer screwed to the front of it. The CZ was well oiled, and I was sure it was loaded. I dropped it on the table next to the bag and sat down heavily in a wing chair with my whiskey.

Suddenly I felt very, very old and all my scars and

bruises were individual aches. The air in the room had somehow changed, and I wasn't sure I understood what I had just stumbled upon. She came out of the bathroom and was saying, "Andy, when this is all over, we should go to Califor . . ." She trailed off. She saw the pistol on the table.

"Andy . . ."

"I was looking for cigarettes," a man said with a voice like mine.

"Why didn't you ask me?"

"You were in the bathroom. I was out of cigarettes."

"Andy . . . I . . ."

"I am sorry. I should have picked up on it sooner. Maybe it was the beating, or maybe I am getting old. Never had a milkshake . . . District of Columbus . . . you definitely aren't from here."

"No. I am from Vietnam."

"But you aren't a refugee or a tourist?"

"I had a talent for languages. A district commissar thought I would better serve the revolution by learning English rather than learning to dig tunnels."

"What was the assignment?"

"Andy, it doesn't matter now."

"It does a hell of a lot to me."

"When the imperialists fled . . . they took a lot of money with them. Lots of gold. We knew that Colonel Tran or men like him were going to set up the counterrevolution. They needed the money. If we could get it back, it would cripple them. The two dead Vietnamese men were an indicator. I was sent to get it or find it. I reported back that I had hired you and what I knew about you. They sent further instructions. They wanted me to kill you if I could. Preferably at the monument at night to make it look like suicide. I would leave a note—you would denounce your war crimes."

My laugh sounded like a sick dog's bark. "You people pay someone to come up with ideas like that? Veterans kill themselves so often no one even notices anymore. Did you kill Hieu? Pham?"

"Andy, I couldn't do it. I'm not . . . I am not . . . like you."

"Not like me?"

"No."

"Now what?" I still had the .38 on my hip. Maybe I shifted or maybe she figured there were not a lot of options. She stepped to the table and the CZ was in her hand, all in one fluid motion. She had moved with the speed and grace of a cat. She pointed the pistol at me but without much actual intent. A .32 ACP isn't much of a round, but I could attest to its lethality. I had shot a man in the face with one once a lifetime ago. I wasn't in a rush to get shot with one.

"Andy. I don't want to kill you, but I don't like the thought of being in one of your prisons. I am leaving. I am taking your car." She flicked the safety off with her thumb. She picked up her pocketbook and my keys.

"Please don't follow me, Andy. I will shoot you if I have to." She backed to the door and let herself out. I got up and slowly followed. I wasn't sure what I wanted to say. I didn't love her, but I liked her a lot. Or maybe I just didn't want this to be why she was here. It wasn't love but I didn't want to be just an assignment. I didn't want to feel like a john with a whore. There had been plenty of that in Vietnam and afterward I felt empty. It was little more than scratching an itch. Maybe she reminded me of Leslie and the possibility of having a normal relationship.

Maybe I was just getting so sick of coming home to an empty apartment most nights that the possibility of something more had become important . . . had clouded my judgment.

I started after her, through the door and down the steps. There was a coughing noise and the plaster by my head erupted in a plume of dust. There was the tinkle of the shell casing on the tile floor. I heard her footsteps moving rapidly, then the outside door opening and closing. I crossed the foyer and made it outside and down the steps. She was pulling away in my Ghia. I made it to the sidewalk when she braked at the intersection.

The inside of the car was lit with an orange light. There was a roar that turned into a whooshing noise, and then I was smashed by the heat and a giant's fist. I sat down hard on the sidewalk and rolled in the gutter between a solid Ford LTD and some New England granite. Pieces of Ghia peppered the cars. Windows were smashed out, and all I could hear was ocean roaring in my ears. I had been near explosions before, just not in Boston's Back Bay neighborhood.

I got up slowly. I started to walk on baby deer legs to the Ghia. It was fully engulfed in flames. The tan interior, the soft top, the green paint . . . all gone, swallowed by intense fire and heat. Thuy . . . Thuy was in the car. . . . Thuy was gone. I had seen enough burning trucks to know. I moved closer to the car, but it was too hot. The smoke was acrid and made me cough, my lungs aching, each cough reminding me of a hundred bruises that I had forgotten I had. I backed away.

I sat down on the steps of a brownstone. I started to shiver as the sweat chilled in the cold night air. Blood was coming down my face from a cut that I just realized I had on my forehead. It came to me that there must have been sounds but all I heard was the sound of surf in my ears.

Because it was an actual fire, the fire department arrived before the police, instead of staging and waiting for the police to tell them it was safe, their red lights turning everything into crazy disco with surf noises in my head instead of music. Then there were some rescue people putting me in an ambulance, then getting mad when I didn't want to stay in their magic bus for a ride to the hospital. I think they were trying to tell me that I needed stitches. I was trying to tell them that I didn't care about stitches. They wiped my face down and put a dressing on my forehead.

Then it was a cop in his blue uniform and the ubiquitous notepad and ever-poised pen. My statement was my girlfriend got in my car to go get cigarettes. The car blew up. He pressed for more, like why I went out after her. Why was I bleeding, and why did I have a .38 on my hip? I showed him the photostat of my license. He wanted me to come downtown. I told him to fuck off, and I would wait for the grown-ups to come by and make my statement. He looked at me. He wanted to hit me in the head with a nightstick, handcuff me, and stuff me in the back of a police car. It was a reasonable response for a cop in that situation. He also had been on the job long enough to realize it wasn't worth it. He knew that the detectives were going to be all over this. He stalked off to talk to someone. Fuck him. He hadn't been blown up tonight.

There was a bar across the street. It was a neighborhood joint that I almost never drank in. I got up and started over to it. The cop tried to stop me, to say something. I couldn't hear him over the ocean waves in my ears. I told him I would be in the bar, and the dicks could talk to me there. My statement would be just as brief after a couple glasses of whiskey.

If the music stopped when I walked in, I didn't notice. I couldn't hear it. It wasn't too crowded for a school night. I put a twenty on the bar. I said what I hoped was whiskey. The bartender held up a bottle of Jameson's. I nodded. He brought me a tall whiskey, neat. He took my money. When he came back it was change, a bowl of steaming water, and a clean bar towel. He motioned to me to clean up my face. In the mirror, someone who survived to the end of a slasher movie stared back at me.

The hot water didn't feel good on my cuts and scrapes, but I didn't care. I daubed my battered face mechanically. I watched my face slowly emerge from the horror movie and thought about what a waste it all was. I was the target, not the girl. She was a spy and it wasn't love, but it had been nice for a time to think it might have led to a few less lonely nights. It was a waste of a young life. All the more so because the bomb had been meant for me.

My face was drying, and I could hear a little through the ringing in my ears. I didn't look so bad, and my second whiskey was helping. I still couldn't make sense of the last hour. Someone wanted me dead, dead enough to blow up my car. It seemed unlikely that Thuy would have blown up my beloved Ghia with herself in it. I was watching the lights flashing in the mirror above the bottles. The fire department was leisurely rolling up its hoses. In the mirror, staring at me, was a vision. A woman. A woman with honey-colored hair.

Special Agent Brenda Watts slid onto a bar stool next

to me. She motioned, and the bartender brought her a glass with ice and poured from a bottle of Jack Daniels. She turned and rested an arm on the bar. I had to pay close attention to understand her, which wasn't hard.

"Are you okay?"

"As good as can be."

"You look like shit."

"Thanks . . ."

"Most of the time you look kind of a disheveled mess, but tonight you look like shit that got run over or something."

"You say the nicest things."

"I have a list of names. Priorities, in case something happens. Shootings, bombings etcetera. Your name is on that list, you and a bunch of mobsters and their friends and a certain lawyer. I had forgotten all about you, Andy Roark. Then my phone rings, my home phone, and only my mother calls me on that. The duty agent called me. Your car blew up. He thought I would want to know." I nodded at her. My head felt like it was going to fall off.

"What'd I interrupt, a hot date with a lawyer or accountant type?" Even after watching my car blow up, I was trying to be a comedian, my new career instead of detective because I obviously was not good at that. She laughed, it made her chest heave, and I appreciated the white blouse, a few buttons open.

"You know what is funny? Really funny, *Mr. I am too short to be Magnum*?"

"What?"

"As I was changing to get here, my home phone rang again, my pager went off. I answered the phone, and do you know who it was?"

"J. Edgar Hoover?"

"No, asshole. It was the deputy director. The number two man at the bureau called me to tell me that this was not a bureau case, it was not of interest to me, to leave it alone."

I nodded, trying to process the information.

"The DD does not call supervisory agents at home, much less lowly field agents, like me. Someone is putting the squash on this. BPD and Metro can fight out whose this is. The bureau officially is not interested in who is trying to kill a Mafia-affiliated PI. You are radioactive."

"Hey . . . thanks." In her career "radioactive" meant I was not someone she should talk to. The bureau has high standards and expects their agents to as well. "Brenda, in the hulk of my car, next to the remains of a Vietnamese woman are the remains of a rare Czechoslovakian pistol with an attached silencer."

"What the fuck are you into?" She had nice eyes.

"It has to do with the dead Vietnamese guys in Chinatown and Quincy. I am just not exactly sure how. She was a communist spy. I know that." It sounded funny coming out of my mouth, overdramatic.

"What, like James Bond? Jane Bond. Jesus. You don't fuck around, do you?"

"Well, if it is worth doing, it is worth overdoing." I tried to smile, but my face was a mess, and my mouth just couldn't make it work.

"I think the Company is behind the squash on this. It might be our counter intel guys, but my money is on the Company." She said *the Company*, the universal euphemism for the CIA, like it was a dirty term.

"Great. I saw *Three Days of the Condor*, and I don't like how it ended for him." Dana Hersey and the Movie Loft on TV 38 were heavily responsible for my cinema education.

"Get serious." Either shock was setting in or the third whiskey was working some serious magic.

"Hey, Watts."

"Yeah."

"Will you tell me how they did it? You know, the technical details?"

"Why?"

"I liked her. I wasn't in love or anything, but it is a pretty shitty way to die. I have a little experience in that sort of thing. . . . It might point me in the right direction."

"Roark, what the hell does it matter?" Maybe it was that her eyes were easy to look at or that her manicured hand was on the only part of my arm that didn't ache, but I told her. I told her everything. Everything except the gold. Gold does funny things to people. I told her a little bit about my Vietnam experience.

"Roark, you are in over your head. I think they're professionals and if you don't back off, they are going to kill you." The slasher movie face in the mirror was ugly and grew uglier as my smile widened.

"No, Watts. I don't think so. I may not look like it, but I am kind of a professional, too." I knew I was going to kill them. Whoever planted that bomb . . . they were going to die by my hand.

Watts had squared it with the dicks from BPD. I would go in after lunch and leave a statement. She insisted upon walking me across the street and back to my apartment. The door was still unlocked, and she insisted upon checking the apartment. She moved lightly from room to room with her .38 held down at her side.

"Okay, Roark. Lock up behind me and be careful. Call me if you find out anything." She put a card down on my table, but she knew I wasn't going to call. I locked up behind her. Thuy's bulky coat was still hanging on the peg by the door. I pulled it to my face to smell her. I went to the couch with it and sat down.

Something in the pocket hit my shin. It was heavy. It turned out to be a tiny Colt 1908, a small .25 ACP that was good at tabletop ranges and fired a round that gave the humble .22 a boost in its confidence. There was almost no bluing left on this one; it was a patina of almost brown. There was a round in it and another six in the magazine. It was well oiled. The pocket had been altered so that it was also a holster for the .25 Colt. The rounds were brass, and the bullets copper, the tips of which looked like they had solder in them. It was a spy's gun, tiny and only good up close. Someone had modified the bullets, and that scared me. Putting a drop of mercury in a small hollow point and then covering it with solder or lead had very, very bad results for the recipient.

I started to wonder what else was in the coat. I started to feel it with two hands, crushing cloth, sliding, crushing, sliding. I found them in the collar. There was something hard, and when I pulled at the loose stitching, it came apart. Inside were two canvas strips. I pulled them out; each held ten gold coins. They were blank . . . and all gold. All in all, I found twenty coins. It was her escape kit. One-ounce gold coins. In today's market, they were worth maybe ten thousand dollars.

Gold was always part of the escape kit. Coins could be

sold or bartered anywhere. That is why we gave them to our pilots and to our Special Forces guys in Vietnam. That and a blood chit, a piece of map paper with a U.S. flag on one side and on the other a promise to pay ten thousand dollars for the safe return of the bearer of the chit. Thuy's coins came out of a U.S. aviator's survival kit; I knew that much.

Chapter 13

When I woke up in the morning my head hurt, and I wished it was a hangover. The cut on my forehead wasn't bad. I couldn't face shaving, but a hot shower and a new large Band-Aid on my forehead set me mostly right. Coffee and some rye toast helped. I still didn't have any cigarettes. My clothes from the night before were in a heap on the floor. They smelled of acrid smoke and blood, and I just pitched them in the trash.

I spent an hour on the phone with the insurance company wondering if the ringing in my ears would ever go away. In the end, I told them to call the police and they agreed to contact BPD. They said they would get back to me.

I dressed in gray slacks, a light blue shirt, a Harvard club tie I had no right to wear but I liked the colors, and a blue blazer. I had recently read a Spenser novel, so I was trying to dress more like him. I even threw on burgundy loafers. He was a spiffy dresser and a lot tougher than I would ever be. I put the Colt Commander on my right hip and dropped the .38 in the left pocket of my raincoat. While I might have been paranoid before, now I was pretty sure that someone was trying to kill me. I wasn't really keen on that.

Outside, it was cool, but spring was in the air. However, I live in Boston, and snow wasn't out of the question until mid-April. There was a scorch mark on the pavement and lots of broken auto glass. I wanted to throw up but turned toward town and did what they had taught me in the army: put one foot in front of the other. I was sore but found that after a couple of blocks I was loosening up. Moving was easier than sitting on my ass feeling bad about things.

I stopped at the first convenience store for a pack of Luckies. I bought two so I wouldn't run out. Outside, I lit the first one and took a deep drag, the smoke welcome in my lungs and the nicotine working its magic. Across the street I saw a cream-colored T-bird. I pointed my index finger at it, thumb cocked, the universal sign for a gun. He peeled out with a roar. We understood each other. We were on the same sheet of music now. It only took me a beating, a blown-up car, and a dead girl to get on theirs. What can I say—I have always been a slow learner.

Police headquarters hadn't changed much. The desk sergeant was another one straight out of Central Casting. This one looked at me and, in a brogue that was only partly affected, said, "Jesus, Mary, and feckin' Joseph, are you here to report your own feckin' murder?" He said *fuck* like an Irishman.

"No, someone blew up my car. Sadly, I wasn't in it.

Some ten-year-old in a blue suit with a tin star said I had to come talk to a dick." When I tried really hard, I could sound like a tough guy in a movie.

"Feckin' town. This is Bahstin, not feckin' Belfast. It's not right, blowin' up a man's car. All right, you'd be Roark, then. I call one of our twelve-year olds in a suit to come talk to you." I was pretty sure that I liked him. He was the type of sergeant you would hope would come to your call when I was a cop. Ten minutes later, a red-headed cop with big hands and thick wrists poking out of his Jordan Marsh suit jacket came to get me. He didn't say anything to me in English, but communicated with a series of grunts that approximated speech. It was like something out of a Bugs Bunny cartoon. At least he didn't feel the need to hug me, squeeze me, or name me. A small mercy given my current state.

He took me up to the detective bureau and took my statement. Then he wasted an hour of my life asking me stupid questions. I answered them as best as my bruised patience would allow. Then he had me sign my statement, which didn't say much more than my car blew up with Thuy in it. When he was done, I was told to go see Captain Johnson.

His office hadn't changed. He hadn't either. It had only been a few days since I was last here. He was wearing a gray suit this time, with a lavender shirt and paisley tie that made my head hurt. The butt of the revolver was still sticking out of his waistband.

"Roark, are you okay?" He looked at me with genuine concern.

"About as good as can be expected under the circumstances." It was a lie we both wanted to believe.

"Roark, is anything else in my city going to blow up?"

He was serious. Boston cops can put up with shootings, stabbings, riots, etc. but they seem to draw the line at explosions. No one wanted Boston to turn into Belfast.

"Not if I have anything to say about it."

"Why a bomb in the car?"

"It was convenient. I was away, and the car was parked on the street. It was easier than breaking into my place or waiting to gun me down. They were being lazy."

"Any idea who it was?" I had to give him credit—he was good at his job. After talking to the mental midget earlier and being questioned by him now, I wanted to share my theories with him. I wanted to talk to him.

"Nothing but theories right now."

"Such as?"

"I was in the army for a while, or I once followed a cheating husband. He was a demo guy who had blasted granite in New Hampshire for the new highway."

"Are you telling me this has nothing to do with the dead Vietnamese guys you were looking at?"

"Nope." I technically wasn't telling him anything.

"How come the FBI isn't all over this? Your car gets blown up, a Vietnamese woman is in it, and other than the agent last night no one is interested."

"Captain, I don't know what to tell you. That is the FBI for you."

"And what about the shady-ass mob lawyer friend of yours? He have anything to do with this?"

"I haven't talked to him in two years, almost three. Pretty sure he is off the list of suspects."

"All right, Roark. If you think of anything, you call me." He handed me a business card. I took it and told him I would. We stood and shook hands, and I made my way out of BPD headquarters to the street.

I shook a Lucky out of the pack and lit it as I walked away from police headquarters. I needed time to figure a couple of things out. I needed a new car, and I had to try to make sense out of what happened and why. People don't just blow up your car for no reason. Not in Boston, they don't. Maybe in Providence or Hartford, but Boston is a civilized town.

I walked with my hand in my pocket on the butt of the .38 snub nose. No one was following me, and I didn't see any cream-colored Fords. I checked windows and tied my shoes a lot and doubled back, and no one was following me. Maybe they didn't care.

I walked back to my office. The weather hadn't shifted either way. The sun was shining, but it wasn't really all that warm. My head hurt. Actually, my whole body hurt in one form or another. In the past few days, I had been beaten up and blown up. Years ago, I was blown up, shot, and burned. I shuddered to think of what the future was going to hold.

Mr. Marconi saw me coming, and there was an espresso correctto waiting for me. He looked at me and said, "Is it the communists?" He thought that the Red Brigades were always after me.

"Not this time." No, this was the other side. The sambuca tasted like warm licorice, and I thanked him and headed upstairs. I walked down the corridor to my office door, the one with my name written on the frosted glass in gold lettering. I had my keys out, and my hand froze. The hair on the back of my neck stood up.

In Vietnam, we were once moving down a trail, and something didn't feel right. Our point man was a Montagnard. He had seen something and halted us. I moved up to him. "What's wrong?" I whispered. He looked at me and then the trail. "I don't know, *Trung Si,* I just know that something is wrong." We rested on our haunches for five minutes, and then he pointed to something on the jungle floor. "There," he whispered, his fishy breath hot near my ear. "That leaf, it is wrong." One leaf, the size of a playing card, was upside down. We carefully and slowly brushed dirt, twigs, and leaves out of the way, revealing a trip wire that led to four 155mm artillery shells. If he hadn't spotted it, we would have been blown to smithereens.

This time it wasn't an out-of-place leaf. It was scratch marks. There were scratches, fresh scratches, on the face of my lock. Someone had picked it recently. It is very hard to pick a lock without leaving scratch marks. I eased the key in and slowly turned it, listening for noises that sound out of place. I opened the door a crack and looked top to bottom, while still carefully holding the door. I almost missed it, a piece of monofilament fishing line running across the path of the door a few inches from the floor. It was clear and made of some sort of plastic. Someone had booby-trapped my office door with a trip wire.

I had seen a spy movie where the hero carried a small mirror on a telescoping handle. He used it to check under and around things, even up a lady's dress at the end. Mine wasn't government issue. I had swiped it from the dentist. Most of the time, it stayed at home, but after the exploding VW Karmann Ghia trick, it seemed like a nice thing to have with me.

I slid it in the door near the fishing line. I rotated it until I saw the grenade taped to the leg of one of my front office chairs. By the looks of things, someone had straightened the cotter pin. A professional would have replaced the delay fuse with one from a smoke grenade. Instead of a three to five-second delay, it would go off right away. It was a simple way of doing things: tape a fragmentation grenade to something, straighten the cotter pin, tie fishing line to the ring, run it across the door, stick the excess through the door above the hinge and pull the slack tight, tie it off to the hinge itself, and clip off the excess line. If I was right and opened the door normally, the door would have pushed the line, pulling the pin out, and I would have been blown up, solving someone's Andy Roark problem. I was starting to think that someone really didn't like me. I hadn't been this popular since I was in Vietnam.

I pulled the door closed and locked it, just to be safe. I went downstairs to Marconi's. He loaned me a pair of scissors without asking any questions. He was pretty much convinced that I was crazy. I unlocked the door and opened it a crack. The fishing line was taut. I held the door handle tightly with my left hand and then took out the dental mirror. The cotter pin was in place; there were no other surprises that I could see. I took a deep breath and took Marconi's scissors out. They were stainless steel, German, and more at home in a sewing kit than defusing booby-trapped office doors.

I took another breath, held it, and slid the partially open scissors through the opening of the door. The scissors were on either side of the fishing line. I let my breath out, inhaled, and snipped the fishing line. The cotter pin stayed in place, and the grenade spoon stayed on. I breathed a couple of long, deep breaths. I pushed the door open slowly. There were no other trip wires. I used my Buck knife to bend the cotter pin ends back so it wouldn't come out as easily. I cut the tape on the grenade and dropped it in my raincoat pocket.

I took off my coat and hung it on the tree. I then spent the next hour methodically checking my office for more surprises. I used the tip of my Buck knife probing here and there as I worked my way slowly from the office door to the door of my inner office. When I was fairly certain that it was safe, I went and retrieved the grenade from my coat pocket. I opened the door to the large safe; it had come with the office. I unscrewed the fuse from the grenade body and put both in the safe. Without the fuse to set it off, it was essentially ugly sculpture.

It was a smoke grenade fuse. Smoke grenade fuses initiate upon being pulled, no delay unlike normal grenade fuses. That was how we made hasty booby traps out of grenades.

The grenade was an M26 fragmentation grenade. It was an olive green, lemon-shaped hunk of death and maiming. It weighed a pound and was filled with six ounces of Composition B explosives. The metal was scored inside to ensure it would create a lot of fragments. Within fifteen feet of it going off, you were probably dead. Out to a hundred, you were going to be wounded. I still had scars from the small pieces of shrapnel from grenades the Viet Cong had thrown at me.

The grenade body itself had little flecks of orange where it had rusted a little. The stenciling on it was in English, the stampings on the fuse body also. This grenade had originally been an American grenade. That wasn't surprising—we had made literally millions of them in World War II and Korea. Now this one had ended up literally at my door.

I picked up my phone and listened to the dial tone. I thought I heard little clicks and put it down. I took out the hand grenade and screwed the fuse in. I got my raincoat and dropped the grenade in the pocket. I returned Marconi's scissors to him.

"Mr. Marconi, did I have any visitors today?"

"Clients, Andy?" Sometimes Marconi ended up with them if I wasn't around.

"Or workmen, anyone?"

"Today, no, but a couple of days ago, yes, there was the guy from the phone company. Then a little while after him a Chinese came by. The phone company man went to the cellar and then to your office."

"And the other guy, the Chinese?"

"He had a briefcase and a bad suit. Not a sharp dresser, like he got his suits at the church bazaar. He went up to see you. He didn't wait long, five minutes, maybe ten."

"Okay, thanks. Oh, hey, can I have one of these?" I motioned to one of the paper bags that he sent takeout in. It had his logo on it.

"Of course. Please."

"Thank you."

I slipped the grenade into the bag. Marconi's eyes got big.

"Andy, is that what I think it is?"

"It sure ain't no meatball." I walked out.

Chapter 14

When I got back to the apartment, there was nothing
waiting for me: no bombs, no grenades, no Chinese, Vietnamese, or men from Ma Bell. I took the Colt
.25 and unloaded it. I put the gun, its magazine, and the
loose round in a small paper bag that I put in the bigger
Marconi's bag. I wrapped tape around the spoon of the
grenade as an extra precaution. The gold coins in their
canvas sleeves went in my pocket. The germ of a plan
was forming in my head.

I took the bag from Marconi's and left. I used the back
stairs and popped out a block away from the scorched
area where the Ghia had blown up. I walked through the
streets at a moderate pace. No one was following and
nothing seemed out of the ordinary. Near the Greyhound
station at the edge of the combat zone, not far from L.J.

Peretti's, was an antique store that I knew that dealt in rare books and coins. I had done some work for them when someone had tried to put the bite on them.

The manager saw me and led me to the back room. He poured me a small snifter of cognac and had one himself. He was born in Germany but became an Austrian after the war.

"Mr. Roark, what can I do for you?"

"I would like to convert these to dollars." I put the strips of coins on his desk. He picked them up and looked at them. I picked up the cognac and sipped it. It was a German cognac that was popular among the Special Forces soldiers and their German wives at Fort Devens. Devens was an hour northwest of Boston. Once in a while, I would go to the Class Six store, the army's version of a liquor store, and bring him back some.

"These are unmarked?"

"That is true." He looked at me and at the coins again.

"I cannot sell these." His Germanic sense of order would not allow him to use contractions in his opening gesture in the haggle.

"Yes, you can, it's gold. One can always sell gold."

"They have no markings." The currency market likes to be able to know where the gold is coming from. They don't love the idea that it is Nazi gold that was taken from the camps.

"They are an ounce each. They are pure. And you know they have a value that is intrinsic." He was known to help the value of his antiques by making them seem older than they were. Now he was looking at twenty chances to make rare, antique coins out of gold blanks.

"I might be able to dispose of them, but it would be at

a loss." He was hooked. We haggled. In the end, I ended up with $8,000 in cash and a meerschaum pipe that caught my eye.

I walked out of the store. The Marconi's bag was getting heavier. There still wasn't any sign of the cream-colored Ford T-bird. He probably assumed that I would blow myself up at the office. Everything still ached as I walked. It had been a rough couple of days. My garage was near the river and just off Mass Avenue, not very far from my apartment.

I was in luck. Carney was there. I had helped him out years before, and he was always good to me. He had been in the army during Korea. Tall and barrel chested, he always had an unlit cigar in his mouth. After we shook hands, he said, "I heard your Karmann Ghia blew up?"

"Yeah, how'd you hear?" He shrugged. Carney had one foot in the underworld. He liked me because I had been in a shitty war in Asia, too.

"Good, it was a piece of garbage. You're better off without it."

"The heater never worked well." I had loved that car. It was the first nice one I had ever owned.

"Yeah, exactly what I mean. What can I do for you?"

"I need a car . . . something older, nondescript . . . and with a working heater. It's gonna get driven here in town, so nothing fancy."

"I got just the thing. Actually, thought of you when I bought it." He turned and motioned me to follow him. We went through the bays and out in the back. There was a breeze off of the Charles River that seemed to push the smell of motor oil around. He stopped at a two-door Ford that was painted a shade of blue so nondescript it defied description.

"It's a '75 Ford Maverick 302, the Grabber. It has low mileage and a paint job no one will remember. It is fast and nimble. Pound for pound, I would take it over a Mustang." He got in and started the engine. It roared, not rumbled, to life. "I've tweaked the suspension and brakes. I had a fellow who was looking at it for a job but his parole officer got him first." He smiled around his cigar and pushed the gas so I could appreciate the roar of the engine.

We took it out for a test-drive. It was fast and nimble, like he said, and I had to pay attention driving it. The 302 was a lot of engine for a car that size. I didn't have to mash the gas pedal. We scared a lot of nice Bostonians before we made it back to his garage. We agreed on a price. I peeled several hundred-dollar bills of my coin money and handed it to him. We agreed that he would install some sort of lockbox in the trunk and put in a discreet compartment behind the glove box. He'd leave the dealer plates on, and I could park it at his place for the near future.

I borrowed his phone and called Brenda Watts and invited her to lunch. She, being a humble civil servant, agreed to lunch at the Union Oyster House if I was buying. Carney loaned me a beater while he was working on the lockboxes.

I made my way through the twists and turns of Boston's streets and found parking not far from the Union Oyster House. It is one of the oldest operating restaurants in America. The list of notable patrons is long and includes U.S. presidents. The food was priced commensurably.

Brenda Watts was waiting for me in a booth. Her honey-colored hair was back in a simple ponytail. She was wearing a cream blouse and a simple, dark pantsuit. I sat down next to her and put the Marconi's bag in between us. There was a club soda with a wedge of lime in front of her. The waiter came and I ordered a Lowenbrau.

"Roark, you look like shit warmed over."

"Thank you, Watts. Getting beaten up and blown up will do that to a fellow."

"What's in the bag?" I reached in and pulled out the smaller bag. She opened it and looked inside.

"Cute. What am I supposed to do, scare someone with its popping noises?"

"The bullets have been modified. Looks like they were drilled, then filled with mercury, then capped with lead or maybe solder. Pretty nasty thing: the bullet is fired, the mercury is thrown to the rear, and then when it hits, it is thrown forward and pops the soldering off. It causes vicious wounds that have mercury floating around in them. Quite messy."

"Where did you get this?"

"It was in the jacket pocket of the girl who took my car. She had that and a silenced Czechoslovakian .32 copy of a Walther. I was thinking that you could run it or test it in your lab and see if it has a history. Probably a long shot, but we don't have much actual evidence of anything."

"The Colt .25 isn't such a rarity, though I haven't ever seen rounds like this. There was nothing left of the gun in the car we could use. The fire was hot. Maybe the metallurgy could tell us something, but we aren't looking. No one seems to care."

"The bullets are an old KGB trick. They usually use cyanide. The .25 is an assassin's gun."

"What does a PI from Boston know about the KGB?"

"Oh, Watts, I have been around." I drew the last word out to give it emphasis. She sipped her club soda. It was done demurely, and she looked up at me while she sipped at her straw. If I was standing, I would have felt weak in the knees, but that also could have been an aftereffect of the explosion.

"What did you do during the war, Andy?"

"I was in Army Special Forces. I served in Vietnam." It is funny that what I did a decade ago was still a secret, such a secret that I had signed a bushel of nondisclosure papers, that I was still subject to their ink-crafted chains. What was even funnier was that outside of the guys who were in SOG or directly supported it no one knew about it.

"Then a cop here, and now a PI. You don't strike me as the type to rub elbows with Vietnamese KGB assassins or have your car blown up." Her tone was a teasing one, almost flirty. I was being interrogated but for once didn't seem to mind.

"We didn't actually rub elbows . . . a bit lower actually."

"Roark . . . !"

"How did the car blow up?"

"There was a Claymore mine. There wasn't much left to work with, but they think it was in the rear wheel well." The Claymore mine was a favorite in Vietnam. One pound of C-4 plastic explosive in a curved plastic shell, 750 ball bearings. It wasn't meant to be used in a car. It was meant to be used in the defense against human wave assaults or to initiate an ambush. It was like lining up fifteen 12-gauge shotguns side by side and firing them at the same time. In the case of the Claymore, the curved case angled the ball bearings into a fan that blasted anything in its path. The blast from the pound of explosives was impressive, too. These guys were lazy or believed in overkill and seemed to have access to military ordnance.

"Roark, are you paying attention? I was explaining the Claymore mine." Gone was the flirty interrogation technique.

"Watts, I used them so often in Vietnam, I could set one up in my sleep. I have blown hundreds of them. Putting it in my car was excessive." They wouldn't have needed a pound of C-4 to touch off the gas tank. They wouldn't have needed the ball bearings ripping through the car.

"Watts, what do you think of this?" I showed her the grenade in the bag.

"Is that what I think it is?" The neat thing about hand grenades is that there was no mistaking them for anything else.

"Why do you want that? It is a federal offense to have it." She was all business until she pushed some honey-colored hair out of her eyes and sipped more club soda.

"Someone left it for me in my office. Booby-trapped my front door. Watts, there is a theme to this thing that has me worried."

"What is that, Roark?" She had nice eyes, and I was aware that her blouse was open one more button than Mr. Hoover would have approved of. Her lips were moist from the club soda, and I was a mess.

"Nam. It starts with two dead Vietnamese, Pham and Hieu, one here in Chinatown and one in Quincy. Then a Vietnamese woman shows up and hires me to go look, then she takes me to bed, turns out to be the Vietnamese version of the KGB and gets killed by a Claymore mine, a staple of Vietnam, which was no doubt meant for me.

This morning I went to my office. Something didn't seem right, and then I realized my door was booby-trapped. Taped to a trip wire was an M26 grenade, rigged to blow up instantly. It is like Vietnam—three tours, ten years later—is still fucking trying to kill me." I finished my Lowenbrau, wished I had chosen whiskey, and ordered another. It arrived, cold and in its green bottle.

"Andy, what are you going to do with it?" She was serious, her brows knit. I wanted to bite her lower lip and make promises that I could never keep. Maybe it was nearly being blown up and killed that brings out the romantic fool in me. She was attractive and not a Vietnamese spy, which suddenly was a lot more appealing than I would have thought.

"Take it to a friend at Fort Devens. Have him check the stock number and see if we can track it down." What I was thinking and should have said was, *Stuff it in the mouth of the murderous fuck who killed the girl, my Ghia, and was trying hard to kill me*. "Then have him take it out and have the Explosive Ordnance Disposal boys blow it up. Or just toss it in the Charles—you can't do much more to that river."

We ordered. We started with oysters. Probably the least romantic time a man and woman sat across from each other and slurped them down. I feel bad for people who don't like oysters on the half shell. They are chewy, taste like the ocean, and with a little cocktail sauce, so much the better. Although I have never found them to live up to their reputation as an aphrodisiac.

"Andy, are you going to tell me what this is about? Really about." She looked at me with pretty eyes and concern, and I almost did.

"Watts, you know that I am radioactive. You know, metaphorically. You seem like you like your career. You might want a little deniability."

"Why? I'm not afraid." She raised her chin at me. It was cute and I could see that if I spent more time with her, I would lose a lot of arguments. I could see how she ended up in the bureau. There was a fierceness to her.

After the oysters came a much less sexy New England boiled dinner for me and a Cobb salad for her.

"Did you ever wonder why you got the call in the middle of the night to tell you to stay out of it?"

"Sure."

"Did it occur to you that they are serious about you and the bureau not being involved?"

"So what? You can't blow people up in Boston." She was on her second martini.

"Watts. I am not sure what it is exactly, but I have stumbled into some sort of Company operation. That is why the deputy director is waving you off the case."

"The Company," she said.

"The Company," I confirmed.

"The fucking Company."

"Yep, which means, for you, nice Fed lady, I am radioactive."

"Radioactive . . . Jesus, I don't even like you that much."

We finished and she ordered the chocolate mousse. I ordered a coffee. There wasn't much more to talk about. I paid, we left, and on the sidewalk she looked at me and said, "Be careful, Roark. You are seriously out of your league." I thanked her and drove to the office. Out of my league? I was wondering what league I was in. I certainly wasn't playing in Fenway anymore. I left Watts with the serial number of the Colt, asking her to see if it had any history.

I parked a street over and a few blocks away out of an abundance of caution. I went in the back door of Marconi's. There was a cream-colored T-bird parked in back. The hood was cold. I stopped debating whether to go in. I needed information more than anything. I stopped in Marconi's bathroom and removed the tape from the grenade and put it in my right outer pocket. A smart man would have left. . . . I was frustrated with being pushed around and blown up.

I made my way upstairs and walked into my office. The same pair who had been arguing with Nguyen in the kitchen of the Blue Lotus were now in my office. Asian Run-DMC was there, holding what looked like a small .45 in his hand. He quickly pointed it at me. It was a Llama, a small Spanish .380. Unlike the larger Colt pistol, this had a ventilated rib down the slide. He had on his silly hat and Adidas tracksuit. Standing next to him was the guy who dressed out of a ten year old catalog. He was holding a Smith & Wesson Model 10 snub nose, with its thick six-shot cylinder, in his right hand. Sitting at my desk, looking like he owned it, was a well-dressed Vietnamese man in his fifties. Unlike the other two, who were pointing their guns at me, his, another Llama .380, was on my desk in front of him.

"Hello, *Trung Si* Roark." He had the Vietnamese habit of over pronouncing the *R*s in my name. It amused my teammates in-country to no end that the Vietnamese thought that I was Sergeant Rock, like the comic book character. "I am Colonel Tran."

"Good evening, Colonel. I appreciate your coming in person instead of just blowing me up from a distance." I

slowly stepped further into the office. Ten-year-old catalog guy gestured toward my waist with his .38. I held the
raincoat open, and he stepped in, snub nose unwavering,
and took the Colt .45 out of its holster and put it on the
desk.

"Yes, it is regrettable that things have gotten to this
point. Please understand, we merely thought you were an
annoyance until you and the communist agent went to
Global Sea Transport. That made us nervous, and now, so
much unnecessary killing. Did you know she was a communist?"

"No, I found out a few minutes before you blew her
and my car up." I had felt tense, the type of tension that is
in the jaw where it meets the neck, before I walked in.

"Dad, we should just off this guy and be done with it."
This from the kid in the tracksuit. His father barked at
him in Vietnamese. Salvation Army realized that my
hands were still in my pockets. He gestured toward them
with his thick revolver.

"I really liked that car, too." I ignored Asian Run.
Colonel Tran smiled, revealing gold teeth in front. It used
to be quite the fashion among wealthier Vietnamese soldiers to get gold teeth. Gold teeth and tailored, skin-tight
uniforms. I never understood that.

"She was here to disrupt my work with the Committee
and to kill you. You see, the communists still consider
you a war criminal, whereas the Committee, men like me,
we see a hero. It is just unfortunate that things have gotten so disharmonious. You should be working with us."

Salvation Army pointed his .38 at my midsection, then
at my left pocket. I looked at him. "It's a gun. I am going
to take it out slowly." Using my thumb and index finger, I
took the Chief's Special out of my pocket and held it out

to him butt first. He took it, his eyes straying from the gun to the ring from the M26 fragmentation grenade. He backpedaled, putting my .38 on the desk next to my .45. and said something in Vietnamese.

"Dad let's just kill this loser and split," Tran barked at him.

"*Trung Si* Roark, what is in your other pocket?" I eased my hand out of my pocket. In it I was the fragmentation grenade, holding the spoon down with my thumb. I felt happy for the first time in days.

"Oh, you mean this. You left it taped to my chair. Would you like it back?" Salvation Army said something in rapid Vietnamese.

"Let's just shoot this loser. The grenade has, like, a five-second fuse. We'll be downstairs before it blows up." Tracksuit was full of good ideas. His father barked a short command at him. I looked over at Tracksuit.

"Boy, this grenade has a smoke grenade fuse, not a regular timed fuse. If I let this spoon go, it blows right away." I smiled at him.

"You're lying."

"If you think that, then you are actually dumber than you look, and you look pretty fucking stupid." It would have been worth being shot, blown to smithereens just to see the look of surprise on his stupid face.

"*Trung Si,* please, let's be civil. He is my son. I wanted to raise him as an American and not the way I was raised. Clearly, that was a mistake. You see, he is like you Americans, impetuous and self-indulgent." He smiled, like we were dads at the playground sharing parenting tips.

"Self-indulgent?"

"Yes. You would think that you were the only ones in the war, that your small sacrifices of blood have any bearing on what happens in and to Vietnam. We Vietnamese lost so many more than you. We lost our whole country. Yet you Americans act as though the war only touched you. It didn't. You would come and fight for a year and leave—war tourists. We stayed, we fought the Chinese, the Japanese, the French, and then you came for a little bit." I have seen cobra snakes spew less venom.

"It is funny, Colonel, but I left my blood on Vietnamese soil; most of my friends and brothers died there. We did it because we believed we were there to fight against a horrible enemy trying to enslave you and your country. We were sacrificed a great deal to defend the Vietnamese people. What was difficult, nearly impossible to watch was the sheer greed and laziness of the ARVN officers we dealt with. The ones who would steal the humanitarian aid we gave out. The ones who were too cowardly to go out on missions with us. Not all of the ARVN or politicians, just a lot of them." I was angry. I had seen so many fucked-up ARVN officers that I was still angry. I had known some great ones, but they were as rare as they were brave. The King Bees, the Vietnamese helicopter pilots who supported us, were braver than brave. They would fly into the mouth of hell to get us out of the shit if that is where we were. I loved those guys like brothers.

"I was in military intelligence, I was a colonel, and I had to work with several American officers. You had no stomach to fight the war. You didn't understand the Vietnamese, the Viet Cong. You would tell us what to do as though we were servants even though it was our country. At least the French brought us some culture. . . . You brought Coca-Cola.

"You had stupid rules and didn't want to get your hands dirty. How could you hope to win? Your government wasn't committed to the war. To winning. Look at how they treated your soldiers. They squandered them." Tran sounded bitter. I had to agree with him about some of it. I had seen the Saigon Cowboys who only came to the field for the mopping up. Even worse were the high-ranking officers who stopped in-country on a junket so they could collect hazardous duty pay for the month. The only thing worse were the Gung Ho types who didn't understand how to fight a guerilla war.

I had seen the ARVN intel people torture enough people to know it was a waste of time. Most of the war was a waste. Villages destroyed and people killed to either protect democracy or promote the revolution. It had been a mess of a war.

"Well, Colonel, looks like it's time. Are you boys going to shoot or leave?" Tran sighed and stood up. He came around the desk, the Llama now tucked into his waistband.

"Trung Si Roark, I don't imagine I could convince you to walk away from this?"

"You blew up my car, you killed a girl, and you tried to kill me here. What do you think?"

"No, I suppose not."

"I really liked that car." They walked out, the colonel, the son, and, last, the Salvation Army man. He smiled at me. His teeth were brown from nicotine and too much of the sweet Vietnamese coffee. He turned back from my anteroom and cocked his hand like a pistol at me, made a noise, and brought his thumb down, like a gun firing. He smiled and laughed and walked away down the hall.

As soon as I was sure they were gone, I put the pin back in the grenade, then found some duct tape, and, just to be sure, taped the spoon down. I put it on my desk and put the .45 back in its holster. I put the grenade back in my pocket and the .38 in my other one. Then I spent the next five minutes shaking and thinking about the effects of fragmentation grenades in small spaces.

Then I called Pan Am to see about flights to San Francisco. They quoted me times and prices. I was not looking forward to folding my sore self into an airline seat for seven hours but there was no way around it.

Chapter 15

The flight from Logan Airport to San Francisco was as good as one could expect. The stewardesses were leggy in their blue dresses, pretty and as impersonal as bank tellers. When the captain came on the PA system, he sounded confident and assured. The food was sealed in plastic and microwaved within an inch of turning it into rubber. The liquor came in small, overpriced bottles. My seat was cramped and uncomfortable. The five-year-old behind me seemed tireless in his efforts to kick the back of my seat. His mother was determined to allow him the latitude to continue to "express himself." In short, it was everything that one could expect from a flight in the jet era.

My head still hurt. Takeoff and the cabin pressure didn't help. My ears still had a slight ringing in them from the car blowing up. I kept wondering what would have happened to Thuy if the car hadn't blown up. I didn't love her but I wouldn't have minded getting to know her better. It was hard to think of her as an enemy agent, but it was also hard to think of her like any other girl.

When I told Watts what my plan was, she told me that I was nuts and that she thought I had a concussion. She agreed to take Sir Leominster in while I was away. No sense in him getting blown up, too. He wasn't as experienced with hand grenades as I was. Junior behind me decided that his foot was tired from his self-expression. I built up a small collection of tiny, empty whiskey bottles. I wanted to sleep but my head hurt too much.

The first time I flew to San Francisco, it had been on the way to Vietnam. That flight hadn't been too cheerful. Tony, Chris, and I had been pals during Special Forces training. We each had different job skills and graduated the Q Course at different times. All three of us wanted to go to Vietnam and agreed to look out for each other. Tony graduated first and was in-country first. I followed a couple of months later. I was hoping that he hadn't forgotten us.

When I landed at Tan Son Nhat Airport in Saigon, someone called my name, and it was an overweight master sergeant. I didn't know they could fit an REMF (Rear Echelon Motherfucker), a Leg (nonairborne), and a lifer all in one person, but his ample belly helped me understand how they pulled it off. He told me I was on the next plane to Da Nang and if I hustled I could make the next C-130. I ignored what looked like a barbecue sauce stain near his neatly starched and pressed pocket and moved out smartly.

The flight to Da Nang wasn't long, which was good. The C-130 was fitted with canvas jump seats. The crew chief was not easygoing enough to let us stretch out and sleep on the floor; the good ones do. The wheels of the plane touched down, and we taxied to the terminal. The engines stopped turning, and the ramp went down. A wave of hot, moist air enveloped us. Already rumpled fatigues, the starch long abused out of them, seemed to wilt even more.

Before anyone could move, a booming voice with a thick New York accent commanded, "Hold it, troops. We have a way of doing things here at Da Nang, and that is the Army way. Due to a priority request, all Special Forces personnel will stand up and debark first. Then officers, NCOs, and enlisted men. Now, SF soldiers, hustle up—don't want to make the officers and men wait."

I stood up, as did a few other guys. I took my duffel bag and walked off the plane. Tony was standing there, his big pearly white grin sheltered by a magnificent mustache that was nowhere near being within the regulation. He pointed out a jeep to the other guys and wrapped me in a bear hug. He was wearing faded Tiger Stripe fatigues, mirrored aviators, and his beret. He looked like the poster child for Special Forces. His voice was deep and gravelly. "Red, it is good to see you. Come get in the jeep before the Air Force gets here and fucks everything up."

I didn't wait to be told twice. I got in, and he drove us to another part of the airfield and let the other guys out by the terminal. He gave the quick instructions but had put a calloused hand on my arm. After the other guys split, Tony lit a Chesterfield and offered me one. While I was lighting it, he asked, "Red, did you have any idea what you want to do here in-country?"

"Dunno, figured get on a team or try to go to Mike force. . . . I just want to be in the shit. You know?" I was young enough to think that it would mean something, getting shot at. That I might make a difference. I was eager to get to it.

"Have you heard of the Studies and Observation Group, SOG?"

"No, it sounds like a desk job. I'm not interested in that shit."

"Red, it isn't what it sounds like. If you really want to be in the shit, do the dangerous shit, you want to be in SOG. I talked to the Sergeant Major. He knows you're coming and will give you a shot, because he thinks I'm not a fuckup. I gotta know right now, because you have orders to go to Saigon to work at MACV headquarters. I had a guy I know at the terminal make sure you got on this plane."

"What the fuck?"

"Someone heard that you're smart and that you can type."

"Fuck that. Where do I sign up?"

"Relax. Just sit back and let your old eye-talian Uncle Tony drive you while you take in the sights of scenic South Vietnam, pearl of the Orient."

"Thanks, man. For a spaghetti bender and a Yankees fan, you're all right."

"Well, we gotta take pity on you simple folk from Boston who actually think that the Red Sox might win a World Series someday."

He handed me a Swedish K-gun, a regular one without

a silencer. I checked the bolt and casually laid it across my knees, facing out. It was comforting to have the compact weapon on my lap, thirty-six rounds of 9mm ammunition on tap if I needed it. Tony slung a shortened version of the M-16, known as a CAR-15, over his neck so it rested on his lap and he could fire it one handed.

We took off as he double clutched the jeep. I had a million questions, but Tony's driving didn't allow for much conversation. Even if I could have talked, I was taken by the scenery. It was lush and green, rolling hills and mountains that reached high into the clouds. There were rice paddies and rivers, and the land by the road was so green I wondered if this was what Ireland looked like. There were roads that were paved, and others were ribbons of red clay cut in the greenery. There were peasants working the paddies, water buffalos, motor scooters, and women in conical hats and *ao dais*. The deep South had been exotic compared to South Boston. . . . Vietnam was like another planet.

On the other hand, it smelled bad, and the heat was like driving through a really humid blast furnace. Fort Bragg had been hot and humid, but that was nothing compared to Vietnam. In basic training, then at Fort Bragg, people noticed that when it got really hot my face turned red. That was how I got the nickname.

It took an hour to get to the camp. We barely slowed as the Vietnamese gate guard raised the barrier, and we were inside the first set of wire driving up a hill. It might have had grass once, but it was long gone. Fields of fire had been cleared, sandbags had been filled, and fighting positions, mortar pits, and bunkers had all been built. They had all taken their toll on the greenery.

There was an elaborate system of trenches and watch-towers that allowed the guards to see the terrain. Every-thing was surrounded by a triple strand of concertina wire, razor sharp and six feet high. Cans with pebbles were strung throughout the wire as an early warning sys-tem. Claymore mines were everywhere, and there were machine gun positions in the towers and bunkers.

As we approached an inner wire wall, I could make out the shape of a Quad-50 that could cover the road in or be swiveled to cover the hillside. The tips of metal fifty-five-gallon drums stuck out here and there facing away from the camp, toward the wire. Foo Gas, homemade na-palm in sealed barrel. The front of the barrel was wrapped in detonation cord, and there was an explosive charge in the bottom or back of the drum. When fired, the det cord went off a split second before the main charge, blasting the can open. The rear charge then went off almost simul-taneously, igniting the napalm and launching it out of the can. It was like a giant single-shot flamethrower designed to stop or slow a human wave attack. It was always im-pressive to see the new and elaborate ways man came up with to destroy his fellow man.

We pulled up to another gate, and a small brown man with an M1 carbine slung upside down saluted Tony, and they exchanged pleasantries in a dialect I had never heard. That was the first Montagnard I had ever seen. Tony drove into the compound within a compound and brought me over to a long, low building that served as the command post and living quarters for the CO and sergeant major. It had a tin roof, and the walls were rein-forced with sandbags. The building was half buried in the ground, and we had to step down into the cool interior.

Everything seemed just slightly damp and mildewy. There was an ever-present droning noise that I found out was the sound of the ten-kilowatt generators.

The camp had two, and one was always running twenty-four hours a day. The generators would run a day then rest a day, alternating the burden of providing what was essentially a small barbed-wire-enclosed town's electrical needs. Inside the building, the generator noise was matched by the constant hum of radios, their static broken only by transmissions. We made our way past crude desks, map boards, and banks of radios to a plywood door. Tony knocked and waited.

"Come in!" We went in and both stood at parade rest in front of a desk. The black man behind the desk had a massive shaven bald head, thick neck, and truly impressive shoulders, arms, and hands. He wore a shiny Magnum revolver in a shoulder holster under his left arm. "This the new guy?"

"Yes, Sergeant Major, this is Sergeant Andy Roark. We call him Red." The Sergeant Major stood up and towered over both of us. He stuck out a hand that made mine look like a small child's in his. He crushed all of the bones in my right while saying, "I am Sergeant Major Billy Justice. Welcome to SOG, you are gonna get the chance to do Recon work. I hope it works out. I think a lot of Tony and hope his confidence in you isn't misplaced. I like him enough to ignore the fact that he is trying to put Yankees on all my teams.

"We will get you trained up and figure out what team to send you to when the time comes. You have to earn your way out here. If you can't cut it, we will find you work: Mike Force or an A-team. Recon work is scary, dangerous shit. It isn't for everyone and not everyone can do it. If you look like Recon work is for you we will find you a spot. That will be up to the One-Zero. If he wants to take a shot on you, then he will. If no one wants you . . . well, I heard a rumor you know how to type. I could always use a cracker house mouse, even one from Bahstin." Billy Justice laughed, and I tried like hell not to be angry. Sergeant Major smiled at me. He had a gold tooth in place of one of his front teeth, and his smile was not comforting or warm.

"Thank you, Sergeant Major. I appreciate the chance." I wanted to tell him I would try my best, that in a few short minutes I knew that I wanted to be in this unit, on a team, or I would die trying.

"Good, good, I hope you do. Tony, get him squared away in one of the team hooches. Get him gear and a weapon and generally squared away."

Tony took me to another low building like the Tactical Operations Center (TOC), also known as The Head Shed. This one was broken up into a series of small rooms separated by plywood partitions, each with two bunks with mosquito nets and crude wooden shelves made of plywood for clothes and gear. There were two wall lockers that had been old when this had been a French war in the early 1950's. I threw my duffel bag on a bunk.

"This was RT Rhino's, but they got beat up pretty bad. For now, you can bunk here until they rebuild the team or assign you to a different one."

"Thanks. What happened to them?"

"Bad luck, bad tactics, who knows? Out here, one is just as fatal as the other. You will see that. Out here, you can do everything right and still get greased. They landed and were compromised shortly after the choppers split. They tried to *di di mau* out of there but got lit up pretty bad. Most of the Yards were KIA, a couple of Americans, too. The team leader didn't make it."

We walked to another low building where supplies and ammo were kept. He helped me draw my web gear, rucksack, and other equipment. It was nice having Tony there, because he helped me take only what I would need. I drew an M-16—twenty magazines each could hold twenty rounds—and a Colt Government Model 45. Tony handed me a bunch of grenades and a pen flare. I noticed that everyone, everywhere was always armed. They had, at a minimum, a holstered pistol. He gave me ammunition and a black windbreaker.

"Right now, take these. You never leave our compound without long gun. Always have a pistol on you. If Charlie attacks, you want more in your hand than your winning personality. Later, we will get you fitted out with whatever weapons and special gear you need for the field. Get used to being armed. Get used to cleaning your weapons religiously. Practice rucking. . . . You aren't used to the heat and humidity yet. Then in a couple of months when Chris gets in-country, you can square him away. We will send you to the next Recon school in a couple of weeks." He was referring to the SOG Recon school we all went to before being turned loose in the field.

It didn't seem possible that I would ever not be green, and it seemed impossible that I would be experienced, confident like Tony. Except two months later, I was sitting in a repainted jeep stolen from the air force waiting for Chris at the terminal in Da Nang. I had survived a couple of missions and convinced everyone that I was not a complete fuckup.

I woke up when the plane started to make its decent into San Francisco. I had fallen asleep, lost in the memories of my war long gone by. The airport there is bordered by buildings, mountains, and lots of red tape. The locals really don't like the jet noises. It was like some sort of ride that let people experience what it is like to land in a combat zone. The plane came in fast on a steep angle, and then flared, and the wheels kissed the runway. The only thing worse than landing there was taking off.

The last time I had flown into San Francisco, it was three years ago. A client felt the need to impress upon me how wealthy she was and how much she wanted my service. She flew me out to convince me to take a job that ultimately had almost taken my life. It had cost me my friendship with Danny Sullivan, my oldest friend.

I liked San Francisco, despite the chilly welcome I received there after Vietnam. I never held the spit and the insults against the city. Hell, some of the fights might have been fun if I hadn't been too drunk to remember them.

I came up the jetway, made my way past the hard, plastic chairs in their legions in the gate area. I went past the check-in area, my canvas mailbag bouncing against my hip. I had packed a couple of days' worth of clothes, a shaving kit, and an Inspector Maigret novel. I hadn't read on the plane because of the headache. Now the bad version of "I'm Always Drunk in San Francisco" that was being piped in through speakers hurt my head almost as bad as the explosion.

I walked out into the main terminal. There were people everywhere: businesspeople, families, nouveau hippies, bikers, and a battered private eye who needed a drink. A tall biker-looking guy in jeans, a dark shirt, and a leather vest peeled himself off of the column he had been leaning against with one black biker-booted foot. He had a beard, mustache, and mess of shaggy blond hair. An earring glinted in his right ear. He headed toward me like he was getting paid for it.

"Hey, weirdo, where the fuck you think you are going?" His accent had been Southern once. He was big, broad through the shoulders and thick in the chest. His hands were big and scarred, and just by looking at him you knew that fighting was part of his life.

"Dunno, where is your sister selling her ass?"

"Probably the same place your momma is." He stepped forward and wrapped me in a bear hug that crushed the breath from my lungs. It would have made my ribs and head ache if I weren't already bruised . . . except I was.

"God damn, Red . . . what the fuck happened to you? You look like you have been to the wars." Chris didn't look anything like the young Green Beret medic I had picked up in Da Nang years ago. His nose had been broken a couple of times. His hands were calloused and had grease imbedded in them that spoke of lots of time working on engines.

"My car got blown up a couple of nights ago. . . . I was standing too close to it."

"That explains your face. Did it do your ribs, too?" Chris had been a good medic. He knew his shit and had seen a lot. While Tony and I had gone into Recon, Chris felt he was doing God's work as the team medic for a Mike force. He would tend to the team, their hundreds of

Montagnards, their families, etc. He had rotated out after a couple of years. I had heard rumors of working for the Company in other parts of Asia, being a hired soldier in Rhodesia and Angola. Then San Francisco. We had kept in touch, sometimes letters, sometimes drunken phone calls where we told war stories and cried over our dead comrades. We each felt that if we had stayed with Tony, he would have lived. It was part of the war freight that we carried. The war guilt that would never leave, but at least we could share it with each other.

"I thought you gave that shit up when you started being a low-rent version of Philip Marlowe."

"Me too. What the fuck are you, one of the Village People?" He looked at me for a moment, then laughed.

"Something like that, ya weirdo. Come on, let's go get a drink and catch up. I was kind of shocked when you called and said you were coming out here."

"Yeah, I didn't mean to impose, but I need someone who knows the lay of the land."

"Shit, brother, I am just glad you are here, and we can catch up." His Alabama twang had softened, and his voice wasn't sad exactly, but he had aged.

"It's been too long."

We started walking out of the terminal. Nice, respectable people looked at us and moved out of our path. The two cops by the door eyeballed us. It was the look that I used to give people who I knew were trouble. It was a look that made the hand you held your nightstick with itch. Cops are like dogs: friendly and nice enough, but violence, swift and sure, was just below the surface. Had I gone that far through the looking glass that cops looked at me like I was trouble?

We walked out to the sidewalk. There was a Harley Davidson in front of us. I looked at Chris and said, "Please tell me that isn't yours?"

"What, you don't want to ride, bitch?"

"Given my luck lately, I think there aren't many faster ways to get killed." Chris laughed and pointed to an older beat-up Ford pickup. It had been green once and was a straight bed, the kind where the wheel wells are prominently displayed on the sides. We climbed in and he started us toward the city proper.

Chapter 16

The drive in from SFO, the call sign for the airport, was fairly uneventful. It was funny to me that in California they referred to the airports not by name but by call sign: LAX, SFO, etc. The traffic was like Boston's at that time of night, early evening, just after work. We bumper-to-bumpered our way to Chris's apartment in the Richmond district. We rode up and down hills like roller coasters. I could see why so many movies loved to film car chases in the dramatic scenery. I was taken by the fact that the Spanish influence was still evident even though it had been a couple hundred years or more. It was hard for me to reconcile palm trees and the raw chill of the March night in San Francisco.

Chris's apartment was actually a small stand-alone building. It was wedged between an all-night laundromat and a run-down duplex. He parked in the laundromat's parking lot and we walked over to a gate made of eight-foot-high spiked metal bars. Chris unlocked it, and we were in a narrow alley between his apartment and the duplex. His front door was twenty feet down the alley, and twenty feet beyond that was a small yard fenced in by a stockade fence.

He let us into the apartment, which turned out to be a large room that made up the kitchen, dining area, and living room. It was probably two-thirds of the structure and had a white tile floor and white-faced cabinets. To the left there were two doors, each close to an exterior wall, each with three steps up. One set of steps led to the bedroom and one led to the bathroom. Opposite that on the other end of the apartment was a door leading out to a small patio. The apartment was spartan in its decoration and I had the feeling that Chris could leave it at a moment's notice.

I dropped my bag next to the couch, where I would be sleeping. Chris went to the refrigerator and pulled open the door.

"You want a beer, Red?"

"I sure do." He handed me something that definitely was not Lowenbrau. The bottle was brown and squat. The label had a picture of a blue ship's anchor centered on it that read, "Anchor Steam." It was cold and had more body and more flavor than the beers I was used to.

"Do you like it? They brew it here in San Francisco."

"It's very good." And it was.

"Are you hungry?" Chris, the biker with the smashed nose, former medic, now turned the perfect host.

"I can eat." That was an understatement. The food on the plane had been unappetizing.

"I made a red pepper and shrimp risotto."

"That sounds great." I had known Chris as a top-notch medic, a Green Beret, and an all-around badass. Now he was also a gourmet cook. He sautéed spinach, dusting it with a bit of nutmeg and black pepper. He then got out two bowls and served out the risotto. It was red, like pasta sauce after someone has poured in a bit of heavy cream. The shrimp were in it, and Chris had dusted it with bonito flakes. The effect was awesome and a little unsettling. As the heat rose from the rice, the bonito flakes wiggled and waved. At first, it reminded me of insects, but then I tasted it, and it was fantastic. He put the spinach on the side of each bowl. Chris had uncorked a red wine to go with it.

"It's a '79 Brunello di Montalcino. It was a good year. Not a great year, but a good year. It should stand up nicely to the shrimp and bonito." Chris was right; it did. The shrimp were fresh and perfectly cooked.

The food was excellent, and we spent some time eating without saying much. After the meal was done, we began to catch up. Other than a drunken night in Boston after Chris had rotated home, we hadn't seen each other since we were in-country. I told him about my brief stint as a cop and then some stories of life as a private detective, mostly amusing tales about infidelity and insurance fraud. He told me about being a mercenary in Rhodesia and Angola.

"What are you doing now?"

"For a living?"

"Yeah."

"Honestly, Red?"

"Sure, it isn't like I'm in a place to judge anyone." I wasn't and certainly not Chris.

"I run with a bunch of guys. Sometimes they need

someone who can patch up a wound without calling the cops. I'm good at patching people up. "

"Probably doesn't hurt that you know a bit about guns and never shied away from a fight in your life." He hadn't. I had watched Chris in more than a few bar fights. It was impressive.

"No, I guess it doesn't."

"So, you're in a bike gang?"

"No, I'm not in it. . . . I'm not a joiner. Not since Vietnam. No, I just hang around, kind of like a consultant. They pay pretty well, I get to spend time on my Hog, and I wasn't cut out to be a cop."

"Hey, man, like I said, it isn't for me to judge. Right or wrong, you paid your dues in Vietnam. You paid early and in full."

"We sure did." He held out his beer and we toasted.

"Red, why are you here, all bruised, beat up, and blown up?"

"What if I told you that I was chasing a rumor, a hint, a suggestion, a fairy tale about some gold? Gold that doesn't really belong to anyone anymore." He stopped drinking and put the beer bottle down on the table.

"Gold. Like as in Miner Forty-Niner? What is it, old Nazi gold, the stuff they disappeared with forty years ago?"

"No. This isn't that, or that old. This is from South Vietnam, their national treasury. Gold bars taken out on a ship as Saigon was falling. A ship that is currently not very far from here."

"Okay, but why would it still be on the ship?"

"Well, I'm not sure it is. I think it is because gold is heavy and the people who pulled it out of Vietnam may not have had any way of disposing of it without drawing a lot of attention to themselves. They didn't have an organization or resources. Maybe they had some contacts in the CIA and the army. Maybe they didn't trust anyone. When Saigon fell, the Swiss barred their banks from taking any gold bullion from Vietnam or Cambodia. It is possible that they left it on a ship, in a safe place waiting for the time to be right to start a counterrevolution. A ship that their good friend Uncle Sugar would provide free maintenance and security for."

"Why not take it to a bank?" Chris asked.

"I think if they tried to dispose of it normally, the communists might be able to make a claim on it."

"Why not just hide it someplace like Fort Knox?" He was asking the sixty-four-thousand-dollar question.

"Because the ship they have to move things on and off of the ship for maintenance reasons. People can come and go. Boats can pull up alongside and heavy cargo can be off loaded. I imagine there is a lot of paperwork involved with anything at Ft. Knox but not so much with the Mothball Fleet."

"The Mothball Fleet?"

"Yep. The ship's last location from '75 till now is in Suisun Bay." I told him about Thuy, the murders in Boston and Quincy, as well as our trip to Virginia. I told him about Colonel Tran and his flunkies.

"They beat you up, blew up your car, and boobytrapped your office?" Chris was shaking his head.

"Yep."

"All because of some gold?"

"Well, in their defense, it might be a shitload of gold. That, and the Committee to Restore the Republic of Vietnam might feel that I had information about some of their dirty deeds."

"How dirty?" Chris had the rare habit of looking at you when talking to you. Not just glancing, but looking at you with the full force of his gaze.

"Shaking down Vietnamese business owners, intimidating Vietnamese journalists, murdering them . . . little things like that that I find very un-American." It was all bad, but murdering a journalist seemed particularly far from American ideals.

"And the bastards blew up your car . . . with your girl in it."

"Yeah, that too. Though I don't know how much she was my girl. . . . It isn't like we had a relationship. I was an assignment to her." I hadn't been in love with her or anything but I didn't like just being an assignment.

"It couldn't have been just that for her. She didn't kill you. She knew that going back to the land of Uncle Ho as a failure probably would land her in a reeducation camp or dead." That was the funny thing about Chris—for a guy who was a devout Southern Baptist when I met him, he had slowly turned into something else. He had mellowed, had a drink or two and stopped judging people through the lens of his church.

"Thank you. Maybe it is easier to think of it like it was just business. On the other hand, I liked her, however little I knew her." It wasn't something that I had wanted to think about. It was easier to deal with her death if she was an agent doing her job. It was easier if I could be more upset about the car than the person. It had been such an unnecessary waste of life. She had been young and vital. In the quiet moments in bed she reminded me of Leslie or more accurately the way I felt when I was with Leslie. It wasn't the same but it was a hint of what was out there. Maybe I just wanted that feeling back again. It could never happen but that didn't mean Thuy should have been killed.

"What are you going to get to replace the Karmann Ghia?" Chris was a gearhead through and through.

"I already got it. An older, well-maintained Ford Maverick, 302." Chris whistled.

"That is a lot of car for a city boy like you, Red." Chris used to regale us with tales of racing his friends down the red clay back roads of rural Alabama. He had lived outside of Anniston, Alabama, not far from the army base.

"Thanks, you aren't exactly country anymore, making fancy risotto and drinking good wine. Educating me about the difference between a good and great year in Tuscany." He shrugged his shoulders.

"You know us old Special Forces NCOs, we are not just content to exist, we must strive to learn, to grow, and to improve." He was quoting an instructor from the Q Course that was infamously tough, not the type to scream and yell but rather to have very high standards, standards that you either met or, more likely, you didn't, and you were out.

"You young Special Forces NCOs, y'all need to learn to expand your minds. You need to understand everything from geopolitics to medicine, to history, to small unit tactics and ballistics. You all aren't just a bunch of leg NCOs who only need to know just what they need to know." We both laughed. The funny thing was that the master sergeant we were imitating was right. SF NCOs had to know and do more—that was why it was so elite. A Special Forces sergeant would lead the same amount of men that a captain in the infantry would end up leading, except that we had to do it in a foreign language, be aware of the geopolitical implications of every mission, as well as be culturally attuned to the taboos of the men we were leading. It was heady stuff.

That was why it had been a colossal waste to lose so many in Vietnam. There had been nothing wrong with fighting and dying bravely, as many of us had. It was just that they, the boys in Washington in their famous buildings with famous names, had squandered a precious, precious resource. They had asked us to make horrible sacrifices for a war that they were unwilling and eventually unable to win. In the end, for what? Chris's voice broke through my bitter reverie.

"Red, what's your plan?"

"What makes you think I have a plan?" I asked innocently.

"Red, I was in the jungle with you. You may not have liked to admit it, but when you were running Recon, you had a plan for everything. You had plans and contingency plans and you were able to adapt and shift gears fast. Shit, you probably don't brush your teeth without a plan." After Tony had been killed, Chris came to Recon. He had been good at it. Better than me, if I was being honest. If I planned and tried to figure out every angle, he seemed to glide effortlessly from one situation to the next. He was able to simply react and react until he was out of a bad situation.

"I was thinking that if you had the time and could put up with me for a few days I might set up a Recon. I want to check out the Mothball Fleet from the shore and then figure out the best way to get onboard the *Adams*. Once on board, I want to look around and see if there is a pile of gold sitting around."

"And if there is? What, are you gonna steal it? You don't strike me as the type to steal."

"I don't know. Part of me would love to be rich, but mostly I don't like how these assholes treat people. I want to hurt them, maybe expose them. I don't know. They blew up my car, and I really liked that car."

"Okay, I get it. I can help you out for a few days. My work is, uh, unstructured."

"Cool. I figure we need to do a map Recon, then drive out and around the bay. Take pictures and look at the area with binoculars. Figure out the method of attack. We have to figure out how to get across the water quietly and onto the ship. Probably take a couple of days to plan."

"You packed light, so you will need clothes and stuff, a piece. I assume you are lying low." Chris was talking out loud but he was planning like any good soldier would—he just did it vocally. We talked about binoculars, boats, and cameras for a good hour or more. At some point in time, my eyes grew heavy, and I kicked off my shoes. I stretched out on the couch and slept. For once it was a deep, dreamless, restful sleep.

I woke up once. I had a wool blanket thrown over me and could hear Chris snoring in the other room. He had put a holstered .45 on the coffee table by the couch. I didn't have to check and see if it was loaded. I knew Chris. Next to the .45 was a bottle of Anacin and a glass of water. I pulled the blanket close and went back to sleep. It was good to be back among my own people.

Chapter 17

The next morning was chilly and damp. It wasn't misty out; it was San Francisco. Chris had made coffee in a Chemex carafe. The carafe looked like a glass model of a nuclear reactor cooling tower. The coffee sat in a special filter on top, and you poured hot water through it. The whole thing took a long time but was worth it. Chris had ground the coffee that morning. The smell of fresh coffee filled the little house.

Breakfast was simple: toasted whole wheat bagels, cream cheese, and lox. Chris offered some pickled red onion to go with it. The tartness of the onion was a nice counterpoint to the saltiness of the fish. It was a simple breakfast that worked because somehow the competing flavors managed to complement each other. A second mug of coffee and a hot shower made me forget that I had spent seven hours on an airplane and almost three in airports.

We went out to Chris's truck in the parking lot of the laundromat. He walked all the way around it, looking for wires on the ground or telltale signs of tampering. Apparently, my friends on the Committee weren't the only ones who liked to blow things up. The bikers Chris was affiliated with had rivals. Those rivals liked to use dynamite and blow up cars and clubhouses. Our paranoia checks done, we got in and headed down to the harbor. We nosed around down by a part of the waterfront that didn't cater much to tourists but to fishing boats and serious boaters.

We parked and got out. Chris figured we should start at a ship's chandlery. As we were walking over Chris said, "I wonder how long this will last?"

"What?"

"This, all of this," he said, gesturing at the area around us. "It is only a matter of time before the real estate assholes buy this up, too, turn it into condos and high-rises with water views and restaurants with cutesy names. There won't be any room left for regular people to work or enjoy the bay."

"I know what you mean. Boston is the same way. Between the yuppies and the college kids, the whole face of the town is changing." I didn't even bother to mention the traffic or the near impossibility of finding a parking spot.

The ship's chandlery was in a small building wedged in between two old industrial buildings. They were made of brick and smelled of saltwater and dried fish. Inside, we were in a place wholly dedicated to things nautical. It was filled with different samples of rope, brass fittings, polishes, preservatives, and paint. They had radios and electronics, depth sounders, radar, Loran receivers, and lots of things that I couldn't afford, to go with the yacht I didn't have. They had racks of foul weather gear, rubber boots, and wool fisherman's sweaters. If I needed a knife with a marlinspike or a flare pistol, this was the place to get it. Lastly, in one corner were several oak barrels with rolled charts stuffed into them.

We picked through them and found the one of the San Francisco Bay and Suisun Bay. They also had regular U.S. Geological Survey maps of the area, and we grabbed 1:50,000 map sections we needed. I spent more on an excellent pair of rubberized Steiner binoculars than I would have if it were my money. I added two portable marine radios. They were like walkie-talkies but made for use on the ocean. We weren't exactly sure why we would need them, but our time in Special Forces left us with a pathological need to call for more guns or ride home.

Next, we went to an army/navy surplus store, where I spent some money on a blue wool commando sweater, the kind with the patches on the elbows, shoulders, and left side of the chest. I added green fatigue pants in my size, a West German Army undershirt, a black knit watch cap, and a U.S. wool long sleeve undershirt to the growing pile of gear. I found a pair of dark blue Converse Chuck Taylor high tops, the cheapest jungle boot and dive shoe in use the world over. I added a used KA-BAR sheath knife, Marine Corps issue, one of the best all-around knives made. To all of this, I added a camouflage poncho, an army issue lensatic compass, two canteens, and a couple of the new army issue MREs in their brown plastic bags.

Chris threw in a camo stick, army camouflage face paint in an aluminum tube, and an angle head three-color flashlight. Some kid at the Presidio probably sold them to make some extra cash to get him through to payday. Sometimes it can be a long ride until the eagle shits, and a weekend pass can make payday seem awfully far away.

I was looking for a camera. I wasn't looking to spend any more than I had to. Chris suggested a pawnshop. We had gone to several down in the Tenderloin district. We stepped around the addicts and prostitutes and made our way past the seedy tattoo parlors, check-cashing outfits, bail bondsmen, dealers, pimps, and downtrodden. The people they don't make television shows about had to end up somewhere. In San Francisco, it was the Tenderloin. They were people like you, like me, like Chris, but they were just living harder and dying faster. Life was hard, and it was harder for these people. Some had made bad choices: crime, drug addiction, etc. Others had it thrust upon them by poverty, victimization, bad luck, or just were born into bad situations. Some of them were there as the end result of a lifetime's series of bad decisions. It didn't matter; they were in the same place at the same time struggling to survive.

After pounding the pavement for a while, we found what I was looking for. It was a Nikon, a waterproof 35mm. It came with a telephoto lens that was more like a telescope and a soft case. It was worth a few hundred dollars to get a camera set up valued at almost a thousand. The pawnshop owner threw in a few rolls of film. It was afternoon by this point, and we decided to go back to Chris's for beer and a map Recon of the Suisun Bay.

When we got back with our purchases, I cleared Chris's table, and we rolled out our maps. The chart was a stark pen and ink: black lines, plus signs, and numbers denoting depth. The USGS map was more familiar territory for me. It was a topographical map similar to what we had used for years in the army. The colors were old familiar friends: green for vegetation, black for man-made structures, buildings, roads, and railways. Red was for contour intervals, weird wavy lines that showed you elevation but also provided clues as to how steep hills were or where you might be able to hide or make a hasty path. Blue was for water, rivers, ponds, and oceans. A love child of green and blue usually meant a swamp or wetland. I loved maps. My time in the army had taught me to appreciate them as excellent tools, but there was more to it than that. Tracing my finger along contour lines, streams, and rivers, I had a sense of the earth beyond what I could see with my own eyes. That was a rare thing. The colors on the maps had meaning, revealed secrets and ultimately had meant the difference between life and death.

I placed cups, saltshakers, and glasses down to hold down the maps and chart. Chris brought us two excellent Anchor Steam beers. We stood shoulder to shoulder leaning over the maps and the chart. It felt like mission-planning sessions when I was in Vietnam. All we needed were the aerial Reconnaissance photos. But this wasn't Vietnam. We weren't at war, and it wasn't god-awfully hot and humid.

Suisun Bay started its life as the mighty Pacific Ocean, whose vastness poured violently into the San Francisco Bay, which flowed almost forty miles inland to the east. It hugged Alcatraz Island in its cold, choppy embrace and turned south to give Oakland some waterfront. Farther south, it was caught in a basin by San Jose. In the opposite direction, it flowed by San Quentin, keeping the tenants cold in the yard during the winter and offering the barest hint of sea air in the cells in summer. The Pacific

Ocean flowed under the I-580 and into San Pablo Bay, moving inland, moving east, invading inland to meet a series of river deltas. It spread north toward Vallejo, but that was just a tease. The bulk of it headed east inland toward Benicia and the Suisun Bay.

The bay was home to sturgeon fishing and the site of the catastrophic Port Chicago explosion during World War II. Port Chicago was on the southern part of the bay. The navy had an ammunition-handling facility where they loaded shells for the war in the Pacific onto cargo ships. One day, due to bad luck, poor policies, or, worse, leadership, there was an explosion that leveled Port Chicago. Scores were killed, and the damage was unimaginable. Most of the dead sailors were black men loading the ships. It was one thing to be killed fighting for your country but another to be killed by a lack of caring.

To the immediate north across the brackish, brown water stirred by the near constant winds were Roe Island, Ryer Island, a whole bunch of marshlands, and Grizzly Bay, and farther north, Travis Air Force Base. Sandwiched between Grizzly Bay and Honker Bay were the marshes. The map showed black lines crisscrossing through them and leading to the water.

To the west was Suisun Bay and the Mothball Fleet. The fleet was anchored off some marshy area, slough for all of the industries, tank farms, refineries, and the Goodyear factory to empty into. Even though it was only thirty miles from San Francisco, the area was a mix of remote nature and industrial splendor. The ships, a collection of Liberty ships, Freedom ships, tankers, and other assorted vessels, were a couple hundred in number and were moored parallel to the northwestern shore, on the Goodyear side of things. It looked isolated and any traffic by land or water would be regular and not tourists. The security forces, the maintenance workers, and Coast Guard ships on patrol were vying for space in the channel with tankers, freighters, and fishing boats.

We started with the fleet and worked outward. We looked at waterways, terrain features, islands, roads and highways. We traced the routes back to San Francisco. We figured straight line distances and map distances, calculated different routes and the time it would take. We talked about what I wanted to do and the best way to do it. We worked the problem inside out and back again, developing a plan of action. It would be a two-phase Reconnaissance. First, find a place to lay up and watch the fleet, then figure out their security measures. Second, get out onto the ship and see if there was any gold on it. The ship was monitored around the clock, and it was U.S. government property, so if I got caught, I was dealing with the Feds, not cops.

The plan was to get on board under the cover of darkness, poke around, then slip back out. I didn't know what we could do if there was gold on board. Gold bars are heavy and there would be no inconspicuous way to move them. It didn't seem feasible, but I was putting the cart before the horse. I had never planned a gold heist before.

We decided that we needed dinner and that Chris didn't want to cook. Chris suggested pizza, and the thought of cheese and sauce seemed undeniably good. Chris said there was a place around the corner, and we stepped outside. The warm, windy March day had turned into a raw, chilly evening. As we walked the few blocks to the restaurant, he told me funny stories from Angola and Rhodesia. Some involved drunkenness while spending time on leave or the difficulties of working in an environment where several different languages were spoken by the soldiers. He told me stories about the monkeys and the mischief they would get into. The monkeys in Rhodesia and Angola weren't much different from those in Vietnam when it came to getting up to no good.

The pizza place was nothing special on the outside, a couple of windows with neon bar signs, but you couldn't really see very far into the restaurant. Inside was an eclectic collection of chairs and tables with red checked oilcloth on them. They had the standard shakers of red pepper flakes, Parmesan cheese, and granulated garlic in the center. The walls were decorated with a mix of posters advertising Fellini films and old rock concerts. The lights were dim, and the floors were made of roughly finished planks. Chris told me to let him order and went up to the counter. No two chairs or tables were the same. They were all refugees from furniture stores, thrift stores, and estate sales.

He came back with a pitcher of beer and two glasses. He sat down, and I poured us a couple of beers. Chris drank deeply from his and wiped the foam out of his beard with the back of his hand. The beer was cold and good, but it wasn't Anchor Steam.

"Red, how come you didn't stay in the army? I figured you for a lifer, Green Beret all the way. It seemed like you were born to do it, being a One-One, then One-Zero, and then riding Covey." A One-Zero was the Recon team's team leader. He wasn't always the highest-ranking man, but he was always the best man for the job, which meant an experienced Recon man who had been a One-One and One-Two. He had to be selected by the CO and the sergeant major. Which meant that the sergeant major told the CO whom he wanted as a One-Zero and the CO signed the orders. It was a real honor. A One-One was the assistant team leader. He usually watched the back trail, was responsible for covering up the team's tracks and ensuring they didn't get caught by surprise from the rear. A One-Two was the team radioman, humping the heavy PRC-25 radio and making sure that the team could call for help or a ride home.

Covey was the Covey Rider, which was a whole different beast from Recon. Covey was an experienced Recon man riding in an Air Force Forward Air Controller's (FAC) plane. Covey was the link on the radio. Covey checked in on you morning and night. Covey was the one you called when shit went south, went bad. Covey coordinated planes and Cobra gunships and, if you were in range, artillery. Covey could, in an emergency, bring every available aircraft in Vietnam to your aid. Covey was the calm voice on the radio telling you that you were going to make it. Telling you where he needed you to maneuver to get pulled out on a chopper. Covey was the cat who saved your team's ass.

When Sergeant Major Billy Justice felt that I was too fried, too far gone to run Recon anymore, he sent me to be a Covey Rider. He saved my life, and I repaid him by helping save other lives on the ground. It wasn't that riding Covey wasn't dangerous. Guys got shot down or crashed. The NVA and Cong loved to shoot at anything in the air. Covey Riders and their pilots did insane shit, like flying through weather Rudolph the Red-Nosed Reindeer wouldn't dream of flying in. Riding Covey was just a different type of danger. Which was funny about Vietnam— it offered a wide variety of ways to get dead.

Everyone started out as a One-Two. Not everyone was good enough or even wanted to be a One-Zero. It was an

awesome responsibility. One-Zeros were wholly responsible for the teams. They decided what training was un-
dertaken. They planned the missions and then led them.
They were responsible for the safety of the men and the
mission's success. They made decisions that were usually
left to company commanders and field grade officers,
captains and majors. Not sergeants.

Small teams were hard because everyone knew everyone intimately. We lived, trained, and fought together. We
ate together, drank together, and became very, very close.
Inevitably, everyone's luck would run out. For most people that meant being killed, captured, or at best wounded.
For a One-Zero, that meant you lost men who were your
responsibility, but they were also your brothers. My great
curse was that I survived. My men were dead; I had failed
them and had had the temerity to live.

It wasn't just the Americans either. We got to know our
Montagnards and trusted them with our lives. They were
like our little brothers. Some teams used Vietnamese soldiers, or in some rare cases, Chinese mercenaries. I could
never trust the Vietnamese we worked with. There were
too many stories about their being infiltrated by the VC.
We trusted the Yards because they hated the communists,
and they hated the Vietnamese. They were so discrimi-
nated against by the Vietnamese that they loathed them
whether they were from the North or the South. They
were loyal to us because we treated them like people. We
ate with them, provided medical care to their families,
and genuinely appreciated them. They were tough, loyal,
and outstanding in the field.

"Shit, man, I don't know. I loved the army. Loved SF
and loved the war. But it was changing. It turned into a
meat grinder. We lost so many Recon men. I lost my One-

One, my One-Two, and half of my Yards. . . . I lived. Toward the end, we were shorthanded, and Saigon kept demanding that we take more and more risks. I started contemplating taking missions that I shouldn't and risks that were insane. It just seemed like we were throwing away our most talented soldiers. I didn't think the war would end. . . . I figured I could always go back, then I couldn't." It had been a while since I had thought about my fortune.

I could talk to Chris about it—he knew. I couldn't talk to anyone else about it. Commanders should not live, and their men die. Our job, after the mission, is to safeguard our men . . . except that war, combat, is fundamentally unsafe. There is an element of randomness to it. You can do everything right and still get dead. I felt like a parent who had outlived his children. I felt hollowed out, carved from the inside, with nothing left but emptiness and raw hurt.

I felt Chris's hand on my shoulder, a big hunk of granite, composed of moving parts that squeezed my shoulder. I would have winced, but I was too busy noticing the tears that seemed to be fleeing from the tyranny of my eyes. Like a rain squall, it passed quickly. I wasn't in Vietnam but in a funky pizza place in San Francisco.

The pizza arrived, giving me a moment to collect myself. It was the size of a manhole cover. Living above Marconi's, I found that my experience with pizza was that they came in two sizes, small and large, not manhole cover. At home, the crust was thick, the sauce was red, and usually they came with pepperoni, maybe sausage. The only vegetables I remember seeing on them were black olives or mushrooms, maybe onions or peppers, but nothing exotic. I had never seen anyone order anchovies

and knew that Marconi kept a couple of cans on hand in
case of small fish-based emergencies.

The pizza that lay before me was like nothing I had
ever seen. It was, as I said, the size of a manhole cover.
The crust was some sort of whole wheat and rolled very,
very thin. Instead of red sauce, it was covered with green
pesto sauce. The pepperoni was nowhere to be seen, but
instead, thin slices of tomato were laid in the green sauce.
There were big globs of melted white cheese that tasted
like nothing I had ever had before. It was fresh moz-
zarella. Then sprinkled in was some sort of cooked, salty
ham. Chris told me it was prosciutto, and I was in love. It
was nothing short of amazing.

When I recovered my senses, I asked Chris, "What
about you? You were good at it. You would be a sergeant
major right now?" He put down the slice he was working
on and picked up his glass of beer. I was impressed that
he didn't accidentally crush it in his giant mitt.

"Red, I loved it. I hated losing guys, but I loved the
war. I loved the army. I was a good Southern boy. . . . I
was from a county that was so Southern Baptist, so Holy
Roller that the county was dry, and anything other than
being married with kids was suspect. The army was eye
opening. I met people from different backgrounds—
weird Irish dudes from Boston or New Yorkers like Tony.
It was enlightening seeing the world . . . going on R&R
in exotic places, the camaraderie. . . . It was all the things
I missed in life. In the end, I knew I had to leave. I couldn't
stay and take Uncle Sugar's pay."

"Why not, man?"

"Red . . . I don't know how to tell you this . . . I'm
gay." Chris was looking down at his beer. It was clear to
me that he didn't know how I was going to take it. It was

a huge thing to tell another guy from our world. Ours was a world where men would fight over someone questioning their word, challenging their integrity. Men didn't lie to each other because trust was a fundamental necessity. Not everyone lived by that code, and there were guys who were subpar . . . but not us. Also, in the sixties, in the army, we were not super enlightened. Homosexuality was taboo.

"Huh." I didn't know what to say.

"Yeah . . . you still want to sleep on my couch?"

"Jesus, Chris, what does your being gay have to do with us being friends? After all the shit we have been through. We became brothers, by choice, by being in that shitty war, years ago." He looked up and smiled, and for a moment I could see the dopey kid with the crew cut that I had met almost fifteen years ago.

"Red, you know . . ."

"Hey, man, you are one of the toughest guys I know. You were always there for me; you saved my ass. You were there for any one of us. We are friends. What does it matter who you love?" Chris had been a fearless medic. He risked himself, literally, countless times to save guys, treating them under fire or volunteering to ride into hot LZs on extraction choppers.

"Where I grew up, gay was not an option. To be gay was worse than being black, and I grew up in Alabama when Jim Crow was a fact, not a historical footnote. Then the army wasn't exactly the place to be gay." The army considered homosexuality a crime when we were in. You could be kicked out or even sent to the stockade. "I didn't even know that what I felt was okay. For a long time, it was the work of the Devil—that was what they taught us in my church. There were no gay people in my town. The army wasn't much better. I didn't want to get busted out of the army. Even worse than that, I was afraid team guys wouldn't want to work with me. The thing of it is, Red, at the end of the day I had to face up to the fact that I was who I was. There was no changing that.

"In the end, I left, got out. Then I went to be a mercenary in Africa. I traveled. I got used to who I am. I became a Buddhist and a biker. I try not to hurt people who don't deserve to be hurt. I earn money the best way I can." He was uncoiling years of fear that his brothers wouldn't understand. That I wouldn't. It had to be a hard burden to carry.

"Hey, man. I won't pretend that at twenty-one years old I was mature enough to not say stupid shit . . . but you were always my brother. I trusted you with my life then and now. Your personal life . . . I am not one in a position to judge. Even if I were . . . I wouldn't know how."

When the waitress brought the check, Chris had wrapped me in an awkward bear hug. It was awkward because we were sitting in the chairs, turned to face each other. I could feel tears falling on me and could barely breathe. She must have thought it was weird, two grown men hugging and crying. . . . On the other hand, we were in San Francisco, a city that had a premium on weirdness. For her it was probably just a slow night.

Chapter 18

I woke up on the couch the next morning to the smell of fresh coffee. My tongue felt like it was made of imitation velvet, and my head felt as though I had lost a fight with Marvelous Marvin Hagler. The whiskey that followed the beers at the pizza joint turned out to have been just as vicious Haggler's straight left jab. We had stayed up late, talking about our war and reminiscing about old and absent comrades we would never again see.

A hot shower and then a hot fresh coffee from the Chemex. Chris had gone out and bought fresh doughnuts from a bakery named Viera's. The combination of all three turned around what could have been a rough morning. The doughnuts were small and brown, and the inside was yellow cake, sweet but not cloying. They were worlds better than doughnuts from any chain back home. They were still hot, and I could eat about a hundred of them. The doughnuts were made by hand. Some guy stood over a hot fry machine and cranked an old-time doughnut machine, dropping moist dough in the hot oil, and cooked it until it was a soft brown on the outside and yellow inside. When they came out of the fry machine, they were either dipped in a mix of sugar and cinnamon or had one side dipped in chocolate. You could get plain ones, but what was the point?

When we finished breakfast, Chris poured coffee into a thermos and we left. We took our maps and chart and got into Chris's truck. He had a .45 tucked into the small of his back and handed me a small revolver.

"We have some trouble with a rival gang. If I am going up north, I have to be careful, heeled."

"Okay, thanks for the piece."

It looked like a Colt Detective Special and a Smith & Wesson Chief's Special had had a love child . . . except this child was uglier than its parents. The cylinder looked like a .22 instead of a .38. The grips were wrapped in grip tape that was bent at the end to form a tab. The idea was, after shooting it, you held on to the tab and dropped the gun. The tape unwound and, voila, no fingerprints on the grip. It had some rust on it, but the internals were well oiled. The trigger was a little stiff but broke cleanly when I dry fired it. Mercifully, it still had serial numbers. The blue tapered barrel had CHARTER ARMS, BRIDGEPORT CT embossed along its right side. He handed me a small box of bullets.

"Here are rounds for it."

"How hot is this piece?" I asked Chris.

"Lukewarm . . . but I figured the tape couldn't hurt." He meant that it had a history but no bodies on it. Maybe stolen or maybe used in a robbery but no murders.

"It is a .22 Magnum. Fires a small bullet really fast and loud. No recoil but a lot of flash and bang. In the unlikely event you don't hit what you are aiming at, you will seriously scare the shit out of them. That little round will make them think you are shooting a real Magnum at them."

"Huh, okay." I would have liked something bigger, but, at the end of the day, it was more about where you put the bullets than how big they were. It was better than just trying to defend myself with my highly developed sense of humor. After all, it was the thought that counts.

"It's a Charter Arms Pathfinder." I loaded six rounds in the cylinder, and put twelve in my jacket pocket. I put the partially full box of rounds into another pocket. I grunted and stuck the gun in my waistband behind my right kidney, which was possibly my favorite kidney.

Today, we were going to drive around the Bay Area taking the highways and byways, looking at the area around Suisun Bay. I needed to get a fix on what we were dealing with. I had a tentative plan formed in my mind, but there was only so much that the maps and charts could tell me. In-country, we had aerial Reconnaissance photos to help with the planning, which was a luxury I didn't have here. The drive could help us figure out what type of boat I would need to get out to the *Adams*.

If I had my choice, it would be a battleship with big guns. Lately it seemed like I was outgunned and outnumbered. Since that was not an option, I wanted a Zodiac with twin Mercury seventy-five-horsepower outboards and a squad of marines to go with it. In reality, it was going to have to be either an inflatable boat with paddles or some sort of kayak. Inflatables were easy to hide and set up. I could row one silently out to the *Adams* and get on board and have a look around. The problem was that they were just not superefficient, they were ungainly, leaked air, and sucked if there was any sort of headwind. Suisun Bay was named for an old Indian term meaning windy.

My best bet would be a kayak. The army had spent some time teaching me and other SF guys how to use them. The problem was that I didn't know where I could get a folding one like the SF used. The commercial ones were fiberglass and heavy. I had to be able to hide it while I was on board the *Adams*. I could tie it off and partially sink it but that meant at some point I would have to get it out of the water and drain it. That was slow, and I might have to leave in a hurry.

I was thinking about all of these things as we took the I-80 east. We crossed over Treasure Island, which was man made for a world's fair; in World War II, the navy took it over. Now, it was a naval base that was innocuously placed between San Francisco and Oakland. Briefly, we were on the I-580 and then back onto the I-80.

I marveled at how different the climate, the architecture, and the feel of the place were from the East, from New England, where clapboard and shingled houses with white trim and blue shutters were the word of the day. Brick was exotic. Here, there were red tile roofs, stucco sides, and palm trees. Here, ranch houses made sense and were the norm. The roads and highways were wider, more clearly marked and straighter. The roads didn't have potholes that could swallow a car whole.

The I-80 took us to Route 4 east. Heading east felt strange. I wasn't heading home but rather heading farther into the country I wasn't familiar with. We picked up the I-680 north, passing through Vine Hill and Mococo at highway speed. I am sure they are nice towns, but we slipped through them too fast to get a feel for them. We crossed the bridge over the part of the bay where the San Pablo gives way to the Suisun. To my right were railroad bridges that support the industrial areas, the Goodyear plant, and refineries.

From the highway I caught my first glimpse of the fleet. There were rows of pale gray ships stacked together bow to stern in groups of ten. Each group was separated by hundreds of yards of water. They were a few hundred yards, maybe even five hundred, off the shore. The navy had chosen Suisun Bay to moor the Mothball Fleet because the water was deep enough for large ships, and it was brackish, which cut down on the rate that the ships would rust.

The shore itself was a wide band of salt marsh with industrial catch basins that were separated from the bay by a narrow strip of marshland. Then farther inland was the industrial area. It was a desolate mixture of industry and nature. There were no houses, no Dairy Queens, no signs of regular life or regular people along that part of the bay. It was the perfect place to store obsolete ships, ships that were waiting for the next war, the next time to be useful, the next chance to have some meaning. I could relate to those boats. Many days I felt as though my relevance ended when the last helicopter left the embassy in Saigon.

We followed the I-680 north, rising through the hills and passing by Lake Herman Road eventually getting off on Marshview Road. We doubled back down Goodyear Road. Mostly, it was just bleak marshland on one side and bleaker industrial hulk on the other. As we moved closer to the fleet, houses and buildings started to spring up. There were boats moored in the Goodyear Slough, which could have also been named Mud River. We came to a boatyard and a marina, both of which looked like they had been built in the late forties or early fifties, offering GIs the dream of boating that didn't involve yacht club snobbery or prices.

On Goodyear Slough, you needed a boat and mooring fees. No Mayflower pedigree was needed. That had been during its height. Now it was as grim, as dented and faded as a crushed can of Falstaff beer. I have nothing against it, but its glory days were long over. The buildings were faded with peeling paint, and the boats in the basin weren't faring much better. They were tied off with care, but all of the brass was spotted with green. The teak on many of the boats sported varnish that had blistered in the sun and salt. They were all power boats, almost all wooden hulled, and the youngest one had been launched when Kennedy was president.

We kept driving south through barren marshland on either side of the road. Gulls wheeled in the sky, and the low tide stank of rotting fish. We passed a marshalling yard and crossed Morrow Lane, still moving south. We turned toward the water and made our way on smaller roads and tracks. They didn't have names, and we ended up dead ended with nothing but marsh in front of us more than once. Finally, we ended up on a service road near the water, and after following that we ended up facing the bay.

We got out, and Chris put up the hood. He fiddled around with the engine while I scanned the rows of ships, moored, straining against their anchor lines in the wind.

We were in luck; the only row of Liberty ships was closest to us, which meant that it was last in the row of ships. Chris scanned it with binoculars while I snapped away with the camera. I was able to make out the name *John Quincy Adams* in fading letters on the stern of the northernmost ship. I made some quick snaps of the patrol boat on its circuit around the ships. The navy seemed quite serious about protecting the fleet. They had regular patrols, and once in a while the boats were armed with M60 machine guns. The occasional Coast Guard cutter with its white hull and slanted orange stripe would tool around the bay. We saw boats that went out to different ships, either to bring out workers to service them or to cannibalize parts to be used elsewhere in the fleet. There were tugboats that were used to push, pull, and tow ships in or out of the stacks as needed.

We spent about five minutes watching and snapping pictures. Any more than that would have seemed suspicious. Chris put the hood down, and we climbed back in the truck. We noticed that a patrol boat started to head our way and then went north, patrolling the coast, then circled back around the ships. We headed south. An older green Ford pickup truck driving down a dusty road, nothing suspicious about that. Occasionally, a car or truck would pass us heading north, but all in all there was very little traffic on the road.

We turned inland, to the west, passing by the buildings used by the navy Shore Patrol. We saw the SP's, the Navy's version of MP's, were hanging around in their white uniforms. They were the ones who were guarding the Mothball Fleet. I noticed that some of them were carrying .45 caliber M3A1 Grease Guns. It seemed like they were toting some heavy artillery around just to watch some old ships rust in the bay. Some of them had holstered 1911 pistols on their hips and white Billy clubs on the other side of their belts. They wore white polished helmet liners with "SP" on the front. Suspicious eyes tracked us as we drove past them, making our way back to the I-680.

We followed the I-680 north. One option would be to put in at Goodyear Slough and follow the coast south to the fleet. The problem with that was they seemed to patrol it well. I could also try to navigate the maze of canals through the marshes, but it seemed easy to get lost in there. That could end in disaster. Also, I had no idea what chemicals were being pumped into those relatively stagnant waters, and I wasn't eager to go swimming around in them.

Instead, we needed to head farther east away from the water. There were two islands in the bay that were a couple of miles from the fleet. They might make a good place to stage and watch the fleet before trying to infiltrate the ship. It seemed like the patrols kept relatively close to the Mothball Fleet, and the commercial traffic, fishing boats, stayed away.

We took the wide, flat, black and yellow ribbon of the I-680 north and traded its three wide lanes that ran more or less north and south for a brief reacquaintance with the I-80 proper. Then we headed west on local Route 12, two lanes each, east and west. It wasn't as wide, and there was more traffic, but we drove by the Jelly Belly factory that made the very jellybeans that the president had sitting on his desk in the Oval Office. Chris drove well, always reading the road ahead of him and constantly checking the mirrors to see if any threats were sneaking up on him.

We turned south toward Montezuma on increasingly smaller, narrower roads. We crossed a dam that bridged the Montezuma Slough and headed farther south into more marshland. We then followed a series of back roads east toward Grizzly Bay. We crossed a rickety bridge, drove on more dirt roads, and ended up at the water on a road that hugged the beach, raised above the marsh. We stopped. Three miles away, bobbing like small toys on the water was the fleet. In front of us lay Ryer Island, and the map told me in front of that was Roe Island.

The islands were far enough away that a lone man with training and experience could lay up and watch the fleet undetected. With a kayak or small, quiet powered boat, I could slip the mile and a half to the fleet in the dark and get on board one of the ships. It meant crossing open navigable water with ships moving around. In the dark, at sea level, I wouldn't even register on a tired watchman's radar screen. I would be invisible, which was cool, but also meant that I could be run over by a tanker, cargo ship, or anything, and no one would know or care. But I was a Recon man . . . and being invisible was my best defense against a security force looking to keep people off the ships.

I could kayak out to Ryer Island at dawn and build a hide, probably little more than a camouflage nylon poncho made into a low tent in the scrub brush by the marsh. I could spend the day there, watching and sleeping. I could shoot an azimuth with the compass to the ship, and then, late at night or early in the morning, kayak out in the dark. The compass had luminous paint on the arrows so it would be simple navigation. I could get on the *Adams,* find a way in, and hide my kayak. I could explore and sleep on board during the day and slip away at night. Then I would head back to shore and have Chris pick me up. If I found the gold, then we could figure out what to do with it.

I told Chris my plan, and he added useful suggestions. We followed the marsh road back to Route 12. It took us to the I-680 back by the Goodyear plant and the refinery. To my right was the industrial sprawl of postwar California. To my left, gulls wheeled over the marsh and bay, whose conservation had been sacrificed in the name of industrial progress. We followed the I-680 south through a valley and took a right onto Route 24 in a town called Walnut Creek. We took 24 up into some hills and crossed over the ridge, then down toward the water. We drove through Rockridge and picked up the I-80, which was to take us back to San Francisco. We drove over the Oakland Bay Bridge; the Alameda Naval Air Station was down to my left and Treasure Island to the right.

Chris nosed the truck through the city, and we found a place to park. It was late in the afternoon, and we had missed lunch. Chris took me to a funky sandwich joint. It was as if in San Francisco there was a city ordinance stating that 75 percent of all businesses had to be funky, quirky, or similarly original in content and style. This place was no different. The front of it was brick faced and a cigar store Indian was out front. Instead of a cigar, the wooden Indian held a bottle of pop. We went in and stood in line to order. Chris assured me that this place would be memorable.

The sandwich options were written in different colored chalk on one wall that was painted to be a chalkboard. There was a wooden barrel filled with half-sour pickles cut into quarters and a pair of tongs on string that was attached to the side of the barrel. You were supposed to help yourself to as many half-sours as you wanted. It is a well-known fact in the greater Boston area, among those who care about such things, that I am crazy about half-sour pickles. You can keep dills and your bread and butter pickles. I am not saying that those aren't fine pickles—it's just that the half-sour is where it's at.

Chris ordered a turkey sandwich on whole wheat bread with mayo, sprouts, Brie, and avocado. I ordered a roast beef with tiger sauce, which turned out to be a mixture of cream cheese and horseradish, with sprouts on pumpernickel. We helped ourselves to pickles while we waited. I had two and took another one to have with the sandwich.

"Gawd, Red, I never knew you liked pickles." Sometimes the kid from Alabama still poked out.

"I could say the same of you." I said it without thinking. That was one of my many curses, having a brain that works slower than the mouth attached to it. He looked at me out of the sides of his eyes, and for a second, I wondered if he was going to hit me. Then he threw back his head and let out a loud, deep laugh. He chucked me on the shoulder, and I winced.

"See, Red, I knew you would get it." Our sandwiches were up at the counter, and we took them to our table with a couple of Cokes. I don't know about Chris's, but my sandwich was fantastic. The dark bread, cream cheese coupled with the heat of the horseradish, cooling sprouts, and superb roast beef were a thing of beauty.

"Red, I've given a lot of thought to your watercraft problem." He said this around a mouthful of sandwich. There were crumbs in his beard. "I think you need a folding kayak. Like we trained with in the army." They had been made of canvas and wood, olive drab throwbacks to the OSS and our fathers' war.

"Where are we going to get one? A museum?" Kayaks were now made of plastic or fiberglass. They were rugged and nearly unsinkable, wide in the beam and good for rivers and rapids.

"Nope, there is a place not far from here that sells high-end outdoor equipment. They still make and sell Kleppers." Klepper had made the first successful folding kayak at the turn of this century. The old Klepper kayaks we had seen were light and elegant thin-hulled creatures. They were made with a light wooden skeleton and had waterproof canvass and rubber stretched over them to form a hull and top.

Klepper was a seventy-year-old company that did one thing better than anyone else, and that was the folding kayak. Chris was onto something. A Klepper would be lighter than a modern one made of space-age plastics. It could be folded and transported in the bed of Chris's pickup and deployed quickly. Also, our pickup wouldn't attract as much attention with the kayak folded in the bed.

"They aren't cheap, Red. But you could pawn it afterward and get some money back, or I might buy it from you. I might have need of one someday." He was smiling, excited. The truth is, we both felt like we were planning for an op, like we were back in Nam. We finished our sandwiches and braved the traffic in San Francisco in search of a special kayak.

San Francisco reminded me of a hilly, palm tree–growing, hippie-infested version of Boston. Both cities seemed to have the same amount of litter, but San Francisco was seriously lagging behind in the pothole contest. The cable cars were running again after an almost two-year hiatus to repair and refit the whole thing; Mayor Feinstein's crowning achievement.

We found the store that Chris wanted and went in. It was full of expensive, high-quality camping and outdoor equipment. You could buy Pendleton wool shirts and sweaters, European outerwear, silk long underwear, or Doxa dive watches. All of it came at a premium price.

Chris knew one of the clerks and explained what we wanted. He was able to find us one in dark blue canvas and a paddle. The store threw in a life jacket that was more like a vest than the big orange affairs found on ferries. After paying for it, my gold coin money was down to a pale reflection of itself. We pulled Chris's truck to the alley behind the store, and the clerk met us with two large canvas bags. There, he showed us how to fold and unfold it. That done, it was packed into its two canvas bags and put in the back of the truck.

We stopped at an A&P for some additional supplies: a couple of liter bottles of fancy French bubble water, a can of salted peanuts, and a can of salted cashews. I also grabbed a box of raisins, a couple of apples, and a box of sandwich bags. I was going to be paddling for a few miles in a windy bay and laying up for the better part of a day watching ships swinging on their moorings. Chris also picked up some steaks, potatoes, and spinach for dinner.

When we pulled into the laundromat parking lot, it was just getting dark. We split the load to be carried inside between us. Inside the apartment, Chris set about making dinner. I laid out the gear I would take with me on the recce. Chris insisted that I should take the gun with me. I didn't have the heart to tell him that I wasn't planning on scaring pigeons. On the other hand, a .22 Magnum was better than no gun.

I folded the surplus store clothes and put them by the couch with the Converses and the KA-BAR knife. Most of the equipment and food went into the dry bag that Chris had loaned me. I left out only what I would need to wear in the morning. I had more than enough food to carry me for a day. I wrapped the revolver in a sandwich baggie. It would ride in a pocket. Twelve loose rounds went in another. I wouldn't need more than that.

I took ten one hundred–dollar bills out of my wallet and put them in a sandwich bag. Money was a tool in this case. It might come in handy when ID wouldn't. I left my wallet with Chris. If I were wearing my Rolex, that would have come off, but I only had the Timex version of a dive watch. I took off my dog tags and put them next to my wallet. If something went wrong and I bought it . . . there was no one who would miss me or come looking. I was disposable and not for the first time in my life.

Chris had salted and peppered the steaks. The potatoes were almost baked. He sautéed the spinach with onions this time instead of nutmeg. When the spinach was cooked, he added a little bit of heavy cream and blue cheese. The steaks were pan seared for exactly three minutes a side. Our potatoes were simply served, split lengthwise with plenty of butter and salt. He opened another Italian wine. This one was from Sienna, and it was good. It had a rooster on the label. It was a meal fit for a last supper.

"Red, why do you do all of this?" He was looking at me over the table, a piece of steak impaled on the tines of his fork, hovering in midair.

"What do you mean?"

"The private detective thing. You have told me nothing but stories about the stuff you have lost: girlfriends, your oldest friend, your car. You get shot at, beaten up, blown up, your beloved Karmann Ghia . . . whoosh. What for? You are one of those guys who could do anything." I didn't necessarily agree with him about that. I was pretty sure that Hugh Hefner was never going to hire me to hang out with him at the Playboy Mansion.

"When I came home from Vietnam . . . I had this dream, this vision that I would be like my friend, Danny. I would go to college, get a degree, get a job, meet a nice girl, and settle down. Start a family, buy a house in the suburbs, have a dog and a station wagon . . . you know, all of it."

Chris nodded, chewing on a mouthful of steak. "Yeah, I know what you mean."

"The problem was that I wasn't normal anymore. I spent three years in Vietnam running Recon, flying Covey. I had seen and done things . . . well, you know. I could fake it for short periods of time, you know, normal. . . . 'Oh yeah, did you see the Red Sox last night? I think the new Fords are just great!' But the truth was I was a guy pretending, mimicking normal. Then I was watching the helicopters taking off from the embassy on TV, Walter Cronkite and Dan Rather talking about it. Then I knew."

"Knew what?"

"That I should have died in Nam. I shouldn't be here. I wasn't normal anymore. I didn't care about the Red Sox or if it was raining or what the latest fashion was. I wasn't going to get a degree, go work in an office, whatever. I tried the cops and for a while it helped. Then I realized that they had more bullshit and rules than the army. In the end, I had to be my own boss. Being a soldier, being a cop . . . that was all I knew."

"That simple?"

"Yeah, pretty much. Plus, I figured once in a while I might be able to help someone, some little guy who couldn't stick up for himself. . . . There is a world full of bullies."

"I know what you mean. Being a merc, fighting in Africa for money and for the guys . . . that was my version of what you are talking about. Being gay, there was no place for me in the army. There was no place left for me in Alabama." He shook his head. "Guys like us don't settle down and start families. We don't get to have the stuff that other people get to. We don't get to go out and pretend that the world is all hunky-dory."

"Too true."

We finished dinner and practiced putting the Klepper together and stowing it again in its two bags. The larger one held the rubber and canvas that made up the shell, the smaller a series of lacquered wooden pieces that made up the skeleton. The pieces fit together to make the bow and stern of the kayak. They hinged in the middle, then were fitted into the skin. The skin had valves that you would blow into and they would inflate, tightening the hull, making it rigid. They also added buoyancy in case it shipped water. It reminded me of a bigger version of one of those wooden dinosaur kits they sell at the children's museum.

After a few tries, we were able to put the Klepper together in about five minutes. We would be doing it in the near dark, cold and damp down by the water in the wee hours of the morning. The idea was for me to get to Ryer Island before first light. That should give me enough time to set up a quick hide using the poncho and the scrub brush. We went to bed a little while later.

Chapter 19

Three in the morning came quickly. I had gotten about five hours of sleep. I had dreamt about Vietnam and Thuy. I kept seeing the Ghia blowing up; then it turned into a napalm strike in the jungle. Beautiful orange pillars of fire against the backdrop of lush green and the sound of screaming. Not for the first time I was thankful that I couldn't smell burning flesh in my dreams. I woke up when Chris turned on the lights and bellowed out like a drill sergeant, "ON YOUR FEET!"

Seventeen years after basic training, after screaming drill sergeants, I rolled out of the couch, my feet hit the floor, and I bounced to the position of attention. I realized what an ass I was when I heard Chris guffawing.

"Oh, Red, you are fucking priceless, man." I said something about him having a relationship with himself.

I went to shower, more to shake the cobwebs off of my tired brain than to get clean. I was probably going to spend the day sweating and lying in low-tide mud, getting nothing but smellier.

When I came out of the shower, I shivered. It was a cold, raw San Francisco spring morning. Based on the darkness outside, it was only morning in the most technical sense. I walked out of the bathroom wrapped in a towel and Chris handed me a steaming mug of coffee.

"Jesus, Red, aren't you taking some real chances, strutting around in a towel in front of the Mercenary Queen?" It was the first time I had heard him make a joke about his sexuality since he had told me.

"Buddy, if I am what does it for you, you definitely need to raise your standards." He laughed. We both could joke about it, just like we could joke about war, death and violence. If there had been any awkwardness or discomfort, we both knew it was gone. I dressed in wool socks; the fatigue pants; the Bundeswehr undershirt with its stylized, not Nazi, eagle on the front; the wool long john shirt on top of that. I would save the sweater and the watch cap till we went outside.

Breakfast was simple, toast and scrambled eggs, more coffee. Chris gave me a Thermos of it to take with me. We loaded the gear into the truck, and by quarter to four we were on the highway. There was no traffic, and we made it to the put-in point southeast of Montezuma, the tip of Simmons island, a little before five. We had the kayak assembled and the dry bag stowed by five. I put camouflage paint on my face, neck, and the backs of my hands. The wool watch cap and blue sweater went on. We shook hands and Chris said, "Good luck." I shivered and, in my mind, heard the sound of Hueys as I slid the kayak into the murky water of the Suisun Bay.

Ryer Island was in front of me, almost a kilometer, a klick, away. Across the bay, the lights of the factories and refinery twinkled in the mist. The map told me that there was a small channel running through Ryer Island from north to south. It didn't take long to get to the island, and by the time I reached it, I was used to the feel of the kayak. It was more stable than a canoe, but much lower in the water. It was nimble and swift, but it was work to paddle. The wind always seemed to be howling, and I was not looking forward to paddling out across the windswept bay to the ship when the time came.

I paddled easterly until I found the channel running through the island and turned east, or hard right. I followed the contour of the island until I was near the tip. According to the map that I had studied, there was a V-shaped inlet, almost a small harbor or, in this case, a scale model of one. I paddled in and beached the kayak.

I stepped out and sunk into muddy silt over my ankles. I freed myself with some effort and dragged the kayak up on shore. I slung the dry bag over my shoulders, stuck the paddle in the kayak, which I then lifted upside down over my shoulders. I walked, stumbling in the growing light, over the uneven ground and scrub brush. When I was close to the eastern shore, I put the kayak down behind some scrub and quickly piled some brush on and around it to break up its outline, then went looking for my spot to lay up.

The spot turned out to be a depression roughly six feet long and four feet wide. It was about a foot deep. It was grave-like. I quickly stretched the poncho across it using the bungees from the four corners to the trunks of nearby bushes. A two-and-a-half-foot stick in the poncho's center propped it up. I quickly gathered scrub and grass to help hide the nylon poncho.

I crawled in. I had enough room to stretch out. I could take off my sweater, and that and the dry bag would make a good pillow. With the binoculars, I could see the *Adams* on her mooring. If I had to guess, she was about a mile and a half away across the choppy bay. I had enough room to get stuff out of my dry bag, like food, water, and coffee.

The grass was damp and smelled of salt and sea. I hadn't brought a sleeping bag or tarp and my pants were soon damp, but the wool sweater, wool long sleeve undershirt, and watch cap were keeping me warm. Also, the poncho's low height soon trapped my body heat. When the sun came up, it started to warm the poncho hooch. While I was rummaging in the dry bag for one of the MREs, I found a paperback book.

It was a Spenser novel by Robert B. Parker, one of the very early ones that I hadn't read yet. In the inside cover, Chris had written in his neat script, "Red, in case you get bored or homesick." He was right. I wasn't going to be able to watch for sixteen straight hours through binoculars or a telephoto lens. It would be nice to have some sort of distraction.

The sun had come up behind my hide. A patrol boat with the M60 machine gun made a circuit around the fleet, then went in and out between the groups of ships that were tied together. It moved quickly through the water and headed in. It was probably shift change, and the SPs wanted to go home, go to bed, get in their racks.

Or they were heading to get drinks, get laid, maybe go on days off. Who knew from a mile and a half away? I hoped for them that it was drinks and women.

At seven, I was getting hungry. I decided to try one of the MREs. In my day we had C-Rations, LRP rations and, for SOG, we had special dried rations that were basically freeze-dried Vietnamese staples. We had cans of mackerel to eat with the rice. If we could, we tried to get LRP rations, through trade or trickery.

In the field, we tried not to smell like Americans. We ate Vietnamese food before missions. Our sterile uniforms were washed in common Vietnamese detergents, no perfumes or smells like American ones. There was no smoking on missions, and we would go hours without speaking, relying solely on hand and arm signals. We never spoke louder than a soft whisper, unless we were in a firefight. Then all bets were off.

The MREs came in two brown vinyl pouches that had black writing on them. One said, "omelet with ham"; the other said, "beef patty with bean component, not to be eaten before flight operations." I decided that omelet with ham seemed the way to go, as it was morning. I put the other one back in the dry bag. Inside were foil pouches and cardboard boxes. I pulled out a box that said "omelet with ham" on it and a brown long-handled plastic spoon. Inside the box was a foil pouch and in that was a yellowish flat piece of what looked like anemic yellow Play-Doh with pink chunks in it. It didn't smell good, look good, or taste good. Not much had changed in the world of army rations except the packaging.

There was a pouch labeled "peaches in syrup" that tasted like the old C-Ration peaches. The crowning jewel was something called "chocolate nut cake," essentially flat, dense, sweet bread with chocolate chips and walnuts in it. It was fantastic. The MRE also came with cocoa powder, instant coffee in a small pouch, a moist towelette, matches, two green Chiclets, the familiar-looking folded pack of toilet paper, and a sleeve of Charms candy. All of the trash went back in the brown vinyl bag and back in my dry bag.

I spent the morning watching the ship for a bit then reading a few pages every couple of minutes. I watched the patrol boats come and go. They didn't seem to be on any particular schedule. Fishing boats came and went as I lay in my blind. I took notes about the navy patrol boats and watched birds dive bomb-ships with shellfish.

By eleven, it was warm enough that the grass was dry. I took off my watch cap and sweater and put them in the dry bag. Around noon, I fell asleep for forty-five minutes. It turned out that the life vest that came with the kayak was fairly comfortable under my shoulders when I was lying flat with my head resting on the dry bag.

When I woke up visibility was good. There was no mist, and the ships in their stacks rode at anchor, turning into the wind. The wind ruffled my poncho. I heard the sound of a halyard beating against a mast in the wind. Off in the distance was the rhythmic sound of cars going by on the highway. Gulls and terns competed for space in the morning sky.

Later in the afternoon, I took out the lensatic compass. I opened the lid and formed a tent with the tops and the sight and held it up to my cheekbone. I lined up the wire sight, through the notch, on the hull of the *Adams*. When I was satisfied, I rotated the bezel until the line of green luminous paint was lined up on the azimuth to the ship.

I passed the rest of the day watching the ship and

keeping track of the patrols. If I wasn't doing that, I would pick up the book and read about Spenser's noble efforts in Boston in the 1970s. He was a lot tougher and a hell of lot more charming than I am. I smoked a cigarette, blowing the smoke out slowly, and then field stripped the butt by separating the paper from the tobacco. Then I scattered the latter in a corner of my hooch.

Around four, the clouds darkened the sky, and the coffee in the Thermos was cold. A little while later, I heard the first unmistakable "plip" of a raindrop on my poncho. I listened as the tattoo of the rain on the poncho picked up until it sounded like an Art Blakey drum solo. I was dry and relatively warm; some water came in the hide but not enough to cause concern. Then the squall passed and the rain just turned into a steady drizzle.

Darkness came. I had finished the Spenser novel and most of the nuts. I wasn't hungry, which was good, because I didn't want to face another MRE. I slept for a bit and woke up at nine. At ten p.m., I put the sweater back on and stuffed the hat in my cargo pocket. I had one last cigarette while I held the flashlight against the compass. After that was done, I put the red lens back on the light and then started about my housekeeping. I reapplied camouflage paint to my face and hands. I packed the dry bag with my gear and the trash I had made. Then with the dry bag on my shoulder, I took the kayak to the water.

I checked my watch, and at ten thirty, I turned on the marine radio. It was set to a channel that was at the far end of the dial. I pushed the talk button and keyed it three times, then waited three seconds and keyed it three more times. I waited and then the radio keyed twice and two seconds later twice more. Chris acknowledged that I was going out to the ship. He had driven home and then back to make our communication window. He was already driving home from the put-in point when I was getting into the kayak. He would be back in the morning to pick me up.

I took out the compass and opened the lid. I double-checked my bearing and found it to be true. From now until I was at the ship, the compass would ride open on my thigh, the green line glowing and the green arrow of the needle swinging as I moved. When the green needle disappeared under the green line, I was on course. It was the simplest and safest way to navigate at night. I pushed off with one foot in the kayak and one foot against Ryer Island. I paddled out into the bay toward the ship. Suddenly, I was a modern version of Sam Spade chasing riches and dreams.

The wind was, fortunately, at my back. I was wet from the drizzle and the salt spray but warm because wool is a miracle fiber. I paddled hard, but the current wasn't bad. It was shift change, and I would have to hustle before the next patrol boat came out. I was aware of how small and insignificant I was on the water in the dark. I was tiny and could disappear unnoticed and that would be it. No more Andy Roark. No one to notice except for Chris, and maybe Brenda Watts. I think if she had a concussion, she might be a little sweet on me.

Chapter 20

As I paddled away from Ryer Island and into the bay, the wind was more noticeable. The compass needle started to drift left of the glowing green line. I corrected by pulling harder, digging the paddle deeper, on the left side. The kayak responded, and the needle drifted back under the green line on the compass face. I evened out my stroke and soon I was warm. The wind and the current were strong enough that I didn't want to pause to take off my sweater.

The night was still, and the noises of the nearby industry were rhythmic, calming, and repetitive. Then there was a soft undertone of highway noises like the bass in jazz. My paddle dipped into the water reminding me of a muted trumpet and the wind tore through like Charlie Parker's wailing sax. The kayak and I sliced through the darkness across choppy, brown water. I was enjoying the quiet and the loneliness. Being on some sort of mission again was like methadone to the heroin that was my life in Vietnam. Just a poor substitute.

I paddled toward the row of ships. Off in the distance to my left, I could see the lights from the refinery. The row that I wanted was in an area near marshland, and there was little light coming from the shore. I paddled steadily, checking the compass and making small corrections to keep the needle under the green line. My arms and chest began to feel the strain of unfamiliar work. I was wondering if this wasn't the year to quit smoking.

The drizzle stopped and the sky cleared. As the stars came out, so did the chill. In front of me, shapes started to materialize in the darkness. They formed a row of metal hills, a ridgeline of sorts, in front of me. Then, looming above me, water lapping at its hull, was the *Adams*. Its gray bulk blending with the sky. I paddled around her until I came to the gangway, which was raised up over a small dock that was tethered to the ship.

The dock was made of a wooden rectangular box that was open on the bottom, where empty fifty-five-gallon plastic drums were lashed inside of it for buoyancy. When the crews came over by boat, they would get off the boat and onto the dock and lower the gangway. Lines ran vertically from it to the davits above so that the gangway could be raised or lowered. The gangway could be left up, but the crews would have a place to get on the gangway from. There was some sort of lockbox on a control to lower the gangway.

I took the kayak's painter and did a graceless half roll out of the kayak onto the dock by pulling myself up with a cleat. I pulled the kayak up onto the dock. I took the kayak's bow line and looped it through my belt behind my kidneys. The lines that the gangway was running on were actually steel cables. I was able to pull myself up with my hands and lock the cable between my feet. I climbed the ten feet quickly and was on the gangway. It bounced slightly under my weight.

I undid the bow line and pulled the kayak up onto the gangway with me. Then I carried it up the gangway onto the deck. I would have stopped to salute and ask, "Permission to come aboard?" but there was no one to answer. There was no one standing watch. She was just crewed by ghosts from three wars or, more accurately, one war, one conflict, and one police action. Not that the dead knew the difference. I put the kayak around the corner of the superstructure. It wasn't well hidden, but someone coming up the gangway wouldn't see it right away. My plan was to head back to Montezuma a couple of hours before first light. I dug my flashlight out of the dry bag and went looking for a way into the ship.

I took the revolver out of my pocket and unwrapped it from the baggie. I stuck it back in my right front pocket. Bill Jordan wouldn't have approved of my carrying it that way, and he had literally written the book on the subject of using revolvers. I started to check the hatches leading into the ship. I worked my way around the superstructure, finding hatch after hatch that I would need tools to open. It was beginning to look like I had made the trip to the ship in vain. Then I found it.

In the rear of the superstructure was a hatch that wasn't bolted shut. It was dogged down on well-oiled hinges. The hatch made no noise when I undogged it and was silent the way well-oiled metal is when I pulled it open. I closed it behind me and did just one latch. I was in a narrow corridor or companionway. Off the companionway were compartments. The bridge, the radio room, and the deckhouse were up, and the cargo holds were down. The ship smelled musty, and I was sure that she was more rust than anything else at this point.

I started to explore, feeling like a ghost drifting in the deserted rooms of a haunted mansion. Real Scooby-Doo shit. I checked some cabins and what I think was a Wardroom. The officers mess was deserted, but the tables were still there, with chairs that were no longer neatly tucked into the table. Next was the galley. It was stripped bare except for an old, industrial flat-top grill and two steam kettles. It still smelled like fried food and the faintest trace of bleach.

I made my way through the galley to the enlisted mess. That is where I found something. I said to no one in particular, "Andy, my boy, this is what we refer to professionally as a clue." We private detective types tend to appreciate a good clue now and then.

In this case, it was a large square covered by a tarp. Under the tarp were bricks wrapped in packing tape and plastic, all of it stacked chest high and about eight feet long. I dug the tip of the KA-BAR into one of the bricks. Heroin came out. I was looking for gold and found drugs. It wasn't the treasure I wanted to find but it was a fortune. I had to know. I had to keep looking.

I started to make my way down to the cargo holds. I made my way to the number five hold in the stern. It was a large, empty cavern made of metal. If I were to cry out, it would echo. Numbers four, three, and two were empty as well. I was in number two when I heard something, feet moving above me. Noises of metal on metal and people talking, not trying to be subtle or stealthy. They were talking in Vietnamese. I wasn't aware that I had taken the revolver out of my pocket, but it was suddenly in my hand. I was in the dark hiding, and there were Vietnamese voices around me. The old feeling of being hunted was with me again.

They were coming my way, above me, somewhere in the ship. I could work my way up, go around them. There was only one hatch in or out, but I was betting that I could find a way out if I went higher. The ship was secured to keep kids out or people who wanted to steal old electronics, but it wasn't a vault. If I split now, there was probably a porthole or a hatch I could slip out of. Except there was one cargo hold left. There could be gold in it. A treasury from a nation that no longer existed.

The smart move would be to try to run, but I had to know. I wasn't the smartest guy in the room, but I was compelled to find out. I had to know. Now that I had embarked on a fool's errand, I had to see it through. There was no point in escaping if I didn't know if the gold was on the ship. That was the problem. My compulsion to know the end of the story would probably get me killed, but I didn't care.

I moved forward to the last cargo hold, number one. I heard the Vietnamese voices behind me, their feet on decking. I heard their laughter in my mind as I was trapped. There was no gold, no nothing but dust. I was looking for someplace to hide in an empty cargo hold. There was nothing to hide behind and nowhere to run to. I had literally run out of ship. I saw a hatch in the deck. It had BALLAST stenciled on it. I had read that Liberty ships were ballasted by lead bars. The ballast was stored next to the hull under the deck of the cargo hold. The ballast area was serviced by a tunnel that ran down the spine of the ship.

I undogged the hatch, and there it was, a long man-sized tunnel running the length of the ship. There was also the unimaginable stench of bilge water that had been sloshing around with fuel and oil and God knows what chemicals for almost fifty years. I could only imagine what else was in there, too.

They had to have found the kayak. They had to know I was on board. They were looking for me. I slid headfirst down into the dark, damp tunnel. There wasn't much room and I was soaked to my chest in stinking water. I wanted to gag but trying to get away from them seemed a more pressing need.

The ship was made up of metal ribs and bulkheads that formed a sort of triangle. I had to crawl over those every few feet. Every time I did, I disturbed the water and the stench with it. I gagged but held it together. I was crawling through a crude metal honeycomb that was filled with lead bars. I was lucky that I wasn't claustrophobic, and I prayed to a god I didn't believe in anymore that the batteries held on my flashlight.

I had made it under cargo hold two. Everything was clearly marked in old stencils from the forties. I passed row after row of honeycombed metal filled with lead bars. I stopped midway down the hull. A few of the honeycombs were empty except for bits of white burlap. The pieces of old burlap had caught on rough bits of welded seams or rough, unfinished metal. The burlap bits were from old flour sacks, the red, white, and blue design with a pale hand shaking another. USAID was written on the material. A hatch opened, and a voice said, "*Mau, mau lem*. Grenade. Come out, *Trung Si* Roark, or I frag you."

I started moving toward the next hatch until it opened.

"Come out, *Trung Si. . . . ,*" was said in a taunting, singsong voice. I made my way to the hatch and hands helped me out. The hands went over my body, relieving me of the KA-BAR and the revolver and the rounds for the revolver. They took my flashlight, and something hard and metal jabbed me above the kidneys. "*Mau, mau lem!*" The words were Vietnamese and meant, "quickly, quickly go!" The unmistakable commands.

I made my way up ladders and through hatchways. There were two Vietnamese in front of me and two behind me. All four had Madsen Model 50 submachine guns, simple, postwar 9mm weapons made of sheet metal that weighed a hair under seven pounds. They were flat with a side-folding tubular stock that looked like a tired rectangle with one corner a bit farther out than the others. Unfortunately for me, one was being poked in my back with some enthusiasm.

We—the CIA, Army Special Forces—had given Madsen Model 50s to trail watchers in Vietnam. Trail watchers were friendly locals working for us. They would wear civilian clothes and carry a sort of local woven basket/backpack on their shoulders. Inside were a folded Madsen, a brace of thirty-two-round magazines, and a couple of grenades. The CIA had handed them out in Vietnam and in South and Central America, anywhere to anyone who wanted to kill a commie for mommy. The CIA didn't discriminate who they armed as long as they were fighting the evil empire. They were effective weapons that didn't scream America when they were found.

These cats were familiar with the Madsen. They were men in their late thirties who seemed comfortable holding and pointing weapons at people. Again, in this case that was me. They had called me sergeant in Vietnamese, so they knew who I was. When we emerged up on deck, we were behind the superstructure. That was the advantage of one way in and one way out—you come out where you went in.

The guy behind me wasn't shy with his Madsen. He guided me to an area not far from the stern of the ship with sharp little prods of the barrel. He, not so gently, nudged me toward a trio of men; two were older Vietnamese, and the other was a white guy in his early fifties. His hair was light, and he was dressed in boat shoes, faded jeans, and a navy blue sweater with horizontal white stripes. He had a red bandana tied around his neck like he was James Coburn or something. He looked like he should have been on a yacht instead of a Liberty ship.

Only the Smith & Wesson 76 submachine gun, slung barrel down over his left shoulder, was out of place with his nautical image. The gun was behind him, but I knew that he could sweep it up with his left hand and shoulder it, ready to fire, in a fraction of a second. We had taught a lot of our Montagnards to carry their carbines that way when not in the field. The submachine gun and the two spare magazines sticking out of his back-left pocket were not yacht club accessories. He probably had a grenade hidden somewhere and an F-14 Tomcat on call, just in case.

"Hello, Sergeant Roark. I have heard a great deal about you." He didn't extend a hand.

"Nothing bad, I hope? I am afraid you have me at a disadvantage. Have we met?" He was lean, not thin, fit. His eyes never stopped for long on anything. He was always scanning the area. "Let me guess, you're a Company man."

"Well, you are astute. My name is Keller." He said it

with a laugh, and his voice had a trace of Virginia in it, not army or navy Virginia but old money Virginia, the Virginia that spoke of horses, boarding schools and cotillions, cocktails that were served on the veranda of a house whose original owners felt that Jefferson Davis was their true president. His accent had been softened by boarding schools in the Northeast and by language schools in parts of Northern Virginia that were owned by the government, but he was old money Virginia. He wasn't some classless, nouveau riche Company man.

"Well, why are we here?" I was hoping that he would tell me something.

"*We*, Sergeant? You are trespassing on U.S. government–restricted property. I am here because we were told that you would be coming. Then there was a bit of extra traffic in the area. There aren't a lot of trucks on the road by Montezuma at five in the morning. Then we watched the ship day and night. We almost missed you. But then you showed up in the Starlight scope on the gangway. It looked like you were exerting yourself, we didn't want to interrupt you."

"You were expecting me?"

"Our associates in Boston warned us that you had flown out here. They also said that you are very persistent and that you are stubborn to the point of foolhardiness."

"Well, that does sound like me. Did they mention my excellent sense of humor?"

"No, they failed to mention that. I think that the colonel grudgingly respects you in spite of the oppositional nature of your acquaintanceship." He smiled in spite of himself. It reminded me of a lizard.

"Does he normally show his respect by blowing up people and their cars?" I was unarmed, and there was no way I was going to fight seven men armed with pistols and submachine guns. I would have to try to talk them into submission with my witty banter. The problem was that, as usual, I was the only one who seemed to find me funny. Maybe I could try to bore them to death.

"Well, Sergeant Roark, at least he takes you seriously. You can tell a great deal about a man by the quality of his enemies. You and he are on opposite sides of this one. And you have become a thorn in his side." Keller spoke as though we were discussing a gentlemen's rivalry.

"They forgot my romantic nature and love of *West Side Story*." The older Vietnamese men were talking among themselves too low for me to hear, but I was pretty sure that they weren't admiring my witty demeanor in the face of danger.

"You do look like you are a Jet, definitely a Jet, instead of a Shark. . . . Sergeant Roark, you have stumbled into something that your government wishes you hadn't." He sounded like a near perfect imitation of someone who was sincerely disappointed.

"I haven't stumbled into anything. I am just a guy taking a look at a piece of history." I didn't try to feign sincerity since he wasn't trying either.

"I wish that were the case, but you and I both know you aren't. The fact that you disturbed the package, poked it with a knife, worries me."

"I am not interested in whatever you have in there." Ironically, I wasn't. I had been chasing a pet theory. Once again trying to prove my brilliance to the world or maybe just myself.

"What are you interested in, Mr. Roark?" I knew Good Cop when I met him. I didn't much fancy the Vietnamese version of Bad Cop. One of the two older Vietnamese had

been a high-ranking officer in the Vietnamese secret police. I recognized him from a trip to Headquarters in
Saigon. Colonel Tran had worked for him. I needed to
play for time. I definitely did not want a guy like that asking me questions. The methods, the ones that I had seen
in Vietnam, were the stuff of nightmares.

"I was looking for gold. Mr. . . . ?"

"You can call me Keller."

"I was looking for gold, Mr. Keller. Through a series
of unlikely events, I developed a theory that the gold
from the Republic of Vietnam's treasury had been smuggled out of Vietnam on this ship." I was moving toward
the railing, away from the gangway. Keller laughed, a
high sound that didn't suit him well.

"Well, Mr. Roark, you are a funny one, I will say that.
How did you come to that conclusion?" I was now leaning against the rail near a large cleat for a mooring line.
Keller didn't have much to worry about; there were at
least four submachine guns loosely pointed in my direction. The older Vietnamese had pistols in their waist-
bands. I explained to Keller, telling him how I had arrived
at the conclusion about the gold, my own version of *The
Arabian Nights*.

"I have to say, Sergeant Roark, you are very astute.
They shouldn't have underestimated you. They told me
that you were reckless and not very bright." He smiled.
He had perfect capped teeth like a daytime TV stars.

"Was there gold?" If I was going to die, I wanted to die
knowing I had been right.

"Yes, there was. Bars of it in the cargo hold. Each day,
each port the pile got a little smaller, but it was still sub-
stantial by the time it got here."

"What did you do with it? Is it financing the Committee and its counterrevolution? Do you mind if I smoke?" I held my hand up, pantomiming holding a cigarette.

"Please do. No, it didn't get used that way exactly. You have friends in the Company." A statement not a question. I nodded; I had made some friends in civilian clothes in Vietnam. "Did you ever hear of Operation Franchise?"

"Nope." I stuck a cigarette in my mouth and two matches later was sucking in a lungful of glorious cigarette smoke. I was thankful for having kept my smokes and matches in a baggie. I hoped that Keller hadn't seen my hands shaking slightly.

"Operation Franchise is a means to help all of our brothers in the fight against global communism. Initially, the Company conceived of it under Nixon. Operation Franchise is a way to lower our expenses and yet still be able to counter the communist threat on a global scale. Under Carter, the funding went away. Then there was a great deal of congressional oversight. Ha, imagine having a bunch of amateurs tell you how to run Recon patrols. . . . These men had no idea about what it takes to fight the communists. None.

"Fortunately, I did. I also knew where there was a source of gold, gold that no one was using and wasn't collecting interest. There was a lot of it. It was conveniently secured, near a navy base, an air force base, a naval aviation air station, and one of the busiest commercial ports in the world. I could have goods brought in and shipped out, and no one would notice."

"You used the Vietnamese gold?" Keller was audacious, to say the least.

"I surely did. It paid for assets and networks and bought weapons in South and Central America."

"You stole their gold? You must have cut them in on it

if they aren't pissed at you. I can't believe the Vietnamese, the Committee, they were just all right with you taking their gold?" I was resting my foot on a large cleat, the type for mooring lines. It was mushroom shaped, a foot in diameter, and eighteen inches high, Frankenstein bolts on the sides of the stem. My right foot was on it, toes flexing and slowly finding the right purchase.

"No, of course not. I didn't just take it. I found a way that they could finance their counterrevolution, a way that they could finance their goals, their dream of a Vietnam that wasn't a people's republic but just a republic."

"Heroin." What else could it be.

"Yes, we had assets in Thailand, Burma, some still in Vietnam, Cambodia, and Laos, all of whom wanted to be rich and had access to a product that was wanted around the world. To include here at home. We sold the Committee a franchise. They would provide people in Asia and here. They would provide security, transportation to shipping and manage the domestic distribution. We gave them the parent franchise and they licensed individual franchises. We would ship and secure it until they were ready to move it to their distributors. Then they would sell it on this end. It was a means to guarantee them a sustainable revenue stream and provide them with arms and equipment, the means to sabotage the People's Republic of Vietnam and to strike a blow to global communism.

"The gold was finite; drug profits grow exponentially. In the end, the gold was a down payment. Those profits from heroin allowed them to buy arms, equip their counterrevolutionary strike force and their propaganda arm. That money finances operations in Southeast Asia, it pays for Vietnamese newspapers here in the U.S., and it funds recruitment of agents and assets in their fight. Our share of the profits allows us to grow and expand, to take the fight to the communists who threaten our very border.

"You see, Sergeant Roark, no one is really interested in Asia anymore. The dominoes didn't fall. Maybe all your collective sacrifice prevented that. However, South America, Central America are close. Imagine a domino effect that involved those nations. Cuba and Nicaragua are bad enough, but imagine a communist Mexico or Guatemala? Imagine if the communists controlled the Panama Canal or the communists in control of all that Venezuelan oil? That would impact us strategically, but it would also impact global trade. Money for my part of the fight has been diverted to a country that most people can't find on a map. We want to show the Ruskies what it is like to have their own Vietnam. That came at the cost of other operations, my operations.

"I had to get creative. I had to find a way to fund a war that no one wants to fight, that no one wants to hear Dan Rather talk about on the *CBS Evening News*. There I was at a McDonald's in Virginia one day. I was eating a cheeseburger, nestled in its Styrofoam clamshell. I was eating French fries and drinking a Coke. What could be more American?

"Then it hit me. McDonald's had a product that everyone wanted, but they could never have expanded to be what they were if it was just two brothers overseeing everything, expanding as much as they could get loans for. But then came Ray Kroc, and he figured out that if they made people pay them to open their own McDonald's he could have one on every main street in America. Then he sold them the product that they would sell. The process, the procedure, the franchise was revolutionary, as revolutionary as Henry Ford's factories. Why couldn't I use the same model to fund our operations?

"Initially, I thought it would be guns. I would sell guns to revolutionaries to fight the revolution. That was impractical. I was talking to a colleague whom I had worked with in Thailand, and he mentioned the vast amount of heroin being moved. He had run a small operation during the Vietnam War and used the profits from heroin to run his operation. It was brilliant, but I needed it to be done on a global scale.

"So, there I was eating my cheeseburger that tasted just like every other McDonald's cheeseburger anywhere in America when I remembered a memo about the gold and the cost to secure it. I saw my version of McDonald's. I would borrow the Vietnamese gold and then use it to fund the weapons they needed and I needed. I would sell them the right to sell the drugs that I need to sell to finance my operations. It was simple. I arranged to take over the responsibility for the gold on board, and the costs came from the head office. I called those men over there and laid out a plan to create a franchise system using their gold as the startup capital. It allows us to bring the fight to our nation's enemies. A nation that you once honorably served."

"So, you sell drugs to Americans to buy guns to arm warlords who deal drugs so that you can buy more drugs to sell to more Americans to buy more arms?" I had known guys from the Company. Most were decent hardworking men and women who loved their country. Anonymous, invisible soldiers, spies, and analysts, none of which was the James Bond type. They were just quiet, hardworking people who were deeply patriotic. I knew men like Keller, too, men who had gone so far down the operational rabbit hole that right and wrong became in-creasingly smaller and smaller concepts. Soon everything, even their meals, was seen through the lens of operational security. After a while, their reality was unreal.

"It isn't that simple. Don't be naïve. You have fought the communists; you know how relentless they are. They are much more ruthless than we are. We have to be will-ing to fight them any way we can, and, Sergeant Roark, you know that your hands are far from clean.

"We created a self-sustaining operation. It is secure and efficient and actually saves the American taxpayer money while keeping them safe. It doesn't matter who is in office or whatever cause du jour Congress falls victim to. We will be able to continue to function whether or not a subcommittee said so. We can take the fight to the com-mies. We can spend more than they can."

"Well, Keller, I will say this: you are passionate about franchising. So, what happens now?"

"I don't suppose you would be interested in coming to work for me? I could use a man like you." He smiled, and I understood how the fish felt looking at the shark.

"Keller, I don't think you know me as well as you think you do." It was the best I could come up with.

"I don't suppose you could keep quiet about this for the sake of your country?" He didn't even say it with a trace of sincerity. If I believed that then I would believe that he would still respect me in the morning.

"I don't know who would believe me if I told them. The issue is that you can't trust me not to." Keller smiled, and it was completely without warmth.

"True. I can't. I appreciate your candor, Sergeant." His left hand was snaking around the perforated barrel of the Smith & Wesson 76.

I took a drag on my cigarette and then threw it left handed across the men with guns. Their eyes unconsciously tracked the glowing red ember. I pushed off with my right foot, up and over the rail. I heard automatic weapons fire and 9mm bullets snapped at me, tugged at my clothes, angry hornets buzzing by me. I exhaled smoke and tried to refill my lungs before I hit the water.

Chapter 21

I turned end over end and hit the cold, dark water with a splash. My landing was awkward, knocking the air out of my lungs and bruising my already sore, battered body. Water hurts when you hit it from a height even when you aren't a walking contusion like I was. I hurt in lots of different places and ways. In the last week I had been beaten up and blown up, found out my lover was a spy, watched her get blown up in my car, and now I had fallen forty feet into Suisun Bay.

Darkness washed over me, pulling me down lower and lower into its inky, cold embrace. Part of my mind reminded me that I could just let the water claim me, that it could offer me peace. I could close my eyes and it would all go away. Except that I am stubborn. I still had work to put in, and I couldn't do that if I gave up.

I opened my eyes. I chose to live. I could see my bubbles going up, heading toward flashlights shining on the water. I could hear rounds zipping into the cold water. I kicked hard with my feet and pulled with my working arm. For some reason, my left arm didn't want to obey commands from my brain. I fought the water with a fierceness like any I had brought to battle.

I swam underwater toward the dock that the gangway was lowered to. My lungs were on fire, and my vision was darkening. I bumped my head on something, another lump for the collection. I felt my way along the bottom of the dock. Between the two rows of plastic fifty-five-gallon drums that kept the dock afloat, there was a bit of space out of the water.

I put my face up to it. I was able to get my nostrils and mouth out of the water in the rounded area between the drums. My feet and legs floated up and I was pinned against the dock by my own buoyancy. But I could breathe. There was just enough air space. I gulped air. It would take them a few minutes after firing on full auto to hear me. After a few breaths, I forced myself to calm down and breathe through my nose. I was trying to breathe shallowly, stay quiet. In my mind, I was like a submarine in silent running. I was alive. My left arm ached, but I was alive. Alive was nice.

By rights they should have killed me. They were over-confident because they had submachine guns and I was unarmed. They should have riddled me with bullets, but they had held their guns casually instead of actually training them on me. I had acted and they had to react. Action is always faster than reaction, and the split second I gained from it saved my life . . . for now.

I had to focus. My motor skills would start to diminish, as well as my ability to think. I had a wool sweater on, but I needed a wet suit or, better yet, to be in Arizona. If I stayed calm, if I kept breathing, I could survive this. Survival was 90 percent staying calm, working the problem, and 10 percent luck. Slow, quiet breaths, I had been breathing my whole life. Now, I had to focus on the process of breathing to save my life.

Even though we were inland in the bay, I couldn't stay in the water forever. I had to outwait, outlast Keller and the Committee. To surface before they left was certain death. The problem was that I could not stay indefinitely without going hypothermic, and hypothermia would kill me as certainly as a hail of bullets.

I was safe for now. Well, *safe* wasn't the right word. Safe-ish? I was hoping they didn't have hand grenades or didn't want to use them if they did. I wasn't worried about the fragments, but the concussion would probably kill me. I had seen too many thrown into rivers as a means to catch fish. It was a much faster method than a pole or a net. The concussion kills the fish, and they float up to the surface. I hoped they weren't fans of hand grenade fishing.

It felt like I was under there forever. It was probably only a few minutes, but I had no sense of time between the adrenaline rush, the fear, and the cold. I started to count to sixty in my head, slowly. Then each time I got to sixty I would add a number in order to keep track of the minutes. I could keep track of how long I was underwater. I had to keep starting over because I couldn't keep track. I was having trouble keeping focusing on the individual numbers in succession.

Once in Phase I of Special Forces training, we were out patrolling, relearning, polishing our land navigation skills, our patrolling skills, too. It was a cold winter day by North Carolina standards: raw, damp weather just under forty degrees. The wind was blowing, and the tall pine trees were swaying and straining above us. We were on a field problem, and moving through the woods, we came to a river. It was still the phase of training when we were accompanied by an instructor/evaluator. We stopped and debated what to do when the instructor said, "Not sure what you ladies are waiting for, but that little bitty river isn't going to cross itself." We only had the uniforms we were wearing and our jungle boots. We decided to strip naked and put our clothes in the waterproof bag in our rucksacks. We still had on our jungle boots and wool socks. We made rafts by wrapping our ponchos around are rucksacks and tying them off. It wasn't perfect waterproofing, but it kept them dry and trapped enough air that they would act as floats for a short time.

We were confident that this was a test to see if we would do it. We figured that once we showed we were willing to go into the water the instructor would stop us. No one wants to lose trainees in training. I was up to my chin when it occurred to me that no one was going to stop us. We were blue and shivering when we emerged on the opposite bank. We did jumping jacks to warm up and shed as much water as we could. We dressed and, still bitterly cold, started moving out. That water was like bathwater compared to the stuff I was in now.

I was shivering badly, and my hands were losing feeling when I heard voices, then steps down the gangway and an engine started. I heard Keller say, "Break up the kayak. Throw his gear into the water with the pieces of the kayak. If anyone finds it, they will think he was hit by a fishing boat or something. Throw that Saturday night special in the water, too. If that turns up in his gear, some-

one might start asking questions." I heard the sounds of
them smashing the elegant Klepper kayak into pieces,
then the splashing of my gear into the water.

Then the sound of an outboard motor starting and they
moved off in their boat. I took a breath and pulled myself
along the bottom of the dock until my head and then torso
was out from under the dock. I got a hand on a cleat and
pulled with all of my waning strength. I lay on my back
on the raft for what seemed a lifetime, but it was probably
a minute, the outboard engine sound growing dimmer in
the night. I flexed my fingers trying to get some feeling
back in them. I wanted to get on board before anyone started
watching the gangway or the ship through a Starlight
scope again.

It took me two tries to grab the hawser and lock it between my feet. What had been easily done an hour or two
before was now nearly impossible. I pulled myself ago-
nizingly upward. My left arm wasn't working right, and it
hurt. Somehow, I made it the ten feet up to the gangway.
I crawled up it. I told myself it was so I wouldn't be seen,
but, in reality, I was too cold and too exhausted to walk. I
pulled myself along the steel deck to the hatch. I crouched
next to it and undogged it, then slipped inside, quietly
closed the hatch behind me. I was shaking, and it was as
much from the cold as it was from coming down from almost being killed.

I walked on unsteady feet down the companionway to
the stairwell up. It was pitch black in the companionway,
and I had to move by feel. It was slow going, and I was
shivering and my teeth were chattering. I was leaving a
trail of water behind me like some sort of sea monster
that had dragged itself from the deep up on shore. Andy
Roark, the creature from Suisun Bay. I laughed to myself

at my own joke as my Converses squelched on the deck. I went into the first cabin I found and stripped off all of my clothes. I wrung out the pants and my German undershirt as best as I could. I wrung out my socks, my watch cap, and my Converses. I spun the sweater over my head a few times and wrung out the long john shirt. The wet wool undershirt, watch cap, and wrung-out skivvies went back on. The sweater, the pants, socks and shoes I hung over an old bunk to dry.

I could feel warm fluid trickling down my left arm. Not a lot of it, but enough to give me an idea why my arm wasn't working right. I found the wound, and I was pretty sure that one of the Vietnamese mercenaries had hit me with a 9mm round. My arm didn't hurt enough to be broken, and it probably passed through the meat of the arm. I wasn't dead, so it probably missed all of the major arteries. I couldn't get a good look it, so there was some guesswork involved.

I took the cotton Bundeswehr undershirt, tied it to one of the many pipes, and ripped it into strips with my good hand. I ripped another piece and put it against the wound. I tied a strip of undershirt around it by holding one end in my teeth and then using my good hand to knot it. I used half the shirt to bandage my wound but it wasn't very neat, but it was better than not bandaging the wound at all.

The sky outside the porthole was turning from black to gray, and then streaking light shone through the sky. The sun came up, and I shivered. I had to get warm or there was no point in surviving last night. I was cold and clammy but wringing out the wool undershirt meant it was damp, not soaking, and I was retaining some body heat. The itchy wool next to my skin was helping.

I started exploring the cabins. I found a musty navy issue wool blanket in one, which went over my shoulders like a cape. In another cabin, I found a bunk with a mattress covered in a large rubber zippered bag. No two cabins seemed to have the same stuff. Finally, I found one that wasn't too musty. Other cabins had an assortment of dilapidated furniture or old paperwork, logbooks, etc. Some had keys, and I found one with boxes of lightbulbs. I briefly thought about a fire, but the paper was damp, and I had no way of venting it and the smoke, if it didn't do me in, would have the navy here in no time. I went back and took my pants and sweater to the nicest bunk I could find. I put the sweater under my head and the pants against the bulkhead. I lay down under the wool blanket and tried to get some sleep.

I woke up cold but mostly dry. My surroundings were chock full of peeling paint and dust, but I had been in worse situations. My left arm hurt, and it still didn't want to work properly. I was hungry, and I was pretty sure that there was no food on board. I would have to stay on the ship till dark. Dusk might be my best bet. I could slip into the water at a time of day that would be too light for a Starlight scope but dark enough to provide some concealment.

I roamed the ship as best as I could. I found graffiti written in Vietnamese that I didn't understand. I could only imagine what conditions on the ship had been like, crowded with refugees, tossing on violent seas, desperate to start new lives away from the turmoil of the communist victory, after the terror of the war. Gold had been packed in the hull, and most of the people on board probably didn't realize it was there. Except one person did. Someone put something wrapped in USAID flour sacks in the ballast section instead of lead. I assumed that it was gold. It would have been hard to smuggle it off of the ship.

I spent the hours until near-dusk walking around and thinking about it. Eventually, my clothes were mostly dry, and I was mostly warm. I found two old orange life jackets in my travels. They were spotted black with mildew, but they would work. I took the rubber bag off of the mattress. I had unzipped it but had raised a sweat getting it off the mattress one handed. I put the life jackets, the wool blanket, my sweater, and my pants inside the mattress bag.

I folded the mattress condom over on itself several times. I rolled the zipper part so that it was covered by several folds of rubber and tied it off with what was left of my German undershirt that hadn't been used to bandage my arm. I managed to form a big rubber loop to slip my good arm through. I found that even though my left arm didn't want to work, I could still use my left hand. I tied the knots by dangling my arm down and using my left hand to hold the strips of undershirt and tie with my right hand. Now, I had a raft, of sorts.

The problem was that I didn't have a lot of good choices. The near shore, with Goodyear Slough and the marshes, was the smartest bet except that it was close to Keller and killer Vietnamese mercenaries. Montezuma was two miles away fighting the current. I could try for the opposite shore, across from Ryer Island to the south, but that would mean crossing several miles of open water. I was injured, starving, and no Navy SEAL. It would have to be the near shore, and let the current bring me to it. That was a swim of a few hundred yards—a few football fields—versus miles in open water, water that I knew only too well how cold it was.

The near shore offered the best chance to survive. It was closer, and there was plenty of marshland to hide in once I made it. I could work my way north of the navy security station and make my way to the highway. I should be able to find a pay phone and call Chris collect. Then I would lie low, waiting for him to come pick me up in his green truck instead of a Huey.

I wasn't looking forward to going back in the water. I didn't want to, but I had the feeling that if the navy found me Keller and his men would end up with me. I couldn't wait on board indefinitely. I was hungry and eventually would grow too weak to swim. Plus, having an arm that had a bullet hole in it wasn't going to help matters.

I took the rubber mattress condom raft to the companionway door. I checked the ties, and when the sun had dipped below the horizon, I carefully opened the hatch. I grabbed the raft and dogged the hatch behind me. The ships had shifted, and now I was far away from the near shore. I could make out white painted arrows on the deck, pointing outboard. The lines led me to wooden steps and a wooden gangway leading to the next ship. I crossed nine more such bridges and I was on another Liberty ship, identical to the *Adams*. I found the gangway leading down to the water.

I carefully went down the gangway and lowered the makeshift raft, dropping it the last few feet onto the dock. It sounded like a gunshot to me, but there were no alarms, no spotlights lit me up. I managed to lower myself then drop onto the dock. My landing was graceless, but I didn't hurt myself or end up in the drink. I put my arm through the loop in the raft and partially slung it over my shoulder. I sat down on the dock, dangling my feet in the cold water, and then scooted off the platform into the water.

It was cold. I was instantly cold. I wanted to get out to wave my arms and call the navy over and give myself up. Instead, I kicked my feet and pushed toward the shore. It was five hundred yards, five football fields away. I kept kicking pushing my ungainly raft along toward the shore. My legs started to burn the more I fought the current, and my breath was ragged.

The current was pulling me south toward the bridges and the industry and the shipping. I was getting closer to the shore but I was also moving south more than I wanted to. South would also bring me to the navy security station. I was in no shape to fight Keller and his goons. I couldn't fight a newborn kitten right now. Instead, I just kept kicking toward the shore. Lights in the distance grew bigger and brighter. I could hear the highway sounds, car horns and the noises of industry as I drew nearer. Then, finally, my knees started to scrape on the sand and silt. I had made it but was too weak to stand. I managed to crawl onshore and collapse in some reeds. My breath was rising toward the newly emerging stars in plumes of steam. Maybe I should see if my giving up Lucky Strikes wouldn't cripple the tobacco industry.

Chapter 22

After lying on my back and contemplating the relative merits of being in a wet marsh I sat up. That didn't kill me or seem to hurt that much. My stomach growled to remind me that I hadn't eaten in almost twenty-four hours. The ship still had had some fresh water and the water fountains had slaked my thirst, but I couldn't find so much as an old can of SPAM onboard.

I got up and took off my wool undershirt and spun it above my head for a few rotations, then wrung it out. I put it back on, and it was followed by the commando sweater, then my pants. I wasn't as cold as the last time I had been in the water, but I had to start moving or I wasn't going to go anywhere.

I stepped into soggy marsh, sinking in over my ankles and stumbling often. It was wet and smelled foul. My efforts to keep my pants dry were mostly useless after sinking in mud and falling into standing water. After forty-five minutes, a lot of cursing, and some sweating, I made my way out onto a dirt road. It was Goodyear Slough Road, little more than a dirt track that cut through the tidal marsh following the slough.

I waited, and there was no traffic in any direction. I stepped onto the road and put my right shoulder parallel to the bay. I started walking north with a purpose. By walking, I mean exhaustedly shuffling at a pace that was less than blistering. My left arm hurt, and it bumped against my side. I slid my left hand into my pocket, hoping to immobilize it. The plastic baggie with my money was still in there. They had taken my weapons and gear but for some reason had missed the money.

I kept putting one foot in front of the other. I had marched—rucked, we called it—literally thousands of miles while I was in the army. It started out in basic training. We learned the skills of a light infantryman, marching with a heavy rucksack, weapon, and ammunition and being able to fight the enemy when we got to our destination. Then in SF, we learned to ruck farther, more quietly, with heavier rucksacks. Then in Vietnam, we rucked farther still with heavier rucksacks, in hotter, more humid weather with more weapons and equipment. Now, here I was, shuffling down a road, moving slowly with no rucksack, no weapon or equipment.

I don't know how far up the road I had gone or how long I had been shuffling along. It could have been yards, it could have been a few miles. It was dark and I was cold. I could smell the unmistakably acrid smell of burning rubber. It came to me on the breeze, and I stopped. I could hear voices and the sound of breaking glass. Off in the distance. I couldn't hear any engine noises. I started walking again. The smell grew stronger, and the voices became more distinct. They sounded like I was right on top of them, but I didn't see anything.

I looked into the night and realized that there was a boat in the marsh between me and the Suisun Bay. It was hard to see at first, because it was screened by some reeds. The hull was facing me. It looked like a thirty-footer, a cabin cruiser, once a rich man's toy now lying on its side in the marsh. It must have broken its moorings and ended up here wrecked after a storm. The voices and smoke were coming from the side away from me, where the deck and cabin would be. There was a narrow path of trampled marsh grass leading around the boat that you would miss if you were driving by.

I waited and listened. It sounded like a bunch of teenagers partying and just screwing around. Hanging out at an abandoned boat was a much better place to drink or smoke weed than mom and dad's basement. I stood still in the darkness listening to them, trying to decide if it was worth the risk. In the end, I had to face up to the fact that I was cold, exhausted, hungry, and had a bullet hole in my arm. Teenagers, even if they turned out to be assholes, were still a better option than Keller and his franchisees. I stepped around the side of the boat to see four unremark-able teenage boys. There were two little Honda 30cc motorbikes leaning up against the deck. They were too small for me to use even if my arm weren't hurt. They were sitting on cushions from the galley and burning rub-ber fenders. The boys were dressed in jeans and jackets or vests. One of them wore glasses, and none of them stood out in my tired mind. At first, they didn't notice me, but then one of them said, "Guys, *guys*, shut up."

"Hi, there. I don't mean to interrupt you, but I'm in trouble, and I could use some help." I could only imagine what I looked like.

"Hey, mister, we aren't doing anything wrong. The boat is, like, abandoned." The boy with the glasses. I could have pointed out that the smashed portholes and windows might indicate that they had been vandalizing. Who was I to criticize boys having good, clean fun?

"I didn't say you were. What I said was that I'm in trouble, and I need your help. Can you help me? I can pay you."

"Help with what?" One of the boys wearing a down vest against the damp chill of the Bay Area in March.

"Nothing that will get you in trouble."

"Hey, man, we aren't into any weird shit."

"No, I need you to call a friend of mine and tell him where I am, so he can come pick me up. I can pay you?"

"Mister, what's wrong with your arm?" From Vest Number 2.

"Yeah, and why are you so dirty?" This from Glasses.

"Some men shot me last night, and I ended up in the bay. I got messy crawling up on shore." It was mostly the truth, but if anyone was to talk to them later, the less they knew, the better.

"Cool. I thought I heard fireworks last night." After that they decided I was okay. I told them I would pay them a hundred dollars. Two would go and call Chris, and two would stay with me. I told them Chris's number and made them repeat it back to me a few times until I was sure that they had memorized it.

"When he answers the phone, tell him the following message: 'Red is declaring a Prairie Fire,' and then tell the man on the line how and where to find me. Or have him meet you someplace and show him the way here." They repeated the message. It was a throwback from our days in Recon. When a team was in trouble, in danger of being caught or killed, they called Covey and declared a Prairie Fire. Covey circled overhead in their plane coordinating the evacuation helicopters, jets, and gunships. Covey was the voice on the radio telling you that you were going to make it. Covey was the ringmaster of the world's deadliest aerial circus.

Calling in a Prairie Fire was bad. It meant you were in serious trouble. You were compromised. The enemy was chasing you. You were in a gunfight or you could be overrun at any moment. Maybe you had been wounded or likely would be. It meant you were in a world of shit. This wasn't Vietnam, but I was in trouble and Chris was the only one who could get me out of it. Hopefully, he was waiting by his phone when they called him. I didn't have a good back-up plan. Or any back-up plan, for that matter. This was a typical Andy Roark production. SNAFU. The old army slang for Situation Normal, All Fucked Up. That could describe my life.

Two of them left on the squat little Hondas with their plump, knobby tires and lawn mower–like engines, like a minibike gang riding off into the night. Only in California. One of the kids left behind offered me a pull from half a bottle of Night Train. I almost said yes, but having some experience with Night Train, I knew that if I lived my hangover would hurt more than my arm.

I made small talk with the two kids, Glasses and the

other one with the vest with a V-shaped maroon stripe. They were fascinated by the fact that I had been shot. They talked a lot about *Red Dawn*. It was their favorite movie and was currently playing on HBO. They loved it when the kids started ambushing Soviet supply columns. I had seen the movie, and it was like a guerilla war training film. Hollywood will probably try to ruin it by remaking it someday.

I was comfortable on the cushions. The burning rubber stank to high hell and made me cough, but I was really warm for the first time in thirty-six hours. The kids seemed like decent, all-American teens, the type who go to Boy Scouts with passion until they realize they want to get laid more than they want to be Eagle Scouts. Then it was all cars, weed, sports, and girls, not necessarily in that order. Then college or maybe the service, but in the post–Vietnam era there weren't a lot of kids joining in spite of the army's urging them to be all they could be.

I had lost track of time. I had a watch, but I wasn't paying attention to it. The hands moved, and I noted the time but then just as quickly forgot it. The teens had left. I think they said something about having to get home before they got grounded. I handed each of them a hundred-dollar bill and said something stupid about staying in school, then sat there alone in the dark with my wool blanket. The rubber fenders had burned out, and I had only clean, cold air to breathe. I tried to remember the words to an army marching cadence about "Christopher Columbo." The words eluded me. Then I tried to think of the words to my favorite Doors songs. Then, somehow, I was singing "Emotional Rescue" by the Rolling Stones to myself in the dark, windy night.

The night was clear, and the stars were bright pinpricks on a panorama of onyx. In the distance I heard thunder. I wrapped the blanket tightly around me. The last thing I needed was to get rained on. I was already cold enough without that. I had been wet enough for the last day and a half. The storm was fast moving. The thunder grew louder, and the very earth trembled. The stars twinkled at me, laughing at their own private joke or my stupidity. Then there were lights dancing in the night, not lightning.

I heard voices and heavy men crashing through the reeds toward me. I tried to push myself up. If I was going to die, it wasn't going to be lying down like some dog that had been kicked too much. Chris and two gnarly looking bikers emerged around the stern of the boat.

"Jesus, Red!"

"Howdy." I felt like giggling; then I was giggling.

"This is my bro from Nam, Red. Let's get him into the truck." Chris was giving orders to the two of the scariest-looking bikers I had ever seen. One stuffed a Dirty Harry–sized Magnum in his belt. The other had slung a Remington 870 pump-action 12-gauge over his shoulder. Rough hands lifted me. Chris had a Ruger Mini-14, the kind with the tubular folding stock, in his hands. They carried me around the beached cabin cruiser to the road, Chris pulling security the whole way, pointing the Mini-14 wherever he thought Charlie might pop out of the brush. His eyes tracked and he pointed the muzzle of the weapon wherever his eyes were looking. He hadn't forgotten a thing.

On the road, the thunder made sense. There were what looked like twenty biker dudes on Harleys. They looked like a band of pirates in their colors. The two with Chris put me in his truck. Chris checked me over quickly and decided that I would make the ride back to the city. With a mighty roar of American-made muscle, we started south down the road. With ten bikers in front of us and ten behind, we rolled down the dirt road and slowed down to turn left by the navy security station. We rolled by slow and loud. Fuck you, Keller! I passed out before we reached the highway.

Chapter 23

Iwoke up in a bed. My mouth tasted like caterpillars had partied in it all night long and left me with a fuzzy tongue. My left arm was bandaged, and I had an IV stuck in the right one. My head hurt and my body was sore. Something in the room stunk to high hell; then I realized it was me. I had been running around, working up a sweat, then dragged myself through the bilge of a forty-year-old unused ship, and then I had crawled through marsh mud and bled on myself, which had only added to the stench.

It took me a few tries to sit up. My left arm still didn't want to work, and I didn't want to disturb the IV in the right one. I managed to scoot into a sitting position when Chris walked in.

"Hey, you're awake. Cool." He checked the IV and

looked at my dressing and then sat down in a chair by the bed. "How are you feeling?"

"A little rough, but I'll be okay. Can I have some water?" My mouth was parched. Chris handed me a glass, and I drank deeply. "How bad is my arm?"

"You took a through and through from a high-velocity round, 9mm?" I nodded. "The bullet didn't strike any major blood vessels, or you wouldn't be here. The bone is intact. The damage was mostly muscular. You'll have to wear a sling, but you should be back to normal in a couple of weeks."

"Well, that's good."

"Yeah. What nearly killed you was the infection. The wound got infected, probably from particles of dirty clothing left by the path of the bullet or your being covered in mud and whatever sewer you bathed in. Who knows? I gave you some antibiotics with the IV. You have a bunch of large bruises, but nothing is broken. I am still not sure what happened, but I am pretty sure that you shouldn't be alive. It seems like you are trying to get yourself killed one inch at a time." Concern showed on Chris's face. "You know, Red, the whole point of surviving the war isn't to get killed at home."

"I wasn't trying to." I was not used to people showing concern for me. My mother wasn't around, and my father was not the type to fuss over me.

"What happened?" Chris unhitched his furrowed eyebrow some.

"No shit, there I was. . . ." We both smiled, because it was a long-running joke that all war stories started with that line. I told him about my adventure aboard the *John Q. Adams*, the heroin. He laughed when I referred to them as Keller and the Vicious Vietnamese. He shook his head

when I told him about hiding under the dock in the cold
waters of Suisun Bay. He frowned when I told him about
my roaming the empty ship and then about my swim to
shore.

He told me that I had been asleep for almost fourteen
hours. He had done a nice job of cleaning and dressing
the wound. He lit a cigarette and put it in my mouth. He
disappeared and came back a few minutes later with a
tray with toast, scrambled eggs, and a large glass of orange juice. Chris put the tray down and then squeezed the
IV bag from the top, forcing the liquids into me quickly. I
suddenly felt cold as the IV fluids rushed into me. Chris
took out the IV and covered the site with a large Band-
Aid.

Chris handed me the tray and told me to go slow. I
started with the toast, which was evenly buttered. There
is nothing worse than toast with just a spot of butter in the
middle. The eggs were soft, almost creamy. He had
cooked them slowly over low heat. Chris explained to me
at great length the advantages of scrambling eggs over
low heat while I ate the very subject he spoke of. It was a
French technique and it was good. When I finished
breakfast, I took a long shower and washed the marsh
stink off me. I took note of some interesting bruises from
where my body had made contact with the water during
my graceless fall.

Chris replaced the dressing on the wound. I could see
the puckered entrance wound. Chris saw me looking at it.
"You probably would have bled more except for hypothermia."

"What do you mean?"

"While you were in the water waiting for Keller and
his folks to clear out, your body temperature was drop-

ping. To compensate, your body started to draw the blood from your extremities and pool it in your torso. That is why people lose fine motor skills when they are cold. While you started to bleed from the wound, your body was actively countering it by shunting the blood to your torso, away from the wound. Then you were still too cold to warm up when you got out, and you were able to put that half-assed pressure bandage on the wound. Hypothermia may have saved your life. You are one lucky son of a gun."

Chapter 24

Boston in mid-March was still wet and cold. There was slush everywhere, and the wind reminded me of why no one moved north to retire. I wouldn't have it any other way. I wouldn't know what to do with myself if I lived someplace with palm trees. I had gotten in on a late flight and slept late into the day. It took longer to wash and dress because I had to do everything one handed. It was late afternoon by the time I got moving.

When I had touched down at Logan, I had taken a few minutes to scan the crowd. No one seemed to be following me or be interested in me at all. People gave me space because of the black cloth sling that Chris had made for me. We had said good-bye at the airport with my thanks, a hug, and an agreement to stay in touch. Chris had saved my life, just like I had his and he mine in the war. We felt no need to make a big deal about it. That was what it meant to be part of a brotherhood. You knew—not thought—that your brother would be at your side no matter how bad, how dangerous, or how certainly fatal the situation was. It was the only certainty in lives like ours.

I had plenty of time to think on the plane. Keller was not stupid, and he would figure out fairly quickly that I was alive. What I was wondering was if he would figure out that I was not a threat to him. I couldn't prove anything and would look like a crazy person if I told anyone. Who would believe that the U.S. government was smuggling and selling drugs to buy arms to fight a covert guerilla war in South America?

Keller probably wasn't a problem, but Colonel Tran and his badly dressed sidekicks were. He seemed to have made a pretty heavy emotional investment in killing me to walk away leaving that unfinished. It wouldn't take him long to figure out that I was alive and well, back in Boston, irritating the shit out of him.

I wanted to talk to Nguyen about the *Adams*. It was neat being on the ship he sailed out of Saigon in. I wanted to tell him about my trip to Suisun Bay. I had a couple of questions and wanted some good Vietnamese food. Plus, I hadn't seen Nguyen in a while, and I was running short of friends in the last few years.

I dressed with care: loafers, because I couldn't tie my own shoes; jeans; blue button-down oxford shirt; and a khaki blazer. I had the Chief's Special, loaded with hollow points, holstered on my right hip. It was riding high, canted forward in a leather thumb break holster. I had a speed loader of hollow points in my right jacket pocket. I slipped Thuy's little Colt .25 into the sling on the side

closest to my body. I was trying to compensate for my in-
juries by carrying a noisemaker. My arm didn't hurt as
much today, but that had more to do with some pills that
Chris gave me than anything else.

I had parked the Maverick three blocks away on the
street. A quick walk around and check reassured me that
no one had planted any grenades or mines on it. It started
up with a healthy roar, and I muscled my way into Boston
traffic. If you looked at the straight-line distance from
Boston to Quincy, it was a ten-minute drive, but the traffic, road construction, and slushy roads meant that it was
early evening by the time I arrived at The Blue Lotus. I
drove past it, parked several stores down, and walked
back.

When I walked in, I was struck with a wave of nostal-
gia. In my mind I could clearly see, smell, and feel what
it had been like to walk in the restaurant for the first time
two years ago. It had been warm, run down, and welcoming, the type of place where you would go with your wife
and kids, if you had them. The smells of exotic food
cooking had been overwhelming, and the atmosphere had
been welcoming. This place had fed me, provided shelter
against the cold, and provided me with friendship, possibly even a sense of family. And as I usually did, I was
about to fuck all that up.

The restaurant was uncharacteristically empty. If I had
been expecting Linh to greet me, I was wrong. Nguyen
walked out of the kitchen. He had a cigarette in the corner
of his mouth.

"Ah, Round Eye Private Eye shows up. What happened to your arm?" He used all of the same slurs but
they were without much humor this time. His eyes took
in the .38 on my hip. Nguyen didn't miss much.

"Oh, some of Colonel Tran's associates managed to shoot me in the arm. The funny thing is that the last Vietnamese man to shoot me was an NVA. I got shot by one of my former allies this time." Nguyen shrugged. He was used to allies turning out to be fickle. A lot of people had changed sides in Vietnam; that was to be expected from decades of war.

"You do have a way of making the Colonel angry at you." He smiled.

"I guess I do, don't I? On the other hand, he blew up my car." And the girl in it. "I really liked that car."

"Car was old. You get new car." He said it the same way he told me about coming to America and starting his life over. You have a country, you flee the country, you have a new country. You start over. It was that simple for Nguyen.

"That car and I had a lot of miles together. I liked that car." I had liked it, also the girl. It wasn't right that she got killed by a bomb meant for me. Someone had to answer for the girl. It hadn't been love, it never could have worked, but she shouldn't have died like that.

"Come on, Round Eye, let's drink to your dead car." He went behind the bar, and I sat down sort of sideways. I wanted to be able to watch the door. I could still see Nguyen. My gun side was to the bar. Nguyen pulled a very old, very dusty bottle of French cognac down from the shelf. He poured us each a snifter. We toasted and I took a sip.

"Why are you here, Andy?" Gone was even the appearance of friendliness. Also missing was the singsong pidgin English and heavy accent. He had stopped pretending to be a poor sailor, a common man. It had been his version of bread rolls and mustard, fake Chinese food, filler material.

"Well, I'm here for a story. You see, when Colonel Tran's associates shot me, I was on board the *John Q. Adams*. The very ship you left Saigon on." Someday I will be able to sit down with a friend for a drink and it won't turn into an interrogation.

"I take it your being there wasn't a coincidence?" He left the bottle on the bar.

"No, it wasn't. I was led to it by a dead journalist named Hieu." Nguyen grunted and shrugged his shoulders. I took another sip of the excellent cognac and wondered what it would do when mixed with the pills Chris had given me. I didn't much care. Today was as good as any day to drink, to fight or to die. I just wanted to hear the story, to know why three people had been murdered. The cognac burned its way down into my belly. Then I started my part of the story.

"It turns out Hieu was from Saigon. He had a friend there who was in the South Vietnamese Navy, named Pham Duc Dong. I have seen pictures of them together in Saigon. Young men, before the war got to them. Pham was a promising RVN Navy staff officer, a logistician. The picture was before Hieu ended up in a communist reeducation camp, and he still could smile at the promise of life. Hieu was murdered, shot several times, not far from here. Pham was stabbed in his car in Chinatown.

"You asked me if I expected you to know all of the Vietnamese in the area?" Nguyen hadn't said anything, his hands flat on the bar, staring at me through his clear aviators. "Except, of course, you did know these two Vietnamese, didn't you?" His eyes met mine, assessing me, trying to gauge how much of a threat I was.

"Yes, I did know them. We were friends in Saigon. We went to the same *Lycée Français*. How did you put it together?"

"You wouldn't believe how many times people have asked me that. You would think that people think me dumb." Nguyen laughed.

"No, Round Eye, you are many things, but dumb isn't one of them." He dragged on the cigarette and the tip glowed. It made me want one, too.

"The answer was on TV last night. I knew you were involved. I just couldn't quite make all of the pieces fit, and then there it was on the TV."

"The answer to this?" He seemed puzzled.

"Yes, *Magnum P.I.* was on, and I was watching hoping to get tips on how to make my mustache look better." Nguyen smiled in spite of the moment. He was still tense, coiled tightly, a human spring under incredible pressure. "It was one of the ones that showed Magnum in his dress uniform and above his left breast was a brass trident clutched in an eagle's talon, the emblem of the U.S. Navy SEALs. Then I remembered a picture I saw in Pham's house. Him in uniform, Hieu clearly a civilian, and another man in an RVN Navy uniform. A man wearing mirrored aviator sunglasses with a brass trident in an eagle's talon above his chest. I didn't recognize you because the glasses were mirrored, you had longer hair, and your face wasn't as drawn as now.

"I am guessing that Pham was in charge of moving the gold out of the country. It was too late to fly it out—the communists had shot the runway at Tan Son Nhat airport all to hell. But there was still the fleet. No one would look at a tired old Liberty ship filled with fleeing refugees. He wanted to make sure it would be safe and that the plan would work. Why not ask his old friend from the *Lycée Français* who was in the RVN Navy SEALs, who had been trained by and worked with the Americans, to watch over it? After all, the ships were going to rendezvous with the U.S. Navy. There must have been someone else watching it, too." Nguyen's shoulders slumped. He sighed and picked up the glass of cognac and took a large swallow of it.

"You know, Round Eye, Colonel Tran and his CIA friends were all very stupid to underestimate you. Yes, you are right, Pham came to me. He offered me safe passage out of Saigon for me and my family if I would guard the gold. He thought that they would offload it, and it would go into a bank either here or in the Philippines, eventually Switzerland. Colonel Tran sent a nephew of his to watch out for it as well. He would never have trusted someone who wasn't family.

"After we left Saigon, and the initial fear for my family, the danger, had passed, I started to worry about the future. I had a family and had nothing that I could do to support them in America. Tran's nephew had similar thoughts, and he suggested that we steal some of the gold. Tran's nephew kept watch while I took the gold bars, wrapped them in flour sacks, and then hid them in the ballast compartment. The plan was that we would go on deck when it was late, and everyone was sleeping and throw the lead bars used for ballast overboard.

"He was a foolish man and liked to drink and liked to

brag. My family's future was at stake, and I couldn't trust him, so one night, we went on deck with the lead bars in a sack. I stabbed him from behind, my hand over his mouth, pulling his head back, taking his balance away from him, the way we were taught by your SEALs. I put lead bars in his pockets and threw him overboard. Everyone believed that he fell overboard while drunk. Which he often was.

"I wanted to get off the ship in the Philippines. The Philippine Islands are big and reminded me of Vietnam. It would be easy to get lost there. My family and I could start again. I had one hundred pounds of gold hidden in the ballast area, so we could live well. But I was supposed to watch over the gold. If I jumped ship then in the PI, I would give the game away. Colonel Tran would know I killed his nephew. He would hunt me for the rest of my life. It had to be America, then. My family could never be safe anywhere else.

"My first sight of America was magnificent. We saw California, growing from a dark line on the horizon to hills and shore. I sailed under the Golden Gate Bridge, Alcatraz off my port beam, and into the navy yard. We anchored in the bay, near the pier. They wanted to keep the refugees on the ship, contained until they were ready for us. We were in America now. Finally, we would be safe.

"I waited till it was late at night and slipped onto the deck. I took the gold, each bar in a flour sack, and I tied rope to the ends. I crawled down the anchor chain, below the waterline. I tied off the sack six feet underwater to the links and repeated the trip four times. Then I swam ashore.

I found a spot onshore. It was several hundred yards

in, a park or parade ground. I buried the gold near a tree that I would recognize easily. I used a statue and the stars as reference. I made the trip four times and was exhausted. I got back to our little cabin and slept for forty-five minutes; then we were taken off the ship and processed as refugees. I was lucky—both An and I could speak English. We were given an apartment, and I was able to find a job washing dishes. Two weeks later, I used a tourist map and found the park. A week after that I made my way to the tree. It took me four nights, but the gold was in our apartment. I had secured a future for my family.

"I laugh thinking of how the cockroaches climbed over gold bars, our clothes that were secondhand. We had long blocks of cheese and cardboard squares of eggs, thirty eggs in a square, that your government gave us. We had a fortune in gold but were living in poverty in a smelly apartment building in Oakland.

"I found a second job in a garage. I did all the worst jobs. I worked day and night at two jobs. An made sure that Linh and Tuan were cared for. I found older Vietnamese and Chinese who had been in America longer and found out where I could discretely sell gold. I shaved pieces off one of the bars. It required great discipline to sell the first bar a little bit at a time. We saved money and I bought a station wagon—it had that imitation wood on the side—and after being here two years, we drove east, toward the sunrise.

"One of the Americans who trained me and went on missions with me and died in my arms was from a place called Quincy. He had told me many times of his home. I later learned that the ship was named for the man who gave his name to the city. I had heard about snow, but it was so much more beautiful than I imagined. The cold was unimaginable. In Quincy, I arrived with the money, which I told everyone was my savings from working two jobs. We never spent too much and I tried to blend in—an average, middle-class American.

"In Chinatown in Boston, I was able to sell more of the gold. We bought the restaurant and finally I felt like we could just live. I felt that we could breathe. We could raise the children. We would never be hungry or scared again. I still had three of the gold bars left. Finally, I felt safe. Even when Colonel Tran came in looking for his contributions, I felt safe. He didn't recognize me. I was just another peasant to him." Nguyen told his story with the easy flow of a natural storyteller. He also seemed to get lost in the past. He smiled to himself, flush with the success of saving his family again. I wondered how often he thought of that sweet memory.

"Then what happened to change all of that?"

It was almost cruel breaking his reverie, dragging him from the success of a father providing for his family. The problem with me is that I have to know. I am driven to know what happened. That drive makes me a shitty person but a good detective.

"Hieu. Hieu happened. He came to America. At first, it was good. We reunited. He was a journalist again, was with his wife and family. Then he started to hate the Committee. Started to write about them. One night, we were drinking cognac, from this very bottle, and I was drunk. I told him we have it good here. I told him not to, as you Americans say, rock the boat. We are alive here. We can raise our families here. I told him I would help him. I told him about the gold. I felt bad for him. He had suffered through so much."

"What did he do?" I felt that internal flush of victory, hubris. My theory had been right. I had been right.

"He grew angry, then suddenly stopped. He told me he wasn't angry with me. He was angry at the Committee. They should have used the gold to help Vietnamese refugees. You must understand, Round Eye, . . . there was much suffering, the boat people and the upheaval caused by war. Hieu was right. I didn't see him for days; then he was shot dead. I was so sad. To have survived the war, to have survived the communists, to come here and find your family again, to have a chance to be happy . . . then to be killed."

"You knew it was Colonel Tran?"

"Yes. Colonel Tran wanted me to help him with the Committee. He knew I had been a frogman, but I told him I wanted to put the war behind me. He would come in and complain about Hieu. Also, I had seen his gun. The same caliber, he carried it all the time. A small version of your Colt .45."

"When did Pham contact you?"

"He called me. He was angry, very, very angry. Hieu had been to see him, and he had told him about my taking the gold. Pham truly believed that we were going to lead the counterrevolution."

"He drove up here to see you?"

"Yes. He was angry. He wanted to meet. He wanted to confront me in person. He came here and we had a very loud fight. We almost fought each other, but we are not young anymore. He left . . . so angry at me."

"Then you called him at his hotel." Nguyen snapped out of his reverie, and his eyes focused on my face.

"Yes." Almost a whisper.

"You agreed to meet. Maybe you told him you would turn the gold over or maybe you said you wanted to explain it to him. You had to see him before he talked to Colonel Tran."

"Yes."

"You knew that he would tell Colonel Tran, and Colonel Tran would want the gold and the man who killed his nephew."

"Yes."

"You set up a meeting in Chinatown. He would take his car and you would take him to the gold."

"Yes." Nguyen was a man who was deflating.

"The knife, a Fairbairn-Sykes Commando knife. Was it in a rolled-up newspaper or blade hidden in your sleeve?"

"It was in a newspaper. The sleeve is too slow; the knife can get caught up."

"You stabbed him in the subclavian artery, between the collarbone and the neck. Just like the OSS taught and we taught our friends in the LLDB and the RVN SEALs."

"Yes, he was a staff officer, with soft hands, clean hands. It was quick. The knife was in my hand, then a push, a little resistance, and I pulled the blade out. He was dead. He never saw it coming, and he felt very little pain." He was trying to convince himself more than me.

"What about his wife? Do you think she feels any pain?"

"You know, Round Eye, . . . I don't care." He had moved so slowly, so subtly that I didn't notice the revolver pointed at my midsection. It was a Smith & Wesson Model 10, a snub nose that held six, and his finger was on the trigger. The barrel was short, and the cylinder was stubby, wider by one bullet than my own revolver on my hip. "I don't care, because I have to think of my family. I have to ensure they are safe, that they can grow up. That is the only important thing. You understand that?"

"Yes. Yes, I do. I am not a threat to you or your family. I would never do anything to hurt An, Linh, or Tuan." I wanted to tell him more, but the bells above the door tinkled and cold air rushed in. It felt like Death's own icy finger on the back of my neck.

Chapter 25

Colonel Tran walked in, flanked by his son, still dressed as though he was the Vietnamese version of Run-DMC, and the henchman in bad clothes. The henchman held a revolver that was the twin of Nguyen's except it was nickel plated. Vietnamese Run held a giant Italian SPAS-12 semiautomatic 12-gauge shotgun and Colonel Tran held his .380 down at his side.

"*Trung Si* Roark, I was hoping that it was you. You are a very annoying man who has caused my colleagues in California a great deal of distress." He was smiling, cocksure. He knew he was going to kill me.

"You blew up my car." I was too tired and beat up for any good tough guy lines.

"Yes, it was a shame you weren't in it with the girl."

"I really liked that car." Then I shot him with Thuy's little Colt .25. I had snaked it out of its hiding place while he was talking. I didn't really aim; he was standing three feet away. I just pointed and pulled the trigger, three rounds in his chest, and I walked the rounds up. One managed to hit him in the throat and three in the face. I dropped the empty gun and stepped to my left off the stool.

I heard the shotgun booming. I heard thirty-eights cracking around us. The restaurant was filled with lightning, thunder, and burnt powder. My hand found the butt of the Chief's Special and my thumb the snap. I saw Nguyen and Bad Fashion Guy empty their revolvers at each other at tabletop distance, each like a perverted mirror image of the other, cigarettes smoking in the corners of their mouths.

Bad Fashion Guy developed a clover pattern in his chest and his face, two extra holes in it. Vietnamese Run was emptying the shotgun, which bucked in his hands, spraying buckshot around. The glasses on the bar were vaporized. Nguyen turned just as Vietnamese Run managed to get his bucking shotgun lined up with him. The blast took my friend off his feet.

I raised the revolver as I dropped into the combat crouch, legs bent at the knees, right arm extended straight out. I shot the kid between his eyes. Twice. Fuck him. Heat bathed my face and hot granules hit it. My left earlobe throbbed. Colonel Tran, Colonel fucking Tran, who had taken a magazine full of .25 ACP rounds in his torso and face, Colonel Tran who was dead except that his body refused to recognize that minor fact, fired his .380 at me.

Actually, he blew off the bottom of my left earlobe. He howled as his son died by my hand. Colonel Tran was trying to kill me, bring me with them, trying to pull me into the dark waters that I had recently escaped from. I shot him, emptying my revolver into his face. Finally, he collapsed—the fight and the life had gone out of him.

My ears were ringing, and my nose was filled with the smell of burned powder and cigarette smoke. I was the only one left standing. I went to Nguyen. I clutched his hand and tried to tell him that I would never have hurt his family. That I didn't care about the gold, I just wanted to know what had happened. I wanted to tell him all of that and more, but my mouth refused to work. Words refused to come out, just sounds.

He wasn't worried about his family anymore. A shotgun blast in the chest had seen to that. I told him he was my friend and brother. I hoped that he and Tony and all my other dead brothers were in Valhalla getting Valkyrie pussy and drinking mead. I hoped that he was at peace. I couldn't speak. I had survived when, yet another friend was killed, and I couldn't even offer words of comfort.

I took the revolver out of his dead hand. I carefully, trying not to leave big fingerprints, emptied the cylinder where he had been standing. I emptied my empties into my palm. Then carefully, holding them by their rims, I slid them into the empty cylinder of his revolver. I put the revolver back in his right hand. I picked up the .25 and wiped it off and put it in Nguyen's left hand. Hopefully, it would look like Nguyen had done all the shooting. There were a lot of rounds that had been splashed around, and cops have been known to get lazy when the answer is right in front of them. I pushed the button that opened the register drawer. I wanted them to think this was a robbery that went wrong. Somewhere in all of it, I reloaded my own revolver.

I took a napkin off a table and held it to my earlobe. When I walked out, I was careful not to step in any blood and left out the back through the empty kitchen. My ear started to throb badly when the cold night air hit it. Feeling empty and sad, I drove back to my empty apartment. My empty life.

Chapter 26

Two nights later, I parked behind The Blue Lotus. I used my picks and rakes to let me into the kitchen. My left arm was working more or less; otherwise I would have kicked in the door. I didn't bother with gloves, as my prints were all over the place. I went to the front, trying to ignore the smell of dried blood and the chalk outlines on the floor where my friend died.

I took the ceramic, gold-painted cat out of the shopping bag I carried. It had cost me five dollars in Chinatown. I put it on the counter. I took out the can of spray paint and sprayed *gooks get out* on the walls. Then I smashed the ceramic cat on the floor in front of the register and knocked over some tables. I unlocked the door and went out front. I broke the plate glass window with a rock.

I went back in and relocked the front door. I lifted the

gold cat from its place on the counter, its one paw in the air in a bizarre feline high-five, onto my shoulder. I grunted. It was heavy and my left arm, while usable, was still not completely healed. I went out the back, leaving it unlocked. The cops would think that the asshole kids had left that way. The cat, much to my relief, went into the trunk of the Maverick. It was another stray cat in a world full of them.

When I got home, I put it down on my coffee table. I watched the Movie Loft with Dana Hersey. He was playing *The Maltese Falcon*. I looked at the cat and drank a tall whiskey. When the movie ended, I half-ass saluted the cat and said in my best Bogie, "Angel, that's the stuff that dreams are made of." I took my Colt .45 and went to bed. It went under the pillow, and I dreamt of yet another dead friend in my collection.

A few days later Brenda Watts called me. "Roark, no one's blown you up yet?"

"Nope, not yet, but the night is young." I was wary of her.

"You wouldn't happen to know anything about an attempted robbery in Quincy? In a Chinese food restaurant, turned into some sort of gunfight? A real bloodbath."

"I think I saw something in the *Globe* about that. I know the restaurant; the owner is a nice guy. I ate there a lot when I was working a case down at the shipyard." It didn't take a genius to see where she was going with all of this.

"Was."

"Huh?"

"He was shot with a 12-gauge in the chest. Picked up a .38 in his side, too."

"Jesus."

"Yep, it looks like a bunch of Vietnamese gangsters have been shaking down local Vietnamese businesses. I guess this guy had had enough. He shot the three guys shooting at him, pretty good for a restaurant owner." She sounded genuinely impressed. "The funny thing is, one of the gangsters had a .380 that matched an earlier murder in Quincy. A Vietnamese writer got popped. Weren't you looking into that?"

"I guess there is no point now." I had all the answers.

"You want to hear something funny, Roark?"

"What's that?" I was pretty sure it wasn't going to be a knock-knock joke.

"For the second time in a week, a Colt .25 automatic showed up. Went my whole career without seeing one, and in the space of a week, you show me one and one is used to shoot a Vietnamese gangster named Tran. What do you think about that?" She hung up on me before I could answer. The case was radioactive two weeks ago and had only gotten more so.

A few days later, I was sitting at the lunch counter at the Brigham's on Boylston Street near the Greyhound station. I was rereading the copy of *The Maltese Falcon* that Nguyen had given me while trying to ignore the junkie half passed out in a booth nearby. I was working my way through one of their famous coffee ice cream frappes and a cheeseburger when Keller walked in.

He wasn't dressed for yachting this time. Instead, he was wearing a trench coat, dark trousers, a tweed jacket, and sensible shoes. He looked like an English professor, so much so that I would bet that his jacket had leather patches. Thankfully, he seemed to have left his submachine gun in San Francisco.

"Hello, Sergeant Roark."

"Hello, Keller. What brings you to Boston?"

"Oh, there was a mess that needed to be cleaned up. One of our associated franchises went bankrupt and seems to be under new management. I was sent to help with the transition." You had to love the CIA—in the movies they talked like spies, and in real life they talked like businessmen. "While I was here the head office asked me to make you a proposal."

"What is that?"

"They would like you to sign a nondisclosure agreement to which you stipulate the classified nature of our franchise operation. If you do, you would be subject to federal prosecution if you disclosed anything about our franchise."

"What is in it for me?"

"We would ensure that the new management of the local franchise wouldn't bother you." I wanted to tell him to fuck off, that I would scream from the roof tops, but I just didn't care enough. Being angry at Keller took more energy than I had. The Company would always have a dirty tricks department; I wasn't going to change that. He took the folded piece of paper out of his pocket, and I signed it. No one would believe me, and I had no proof of any of it. I wasn't even worth killing anymore.

"Take care of yourself, Roark. Not everyone is always going to underestimate you." He left, walking out the glass door, an anonymous man disappearing into a crowd, swallowed up by the crush of people. I sat and finished my coffee frappe. The junkie groaned in his stupor, and I had had enough of Brigham's for one day.

The weather was warm and sunny. It wasn't full spring

yet, but it wasn't the cold New England monsoon that is April either. I was wearing the battered trench coat that Leslie had given me years ago. Like me, it was starting to show its age and was a little frayed at the edges. I pulled it a little tighter when I stepped outside. I had the Colt Commander on my hip. For legal reasons, my Chief's Special was in my safe deposit box at the bank in Providence, Rhode Island, next to my old Colt .32 automatic. If I kept shooting people, I was going to need a bigger safe deposit box.

I took my time walking with no purpose and no rush. I stopped to look in the windows of the nice stores on Boylston Street. I looped and doubled back. I stopped in L.J. Peretti's and bought a couple ounces of pipe tobacco. I made my way out to Boylston Street and then to Charles Street. I went through the wrought iron gates into the Common and found my way to the Soldiers and Sailors Monument. My circuitous route left me confident that no one had followed me.

"Hello, Andy." Linh found me sitting on the bench I had told her I would be on.

"Hello, Linh."

"My mom thought you would be at the funeral." Her eyes were moist, and she was dressed in heels and slacks, with a soft camel hair coat. She was wearing make-up, and it occurred to me that she wasn't a teenager anymore. In grief, she had matured, and now the outward trappings were reflecting that.

"I'm sorry. I couldn't. I wanted to, but I couldn't go."

"Andy, Mom thinks you know something about what happened. None of this makes sense, Colonel Tran and his son trying to rob my dad and getting into a gunfight with him. Then someone broke in and vandalized the place. Andy, nothing makes sense anymore." She sat down next to me and cried quietly into my shoulder for a few minutes. After a bit, she collected herself and sat up.

"Linh, can you tell me what your dad wrote in this book?" I handed her the copy of *The Maltese Falcon*. She looked at it and wrinkled her brow.

"It doesn't make much sense. It says that you will find your Falcon by the cash register. Then he says to take care of me, Tuan, and Mom."

He had known that trouble might be coming his way. He must have written it when Hieu started asking questions.

"Andy, what does it mean? What is this all about?"

I told her about the *John Q. Adams*, the flight from Saigon, and the gold. I told her a little about Nguyen, Hieu, and Pham. I left out her father's role in their deaths. She didn't need to know that her father had murdered men, not out of greed but to ensure that his family could have a life, a fresh start in the land of the big PX. I didn't need to poison what he had sacrificed his life for. She didn't need to carry the guilt for his sins, and Linh, being one of the world's genuinely sweet people, would.

"Linh, I was there that night."

"What night?"

"I was there when they murdered your father. I hadn't seen him in a while and went in for a drink. While we were having it, Colonel Tran and his flunkies came in. They started shooting and we shot back. When the dust settled, I was the only one standing. Your dad was still alive. He told me with his last breath to look out for you and your family."

It wasn't the whole truth, the literal truth, but it was the kindest version of the truth I had for her.

"I knew about the gold and figured out that he had melted it down and recast it. He knew he couldn't take it to the bank, and he couldn't sell it all at once. He didn't trust many people, so he decided to put it where he could see it every day. He made it into something that no one would look twice at in a Chinese restaurant. He recast it into a cat, with its paw up, by your register. Every Chinese restaurant has one. I vandalized your restaurant and took it. I knew that you guys wouldn't know how to dispose of the gold." I handed her the bank book in her name. "There is about two hundred fifty thousand dollars in there. Use it to take care of your family. That was all your dad wanted." I didn't tell her about the cashier's check that I gave to Hieu's widow that was financed by her father's theft. The fifty thousand dollars would give them a chance after so much grief and loss.

"Why did you . . . ?" she trailed off.

"Your dad helped me in ways you can't imagine. After they opened the Vietnam Memorial in Washington, I went to go see it, except that I couldn't bring myself to go. I figured a drink would make it easier. One turned into fifty, and I lost track. I got stinking drunk. I wandered around Washington and got into fights and drank more. I figured that I would go to the wall, see my old buddies. There were more of my friends on that wall than there were alive. Then I was there, in front of my friend Tony's name on the wall. If I had been faster, better, he would have lived. Tony, the others were all outstanding soldiers and men, and despite that, they were killed, and I lived.

"I decided that I would join them. I pulled out my .38 and put it to my temple and started to pull the trigger. Then out of nowhere, this mangy-looking vet starts talking to me. He was homeless, living in the park and guarding the monument. He was one of a handful of guys who did that. He told me I didn't have to kill myself. He asked me to join them, live on the streets or in the park. Spend my nights protecting the Memorial. To me that was just a slower means of killing myself."

"What happened?" She was concerned and horrified all at once.

"I realized that it was my fortune, my curse, to have survived. It was up to me to learn to deal with it. I met your dad a short time later and was impressed with the fact that he had lost so much. He lost friends, his home, his country, and yet your father seemed happy. He had a purpose, and he seemed to have put the war behind him. He came to terms with it. It made me think that maybe I could, too. He told me that he and I were like stray cats, no homes anymore. But what he didn't say was that we had found each other, we were friends. For a couple of years, I didn't feel like a stray anymore." There wasn't much more to say. I couldn't figure out a way to tell her that my dream died in the family restaurant in Quincy. Linh leaned over and kissed me softly on the cheek.

"Good-bye, Andy."

"Good-bye, Linh."

I had almost had a family. I had a friend and then the ghosts of my long-ago war blew it all apart. I knew my fortune: I was destined to be alone. Not lonely. Alone. I was always going to be the only one left. I would carry my pain and loss on my shoulders, bear my burden until it was over. My friends would live only in my nightmares of our war. I would simply mark time, march until I could join them again. I had woken up from one more dream that wasn't to be. I watched Linh walk away from me, becoming blurrier and blurrier through my tear-filled eyes.

Connect with

Visit us online at
KensingtonBooks.com
to read more from your favorite authors, see books
by series, view reading group guides, and more.

for sneak peeks, chances to win books and prize packs,
and to share your thoughts with other readers.

facebook.com/kensingtonpublishing
twitter.com/kensingtonbooks

Tell us what you think!

To share your thoughts, submit a review,
or sign up for our eNewsletters, please visit:
KensingtonBooks.com/TellUs.